BACKSTAB

I much prefer the three-day ordeal of a St. Louis funeral. It lets you get used to the idea the person is dead. By the time you finally get to the burial, you're happy to shovel the dear one into the ground and go on living. After the funeral, everyone comes back to your house and there's baked ham or roast beef and hearty heavy food like casseroles and mostaccioli, potato salad and chips, and lots of beer and wine. Then you sit around and talk about the dead person and all the funny things and kind things she did, and for an hour or two she lives again, and you know that she will live in everyone's memories.

BACKSTAB

A Francesca Vierling Mystery

Elaine Viets

Published by
Dell Publishing
a division of
Bantam Doubleday Dell Publishing Group, Inc.
1540 Broadway
New York, New York 10036

ISBN: 0-440-22431-4

Printed in the United States of America

Published simultaneously in Canada

October 1997

10 9 8 7 6 5 4 3 2 1

OPM

To my husband Don and his enormous . . . gray cat.

ACKNOWLEDGMENTS

Many thanks to my agent, David Hendin, and my editor, Jacquie Miller. This book wouldn't be possible without them.

I also want to thank Father Patrick S. McDonnell, pastor of St. Sebastian Church, Fort Lauderdale. St. Louis Police Officer Barry Lalumandier. Anne Watts and the staff of the St. Louis Public Library. Richard Buthod of The BookSource. Susan Carlson, Karen Grace, Jinny Gender, Debbie Henson, Marilyn Koehr, Cindy Lane, Robert Levine, Betty and Paul Mattli, Sharon Morgan, Dick Richmond, Kathy Rethemeyer of the Fortune Teller bar, and Janet Smith. Finally, thanks to all those helpful folks who must remain anonymous, including my favorite pathologist.

1

Newspapers have always used the language of death and violence. We kill a story. We spike it. Or bury it. We keep old stories in the morgue. Reporters complain that editors slash and cut their copy. Now, with the new computers, we've added more deadly words. We can abort and execute. For us, the pen really is mightier than the sword. But we writers are mostly mild types, content to take out our fury in back-stabbing.

That's why, when the killing started, I knew no real newspaper person was behind it. They would never take those words literally. They wouldn't kill my readers. When I look back now, I blame myself. I should have paid attention to what the two women told me that cold gray February day. Maybe those people would still be alive. Or maybe not. I didn't take the time to find out. I was struggling with the most violent newspaper word of all.

A deadline.

Let me introduce myself: Francesca Vierling, columnist for the *St. Louis City Gazette*. Six feet tall. Dark hair. Smart mouth. Dumb enough to write for a newspaper when anyone with any sense was getting out of the business.

It was three o'clock in the afternoon on February eighth, three hours from my final deadline, and I still didn't have a column. Instead I was sitting in a dark bar in South St. Louis, and a woman was holding my hand. Gina had long silver earrings, a nice set of laugh lines, and a purple fringed top. She had the courage not to dye her reddish-brown hair, now that it was going gray. I liked that. Not that I *like* women. Don't get me wrong. Gina was holding my hand because she was a palm reader. She was also the owner and bartender at a joint in my South Side neighborhood called the Crystal Ball Bar. Like most neighborhood bars, Gina's had hot dog nights, baseball nights, and two-for-one happy hours. But her place had a little something extra. Free palm readings one day a week. Gina read the palms herself, just like she barbecued the dogs on Hot Dog Night.

The Crystal Ball Bar had been designed back when saloons were the working folks' social clubs in this old German neighborhood on the city's South Side. For a quarter, the customers bought a beer and sat in the most luxurious surroundings they would probably ever see. The Crystal Ball had a twenty-foot oak bar, a mirrored back bar, and cozy dark booths lit by the golden glow of tulip-shaded art-glass lamps. The luxury was long vanished. The bar was covered with cardboard racks selling aspirin and Alka-Seltzer and beef jerky. Even in the dim light, you could see that most of the customers were retirees who could barely afford the price of a draft, or worn-out hookers and run-down vice cops. The place smelled of Pine Sol and stale cigar smoke and the booths were harder than a bill collector's heart.

To me, it felt like home. I grew up in bars like these. My first words were "orange soda." Writing any column about a bar was an easy out when I was under pressure. Two columns had gone dead on me in thirty minutes. One subject was out of town, so I couldn't check a vital fact by deadline time. Another column went belly-up when the guy who said his children were unjustly taken away from him turned out to have a conviction for assault and battery. He beat up his wife when she wouldn't let him take their son one weekend. So much for the story of a hardworking divorced dad denied his rights. I rushed down to the Crystal Ball on Palm Day.

Gina said she would read my palm, but she wouldn't take any money for it. She never did. She didn't think it was right to make money off something she said came naturally to her. I didn't feel that way about writing, but I admired Gina just the same.

"If conditions aren't right, I won't be able to do it," she said. But she was a kind person who recognized a desperate woman—me—and she ushered me into the first booth by the door, where she could keep one eye on my future and another on her customers. She closed her eyes, and pulled her concentration into herself, the same way I'd seen athletes do. Then she turned my palm over and looked at the lines on it.

"You have a very old soul," Gina said.

"I'm not surprised. The rest of me isn't getting any younger," I said. I'd just turned thirty-seven. It was traumatic.

Gina ignored the wisecrack. She was taking this very seriously. Her long earrings swayed like chandeliers in an earthquake as she studied my palm. "You have a long lifeline," she said.

That was probably true. The women in my family lived into their nineties. When my grandmother died at seventy-three, instead of the usual ninety-three, the family carried on like it was a crib death.

"But there will be an abrupt change soon," Gina said. She pointed to a spot where my lifeline zigzagged. "I see much turmoil and crisis."

"I work for a newspaper. There's always turmoil," I said.

"This crisis could end your career," she said.

I could feel my palm sweat, even though I didn't believe a word she said. I just needed a column.

"I see you in Washington."

"D.C.?" I said, hopefully. Finally, after fifteen years, I was going to get some national recognition for my work.

"Missouri," she said.

Oh. Washington, Missouri, is a town fifty miles outside of St. Louis, best known for a sausage shop and a bakery. I go there every October because Jim Hanks, a vet friend who lives there, has his annual nut fry. Doc Hanks is the Lorena Bobbitt of the bull world. Whenever he castrates a bull, he freezes the testicles, then in October dredges them in flour and fries them in deep fat. They taste like mushrooms. The best part is watching the guys at the fry. They drink a lot of beer and keep their legs crossed. After about four beers, they start downing nuts at a great rate, with silly smiles on their faces.

But no matter how late Doc Hanks's nut fry lasts at the local VFW hall, I never stay in Washington more than a weekend.

"What am I doing in Washington?" I asked.

"It will be your refuge when your world collapses. In your time of crisis," Gina said. "I'm sorry I can't help you any more, except to tell you to be very careful in the next few months."

I was always careful. I loved the city neighborhood where I lived, but I could get mugged walking to the supermarket.

I came away with the impression that Gina was a decent person who honestly believed in what she was doing, but I hadn't seen a bigger load of garbage this side of the city landfill. Take refuge in Washington? Ridiculous! St. Louis was my city, and I knew it better than she knew my palm. If I ever needed help, it would be right here in my hometown. Oh, well. At least I had a column.

I thanked Gina, grabbed my purse, felt around with my foot for my shoes (I'm one of those women who slip off their shoes the minute they settle in), and went outside to see if someone had ripped off or ticketed my beloved blue Jaguar. Most reporters drive a modest Honda or Toyota. Not me. Modesty is for those who need it. I loved my fifty-two hundred pounds of blue flash. A used Jag costs less than a new Buick, but god, it goes fast.

There is one drawback to owning a Jaguar. You have to listen to a lot of lectures. "Jaguar, huh?" they'll say. "You might as well own two—one to drive while the other one's in the shop." I bought one from the vintage years, '86 to '88, and it was the most reliable car I ever owned.

I stepped over some gray rags of last week's snow and slid into the Isis blue leather seats. The car started up with a low sexy growl. I turned up my FuzzBuster and poured on the gas. I had to get back downtown to the newspaper office.

The Crystal Ball was twenty minutes from the newspaper office. That's what I liked about St. Louis. It was convenient. Everything was twenty minutes from everything else. If it wasn't, we didn't go there. Another thing I liked was the city air. On the South Side, it had that sharp-sour smell of fresh-brewed beer. This part of the city was perfumed by the Anheuser-Busch brewery. If the stuff tasted as good as it smelled, I'd be in a detox ward.

My good fortune was holding. There was a

parking spot in front of the building. I found some quarters in the bottom of my purse, fed the meter, and ran into the lobby. It looked like someone had overturned a junior high. Young teens, with that wet, newly hatched look, were everywhere. They giggled and poked and picked at their zits and picked up everything on poor George's desk. George is the perpetually worried security guard.

George looked more worried than ever, with the students all over him. "Hi, George, how are you?" I yelled as I ran for the elevator. George managed a wave. He was signing in eighteen students for a newspaper tour, putting each kid's name on a pass. The *City Gazette* made visitors wear these awful sticky tags with a picture of the News Hound, the newspaper's doggy mascot who didn't look bright enough to bring in the paper off the lawn, much less dig up stories with his "nose for news."

Adults who made the mistake of putting the passes on a silk blouse or briefcase would never get the sticky stuff off. But kid visitors delighted in sticking the tags on subversive places throughout the building. My favorite was the young vandal who made his pass into a bow tie and stuck it onto the painted bow tie on the oil painting of our managing editor, Hadley Harris the Third. Hadley had to call in an expert from the Art Museum to clean and remove it.

When I started at the *City Gazette* fifteen years ago, the newsroom was the most romantic place in the world. We had these army-green desks, piled high with yellowing newspapers, and beat-up beige file cabinets, gray Royal typewriters, and, I swear, brass spittoons. Nobody used them for spitting. The staff poured their old coffee dregs and dropped their cigarette and cigar butts into the spittoons. The janitor had the awful job of emptying those brass slop jars. My worst day at the paper was when I tripped over one of those disgusting things.

They're all gone now—the spittoons, the gray typewriters, and the army-green desks. Now we sit in mauve-and-gray ergonomic pods and type on beige IBM computers. It's faster and more efficient, but it has all the romance of an Allstate insurance office. Not that I get too sentimental over the good old days. I'd still be writing fashion copy in that world. That's all "girls" could do at newspapers then.

The newsroom had that predeadline hum. It started about three in the afternoon. It was a blend of constantly ringing telephones, small staff meetings, and phone conversations that got more frantic as reporters tried to pin down people for statements before the six o'clock deadline. I could hear frenzied fragments of conversations:

"When do you expect him back? Would you tell him we need his reply for the first edition?"

"When does Detective Connor get in? Not till five o'clock? Will you tell him I'm looking for him? Can I leave a message on his voice mail?"

"Do you think she dyes her hair?"

"At her age, she has to. And speaking of dyeing, get a load of that black suit. Who died?"

I tuned in to those last two remarks, and I smiled. Two female reporters hidden behind a stack of phone books were talking about me. Forget *Front Page* and *All the President's Men*. The emotional age of a newsroom is freshman year in high school. By their comments, I could tell my short black Donna Karan suit had hit the mark. I must be looking good to make them talk so bad.

I waved to Tina, my friend who covered the city police beat, but all I saw was her dark brown curly head and her hunched-up shoulders. She was busy on the phone.

My own phone was ringing when I got to my desk. I found the phone under a pile of legal pads and old feature sections, removed the two yellow Post-it notes I'd stuck on the receiver to remind me to make some calls, and looked at the clock: four-fifteen P.M. It had to be Rita the Retiree, calling me to critique the newspaper. She called me at the same time every month.

Rita got her Social Security check, cashed it, and went down to the Peppermill bar for two draft beers. Then she went home and called me to complain about the paper. I liked Rita and I liked her comments, even if I couldn't publicly agree with her. One sixty-six-year-old woman had figured out what was wrong with the paper better than all the focus groups and survey takers. Of course, she had one up on the high-priced consultants: Rita actually read the newspaper. I'd met Rita a couple of times. She was a good source of neighborhood information. She always looked the same. She wore a pink polyester pantsuit and had her gray hair sprayed into a helmet once a week at the Powder Box Beauty Salon. She preserved her hairdo for a full seven days by sleeping on a green satin pillowcase. She painted her nails red and smoked unfiltered cigarettes.

Rita called me from her home on Gannett. She lived in a brick one-story shotgun house, so called because you could fire a shotgun through the front door and hit all three rooms. First there was the living room, with a huge TV and a maroon three-piece furniture suite, protected by plastic slipcovers. The TV had a rabbit-ears antenna, with aluminum foil on the ends for better reception.

Next came the bedroom, with a Bassett bedroom set and a pink chenille bedspread. She bought them when she married Ray, who'd passed away ten years ago last March, God love him.

But she lived in her warm cozy kitchen, with the big Chromcraft kitchen set, the permanently percolating coffeepot, and the pride of Rita's life, her collection of salt-and-pepper shakers from all fifty states in a tall glass display case. She'd spent a lifetime collecting the twin igloos from Alaska, the cacti from Arizona, the pair of red barns with corks in the bottom from Connecticut—all the way down to twin cheeses from Wisconsin and two buttes from Wyoming. Every week Rita took them all out, dusted them and admired them and put them back in their proper places. When she talked on the phone, she fixed her rocking chair so she could watch them glitter and sparkle, especially the ones made from Arkansas fool's gold.

Rita's smoke-cured voice rasped through the phone line with her usual opening, "Honey, did you see the paper today?"

"Yes, Rita." Here it comes.

"How can they call it a newspaper, when it doesn't have any news? The whole front section is six pages, and four of them are department store ads. And the two big front-page stories are a disgrace. One is called 'Over Easy: 9-Year-Old Boy Breakfasting at Shoney's Saves 6 Kittens Loose on the Interstate.'"

I'd wondered about that one myself. The kitten story was about a Chesterfield kid who was staring out the window, eating pancakes and tuning out a lecture from his mother, when he saw a semi make a left turn into a vet hospital van on the access road. The doors popped off, and six frightened kittens popped out. The kid left his breakfast to get cold, ignored his mother when she told him to sit back down, climbed a chain-link fence, and ran into rush hour traffic to save the kittens from being run over. The smiling blond boy was photographed on the front page with a rescued kitten on his head.

"Who the hell cares?" said Rita. "I mean, I wouldn't want the kittens gettin' squashed, but should your paper encourage children to run into traffic?"

I didn't have to answer that question. Rita went straight into why the other major front-page story bothered her. It had a four-column photo of a weeping black woman, collapsed in the arms of eight of her children, after she heard that her twelve-year-old son was shot in a police raid on a North Side crack house. The story said the kid fired an Uzi at a cop, and the police fired back.

The story began, "Etta Mae has endured much, including her first pregnancy at age 15 and the misery of living on welfare with nine children. But today she had another burden laid on her ample shoulders. Her son, Tyronne, 12, was gunned down, possibly by St. Louis police, during a raid on an alleged crack house. . . ."

Rita was not going to grieve about a dead crack dealer, even if he was twelve. She hated them all. Their desperate young customers had mugged her twice on her way home from her afternoons at the Peppermill. The second time, she held on to her purse so hard she broke her wrist when the kid yanked it out of her hands. Now her afternoons included the added cost of a cab. A tipsy retiree was a target.

"And then they're putting that trashy woman with her dead drug-dealing son on page one," Rita snapped. "Doesn't your paper do any stories about churchgoing black people? I worked with a lot of them at City Hall, and believe me, they held down two and three jobs to send their sons and daughters to college. They raised up fine doctors and lawyers and accountants. But not if you read the *Gazette*. All black people are drug dealers and suffering welfare mothers."

She was warming to her subject. I glanced at the clock: four thirty-five. I had to go soon. I had less than an hour and a half to finish my column.

"Where's the news in my newspaper?" raged Rita. "What's going on in the Middle East? What's Congress up to? What's happening in Mexico after we signed that stupid trade agreement? Why can't I find out what's going on in the world?"

Because the *City Gazette* paid half a million dollars to a group of consultants, who concluded readers wanted local news. If the paper had spent half a million dollars on news staff, they could have had outstanding local stories. But the *CG* didn't want to hire more reporters. So they stuck to murders and kitten rescues, which were cheap and easy to do. They also played to some readers' prejudices: White suburban kids saved kittens. Black city kids sold drugs.

But I couldn't tell Rita that. I didn't have to. She answered her own question: "They're too cheap to do real reporting," she said. I was always amazed at how much readers figured out by themselves.

"And they've missed the real story. It's right there, right in front of them, buried in their own paper."

"Where?" I said. If there was a story going loose, I wanted it.

"Check the 'Police Notes.' The second item under 'City Murders.'"

I hunted around for a daily paper, turned to page five-A, and read the single fine-print paragraph: "Police found the body of a prostitute in a Dumpster in the 700 block of Bedler St."

Hmmm, that address was right by the paper. Also right by the projects. It was a desolate area with empty weed-and-brick-studded lots and soon-to-be-razed buildings. The burned-out shells had the intense blackened look of insurance fires. A lot of bodies were found around Bedler Street.

"An autopsy showed the person had been beaten and strangled and was undergoing a sex change," the article said.

"Wow!" I said, "That would put a strain on anybody."

"Don't laugh," huffed Rita. I could almost see her chin wobbling indignantly. "It says here the deceased was twenty-two, had bosoms, was taking female hormones, but still hadn't had his whatchamacallit cut off."

That's not quite how the paper phrased it, but Rita caught the spirit. The managing editor, Hadley Harris the Third, was a nineteenth-century prude in a twentieth-century job. He wore hand-tied bow ties, parted his thinning hair in the center, and wrote editorials about family values, Republican virtues, and the joys of raising his two daughters.

What most readers didn't know was, Mr. Family Values ran around on his wife. At first I dismissed the gossip about Hadley. Sure, I'd see him with a female staffer a few times, and then she'd be promoted, but I just thought he was getting to know her. He was. I didn't know how well until I covered an undertakers' convention at the Riverside Inn downtown. I was supposed to interview a "grief counselor" in a seventeenth-floor suite. As the elevator doors opened, I saw Hadley and a mousy-looking city desk reporter coming out of suite 1710. Hadley was tying his bow tie, so I knew it wasn't a clip-on, and smooching Miss Mouse on her round little ear. I ducked back into the elevator, hit the down button and hoped they didn't see me. Three weeks later Miss Mouse got the coveted job of consumer reporter. I wondered what she consumed to get that promotion.

A true Victorian, Hadley felt what you said was more important than what you did. Hadley treated readers as if they were sheltered maidens, too delicate to withstand modern life. Nothing improper—i.e., interesting—was allowed to sully the *City Gazette*'s pages. With Hadley on one of his prude watches, I was surprised the sex-changing prostitute made the paper at all, even a paragraph in the "Police Notes." Hadley was constantly lecturing me on good taste. Our latest run-in was when I mentioned in a column that a grocery store clerk found a used condom draped over a grapefruit. I thought this was a funny vignette about city life. Hadley Harris read it on a page proof and almost needed smelling salts to revive.

"Not in my newspaper," he screamed. "Get it out. Out. Out." You'd have thought a rat had run over his desk. I could see his scalp turning pink through the thinning hair. That was a bad sign.

"Hadley, don't cut the condom," I said. "It will be talked about."

"That's not the kind of discussion I want my paper to create," he said. "A Hadley Harris paper has principles. We don't pander to interest in smut."

I wondered if Hadley used condoms for his assignations. I wondered if I could still make my Visa payment if I told the skirt-chasing hypocrite to stuff it. Sigh. Why did I argue? It was useless. There was no way I could explain to Rita we were lucky to see one paragraph on the dead prostitute in Hadley's paper. There was no way to explain Hadley.

"There's a story there. Aren't you curious?" said Rita.

"The victim is a prostitute. Lots of them get killed."

"I still think it's a story," grumped Rita. "I bet a customer found out she was a he and killed her. Remember BJ Betty?"

Rita couldn't bring herself to say Blow Job Betty, as BJ was really called, not even after two beers.

"Of course I remember Betty," I said. "I told you the story."

"Tell it to me again," she said, like a teacher

prompting a not-very-smart student. "Maybe it will convince you this is a story."

"It happened last summer," I said. "Betty hung around the Last Word."

"The newspaper bar," said Rita.

"Right."

"I've never been there," she said.

"You haven't missed a thing. The Word is a dingy place where the staff goes to complain about editors and talk about what they would do if they ran the paper. The draft beer tastes off because Terry, the bartender, doesn't keep the lines clean. The tables wobble and have match-books under the legs. The tops are sticky with old spilled drinks and the ashtrays overflow. The floor crunches and rustles with empty peanut bags, spilled chips, and dropped pretzels."

"Sounds like a lot of old bars," Rita said.

"It's not. It has a mean and nasty atmosphere. You go there to gripe and grouse, get drunk and cheat. I stay away from the Last Word, unless I want to get really depressed. But I was there the night BJ Betty's story broke. Betty was a brassy little blonde with a haystack of bleached hair. She always wore a tight black skirt and red spike heels. She had knobby knuckles and long red nails. The red-painted nail on her little finger glittered with a rhinestone. Betty had oddly big, bony feet for someone so small, but I doubt the guys got much past her bulging blouse."

"They never do," sniffed Rita.

"Betty's name was her specialty. She had oral sex with a lot of reporters, copy editors, phone clerks, and even a few printers in the back of her white Cadillac. It was kind of a ritual. Betty would come in, order a strawberry daiquiri, which Terry the bartender always grumped about making. Terry hated froufrou drinks."

"He probably didn't want to clean the blender," said Rita, who used to work part-time at a bar.

"Betty's order was the signal for one of the guys to sit down beside her. If Betty liked him, and the woman made Will Rogers look like a snob, she'd let him pay for her drink. After a couple of rounds, the guy would ostentatiously escort Betty, a little wobbly now on those red heels, out the back door to the parking lot. About half an hour later, he'd come back alone, grinning."

"Hah. Men. They're all alike," said Rita.

"Charlie was one of her regular escorts," I said, trying to continue. The beer was definitely taking its toll on Rita.

"Is he that little short, balding shit I met that time I toured the paper?" growled Rita.

"Some of my best friends are short," I teased her. "Anyway, these days we say Charlie is vertically challenged."

"That's not the problem. He has mean, shifty eyes. I don't trust him."

I didn't either, but I'd had to find out the hard way. I never could figure out how Rita sized the little creep up so fast.

"Charlie said he liked BJ Betty because he didn't have to lie to The Wife. I never heard

Charlie use the woman's first name. Maybe she was baptized The. 'If The Wife asks me if I've ever slept with Betty, I can tell her no. Well, I didn't sleep with her, did I?' he said, winking. 'I didn't go to bed with her, either.' "

"See, a sneaky little shit," said Rita. It sounded shocking coming out of her mouth. She used the S-word only on her Peppermill afternoons.

"Some guys would ask Betty for a little more than oral sex and she would say, 'Oh, no, honey. Not today. It's my time, you know.' Few complained. They'd rather have Betty's specialty anyway.

"One night five or six guys got to bragging in the bar about Betty's talented tongue. One of them mentioned he wanted to go all the way, but Betty said it was 'her time' this week.

" 'Yeah? She told me it was her time last week,' said Dick.

" 'She told me it was her time the week before that,' said Jim.

" 'Who cares?' said Charlie. 'She'll never come whining to you that she's pregnant.'

"A fat old beat cop who used to work the Stroll was listening to this conversation. He started laughing. I suspect he was ticked off because the *Gazette* had just done its Doughnuts to Diners exposé, revealing some city cops had free doughnuts or dinners at local diners. The owners gave them free food because there were fewer holdups in a diner full of blue uniforms."

"That series was a real revelation," said Rita,

sarcastically. "A lot of good cops got stung because they ate a burger."

I didn't want to hear about it anymore. I continued my story.

"Anyway, the fat cop said, 'If you get Betty pregnant, you'll wind up in the *Guinness Book of Records.*'

" 'Why?' said Charlie.

" 'Guys can't get pregnant,' said the cop.

" 'What's that got to do with Betty?' said Charlie.

" 'She's. A. He,' said the cop, punctuating each word with a mean smile.

"Charlie's face turned the color of pork fat.

" 'A guy?' Charlie croaked, and drank his draft in one gulp.

" 'Betty's a bouncing boy, just about ready to get his final operation,' said the cop, enjoying every word. 'That's why he never gives anything but blow jobs, he-man. You've been getting sucked off by a she-man.' "

"Hee, hee, I loved that part," Rita said.

"Charlie's smile did sort of curl up and slide off his face like a dead worm. He put some money on the bar and left. A lot of guys went home early that night. The men who stayed were the ones who'd never been with Betty in her white Cadillac, and they looked relieved. They claimed they could tell when they saw her Adam's apple. But they couldn't. Betty was darn good."

"Here's the part I want you to pay attention

to," Rita said, still prompting her pupil to learn this lesson. "What happened the next night?"

"The next night, when Betty's Cadillac showed up on the back lot, Charlie and some of the guys were waiting for her. Or him. They beat up Betty so bad, Terry finally came out and made them stop. Betty's blouse was ripped and she had bruises on her face and arms, but she'd managed to do some damage with her long fingernails and spike heels. Terry wanted to call an ambulance, but Betty didn't want any trouble. She drove herself to the emergency room, bleeding all over the white interior. I heard Betty didn't work her specialty for some time. She had to have her jaw wired. The cops asked if she wanted to press charges, but she said she fell in the parking lot.

"She certainly fell from grace at the Word. Betty never showed up at the bar again."

"See what I'm saying? Those guys at the Last Word almost killed poor Betty when they found out what she was," Rita said.

"Yeah, if Terry hadn't come to her rescue with that lead pipe he keeps under the cash register she would have been a goner," I said.

"I think that's what happened to the poor thing they found on Bedler Street," Rita said.

"Why do you say that?"

"Because of what happened when those guys at work found out about Betty."

"It doesn't mean that's what happened to this person."

"It's worth looking into," Rita said.

"It's just another dead hooker," I said.

"I'm trying to give you a good story tip, but you're not listening," Rita snapped. "I better go. Thelma is at the back door." Thelma was her next-door neighbor, eighty-eight years old. I knew she wasn't really there, or I would have heard her yelling and rattling the door knob. Rita was irritated with me. She was also right. This was the second time I'd ignored a woman's good advice. I would regret it.

I finished my column by deadline, but I missed the story.

2

"**B**eing a columnist is like marrying a nymphomaniac. As soon as you finish, you have to start all over again."

A reader told me Ellen Goodman said that. Maybe she did, but Ellen always looked too prissy in that column photo to know much about nymphos. Besides, it sounded awfully politically incorrect. There's no such thing, medically speaking. A nympho is what scared men call an unsatisfied woman.

Still, I know what she means. A four-days-a-week column is insatiable. The thrill of servicing it is almost as good as sex. As soon as I finished one column, I needed another. And another. And another and another and another, until I was panting and exhausted. No wonder they say you put a newspaper to bed.

I love it. I'd hate to have a *real* job. Talking to a palm reader in a bar beats digging ditches and working in factories, and I have relatives who do both. When I finished my Crystal Ball column five minutes before deadline, I was a happy woman. Today's work was done. I could look forward to tomorrow's with satisfaction. Because I had another fantastic subject, a hot and juicy one. I grabbed my briefcase and a fresh legal pad and headed out to the Louie the Ninth Motor Inn, near the airport.

St. Louis is named for Louis IX, the saintly French warrior-king. If a saint who led two crusades to the Holy Land had to do any time in Purgatory after he died, I figure he spent it at the motel named after him, the Louie the Ninth. The decor was punishment enough. The Louie started out as a basic airport motel. It had a big high-ceilinged lobby fronting for a hollow two-story square of rooms. But the motel went slightly wacky when the present owners gave it a medieval theme.

Now aluminum suits of armor stood in the lobby next to the standard motel overstuffed sofas and silk ficus trees. The Sheetrock walls were painted like gray castle stones. The high ceilings were hung with colorful banners, which made the place look more like a gas station tire sale than a medieval court. But most of the activities in King Louis's namesake motel were far from saintly. The Louie was the site of swap meets for bored married couples, swinging singles conventions, and gatherings of S and M aficionados, who loved the Dungeon cocktail lounge.

The motel also hosted the conventions other motels wouldn't touch: scary-weird sci-fi gatherings, comics conventions, and cat shows. Many hotels won't take cat shows because nervous cats shed huge amounts of hair. The Louie's ballrooms had a light layer of cat fluff in the corners. The people who used the Louie never complained. They were happy to find any place that would host their events. I think the Louie's semimedieval staff uniforms contributed to the louche atmosphere. They certainly made me think about sex. The women employees were dressed like Lady Macbeth in long, trailing gowns that emphasized their breasts. The men wore tabards and hose. I have a theory that most men have great legs. The Louie proved I was right.

I tried not to stare at the bellperson with the muscular legs set off by dark green tights. Instead, I went straight to a pale, ponytailed blonde behind the information desk. A Gothic plastic name tag announced that my informant was Tiffany. Tiffany wore her cheap blue gown with the dignity of a Plantagenet princess. Princess Tiffany was talking on the phone to a friend. She looked at me disdainfully, and rightly so. If I was at the Louie, I was probably up to no good.

"I'm looking for the Miss American Gender Bender Pageant," I said, confirming her suspicions.

The pale princess pointed around the corner, not deigning to speak to me. The noise guided me the rest of the way—shrieks, squeals, and shrill girlish laughter. Standing in front of the Crusader Ballroom were some of the tallest

women with the biggest hair I'd ever seen. The
sequins on their dresses were as blinding as
searchlights. They wore more mascara than a
Barbie doll. In fact, they looked rather like giant
Barbie dolls, with exaggerated busts, major
makeup, dangly earrings, and drop-dead gowns.

I've always had my suspicions about Barbie. I
knew for sure *these* weren't real women. They
were fabulous female impersonators hailing
from Maine to Mississippi, here for the annual
Miss American Gender Bender Pageant. They
dragged U-Haul trailers filled with sets for their
talent numbers. They packed eleven-thousand-
dollar Bob Mackie gowns. They brought hair
stylists from Elizabeth Arden and a queen's ran-
som in rhinestones.

A successful female impersonator always trav-
els with an entourage, and these brought their
wardrobe advisers, set designers, and lovers. The
men who accompanied them were decidedly
gay. They wore a lot of black, leather, and
chains. One of them was my friend Ralph the
Rehabber. Ralph had traded in his daytime wear
of paint-spattered, plaster-covered jeans for
something a lot more interesting. He was going
to be my guide for the evening.

Ralph was tall and lean. With his Vandyke
beard and longish blond hair, he reminded me
of those museum portraits of English aristo-
crats. Tonight he wore a silk pirate shirt, a stud-
ded black leather vest, and tight black leather
pants with silver chains going places I probably
shouldn't look. The orange-and-yellow Proventil

inhaler sticking out of his vest pocket spoiled the devil-may-care effect slightly. But Ralph had had a near-fatal asthma attack last December, and since then he didn't go anywhere without his inhaler. He even kept one in a pouch on his ladder when he worked on houses.

My readers knew Ralph the Rehabber as a regular source on how City Hall worked—or didn't. St. Louis is one of the rehab capitals of the country. We have some gorgeous old brick homes in the city, and they go cheap. You can buy what would be a million-dollar mansion in any city on the coast for less than one hundred thousand dollars here. A lot of people fled St. Louis for the new, boring burbs. They saw those areas as crime-free. People like me feared we'd die of boredom if we lived in the suburbs. We stayed in the older parts of town, rehabbed the handsome houses, and lived in luxury on the urban edge.

It takes skill and nerve to finish a rehab project, get the required bank loans and permits, and outwit the city inspectors, and Ralph had all these skills. I think my favorite Ralph story was about when he was fixing six bungalow breezeways in a postwar subdivision on the edge of St. Louis. The city code required a fire door between the kitchen and the breezeway, which spoiled any chance of enjoying the breeze. Ralph rigged up a fire door that could be hung just before the city inspector arrived, then removed. It traveled from neighbor to neighbor, painted six different colors.

I knew Ralph the Rehabber was gay, and had lost his heart to a three-hundred-pound drag queen named Bambi. Bambi was a southern belle trapped in the body of a sumo wrestler. Imagine a simpering sumo wrestler, and you had Bambi. She had doelike brown eyes, a charming giggle, long red hair, and thick, rubbery lips. She shaved her face and her legs. She loved green satin and wore the biggest pair of dyed-to-match green heels I'd ever seen—and I'm six feet tall in my panty hose and wear a size 11 shoe.

Ralph designed all of Bambi's prizewinning outfits, including a green satin wedding dress with a twelve-foot train that made her look like Scarlett O'Hara on steroids. I thought Bambi loved Ralph's work, but not Ralph, and was only using him while she made out with a hunky bodybuilder whose sole talent was flexing his pecs. But I never said anything to Ralph. You can't tell a person the truth about the one they love.

The pageant had been going on for four days. Like most beauty pageants, this one had contestant interviews, rehearsals, bathing suit competitions, and judging for poise, posture, and presentation. Tonight was the climax, with the two most important competitions: talent and evening gown.

The whole event was a flashback to 1957. Female impersonators put on the things many women have cast off—tortured and teased hair, ballistic breasts, hurting high heels. The natural look is not big in this crowd.

Ralph was my guide into this world. Unlike some gays, he never played "shock the straights." Talking with Ralph was like watching a National Geographic special. He narrated the most astonishing facts in a professional, didactic manner. "I got us both passes for the whole show, including backstage," Ralph said. I wondered how many strings, or chains, he had to pull for that. The straight press usually wasn't allowed in these pageants, for good reason. We tended to cover them like freak shows, and displayed all the sensitivity of high school jocks.

"What about the *Gazette* photographer?" I asked.

"He's allowed in, too," Ralph said. "But we'll have to stay with him." I knew that would be fine with Jimbo. He was about twenty-five and looked like Beaver Cleaver, right down to the freckles. He'd react to this assignment the same way as the Beav. He'd give a gulp and a golly. Then he'd grab his cameras and do his usual good job. While we waited for Jimbo, Ralph began his lecture:

"The subject of female impersonators is very controversial in the gay world," Ralph said, and I almost expected him to pull out a pointer and a blackboard. "Some gays feel that men date drag queens because they aren't fully out of the closet and haven't completely accepted their gayness. In other words, we're going out with men who look like women, rather than accepting who and what we are, and loving men who look like men.

"My own theory is that female impersonators let us show our creativity and our need to walk on the wild side. We go for the outrageous."

Ralph certainly did. Dating the Jolly Green Giantess was as outrageous as you can get.

"You won't hear it from the Chamber of Commerce, but St. Louis is a center for female impersonators. It's estimated we have some two hundred fifty in the area." And now, thanks to the King Louie, we had a whole lot more.

Impersonators may look cheap, but they aren't. "It costs thousands of dollars to get up on that stage," Ralph lectured. "The twelve finalists spent a total of a hundred thousand dollars for their dresses. Some losers wind up with colossal debts. Many bet the rent and the utility money and don't even place."

"Then why are they doing this?"

"Often it's a way out of the ghetto or the trailer park," said Ralph. "Many of them are poor boys who have pretty faces and not much else. If they win, or even place, they get a ticket to the gay club circuit. They can make two hundred fifty dollars a night at a cabaret and three hundred to five hundred dollars in tips. It's more money than those boys have ever seen in their life."

"Do they put it away for their old age in securities and real estate, like smart call girls?"

"Most of them don't have an old age," said Ralph.

He pulled out his Miss American Gender Bender Pageant program and showed me the back pages. They were loaded with tributes to drag queens who'd died of AIDS. In their photos, the dead queens shimmered and simpered, and looked pitifully young. Their epitaphs were short and sad. "Beautiful Bettina, 1993 AGBP Runner-Up. 1975–1995. We love you."

I flipped through the fat five-dollar program and found a happier section. It proved a beauty queen is a beauty queen, regardless of sex. These gushed just like female contestants and wrote girlish congratulations to their competition in the program. Last year's title holder, a glamorous brunette named Sweet Cherry Whine, wrote this: "To the contestants—remember to be the best that you can be. While only one of you will wear the Gender Bender crown, you are all unique!" I couldn't agree more.

That's when Jimbo showed up, looking weirdly normal in jeans and a baseball jacket. He was wide-eyed with disbelief.

"We can get you backstage, Jimbo, but you have to stick with me," I said.

"I wouldn't think of wandering off," he said, clutching his cameras like a lifeline.

Ralph led us through the stage doors, where the medieval theme made way for makeshift modern. The backstage dressing area was a long room with scuffed unpainted plasterboard walls and rolling racks of costumes. Wigs perched on stands like small animals. The drag queens put on makeup at long folding tables or poured themselves into their dresses in front of portable mirrors.

"To look beautiful, female impersonators suffer even more than real women," said Ralph.

I wasn't sure I agreed, but I was willing to listen to his arguments.

"Some have silicone implants or take hormones. Others go through worse tortures. They may wear six pairs of panty hose to keep their hip and rear pads in place."

I was impressed. One pair of panty hose is often beyond me.

He pointed to one impersonator struggling to zip up a blue sequin gown while he stuffed his lush foam tush back down in his sheer blue panty hose. I hoped he wouldn't have to use the john in a hurry.

"Should I refer to them as she or he?" I whispered to Ralph.

"It's polite to call an impersonator she when she is in costume," he said—a bit of etiquette I haven't seen yet in "Miss Manners."

We walked through thick clouds of hair spray and heavy perfume. Feathers floated in the air, lost sequins sparkled on the chairs and floors, and there were cries of "Has anyone seen my eyelash curler?" and "Who the fuck unplugged my curling iron?"

I watched a platinum blonde apply false eyelashes one by one with a tweezer. She was better at it than I was. She wore black stockings and a fetching black satin merry widow, which pushed up a pair of foam hooters the size of honeydews.

Jimbo was nearly pop-eyed. I guess he'd never realized beauty was only skin deep.

The Merry Widow grabbed Jimbo by the thigh and said, "Oooh, you're cute."

"I'm married," quavered Jimbo.

"That's how I like them," the Widow said, merrier than ever.

Jimbo put his camera firmly to his face and started snapping. He aimed at a feather fan as big and bright as a jukebox. The sequin detail on a Bob Mackie dress. A large, sexy foot in a large, sexy shoe.

He spent a lot of time shooting a stunning impersonator the color of creamed coffee, in a rhinestone dress just a shade darker than her skin. She wore a pheasant feather headdress and glided gracefully on four-inch heels. Most women I knew couldn't have managed that getup. Most wouldn't want to.

"That's the favorite, Chocolate Suicide," Ralph told me. "She's expected to win this year."

She looked scrumptious, but a shade too short and plump to be a beauty contestant. "She'd have to lose twenty pounds to compete in a female pageant," I said.

Ralph looked hurt. I didn't fully appreciate Chocolate's artistry. "This is one beauty contest where it's good to be short and a little chubby," he said. "They look more like real women. A little natural padding gives them curves and breasts."

I thought the female impersonator standing next to Chocolate Suicide made a better woman.

Sharlot Webb was slender and wore soft makeup. Her shoulder-length hair was a natural brown. Her black velvet dress with the big shoulder bows had hardly a sequin anywhere. I could imagine wearing it myself.

"How about Sharlot Webb?" I asked Ralph.

He shrugged. "Sharlot's okay, but she's not Chocolate Suicide. Let's go out and see some of the talent part of the show."

Jimbo looked relieved to leave backstage. We three made our way through the dusty velvet stage curtains to the ballroom. The stage and runway were decorated with mounds of flowers. The ballroom was jammed with folding chairs, and more people were standing.

The audience was part of the show. At first glance, it appeared to be almost all women. At second glance, some of those women had five o'clock shadows. Others looked distressingly good. After a while I could pick out the impersonators. They were glamorous. The real women looked dowdy, like brown sparrows among the peacocks.

A tall redhead in a black satin gown cut to there made me feel like maybe I should check into a salon for a makeover. I mean, if makeup and padding could make a man look that good, think what could be done for me with the right equipment. "Is she in the show?" I asked Ralph.

"No. Some of the best impersonators never compete. They just do it for fun. I know one who is a banker by day. Another is an accountant. A few are hookers."

A brunette in a red dress slithered by. "That one has a pretty face and a beer gut," I said.

"That's a real woman," Ralph said.

Onstage, things were dull. The talent competition was the slowest part of the evening. Many of the sets were fantastic. There were dungeons and harems and enough fake fog to cover London. But too many contestants simply lip-synched and paraded in flashy outfits. Watching men pretending to be women pretending to sing was boring. "How much longer does this go on?" I asked.

"One more to go," said Ralph. "You're lucky. They scratched the Ass."

I blinked.

"Maria Callous, the Ass with Class. She looks a little like Princess Di and plays on it. She wears these dresses you could wear to Buckingham Palace, with a little rhinestone bow over the butt. She's always escorted on stage by a guy with big ears who wears a tux.

"Last year she was Second Runner-Up. This year, she didn't show after the first day. Rumor is she knew she hadn't added anything to her act this year, couldn't afford a hot new outfit, and didn't have the club support. Rather than risk her title, Maria dropped out. Now she can still call herself 1995 Second Runner-Up, rather than 1996 loser."

"Does dropping out midpageant happen often?"

"All the time. On Tuesday, the Shady Lady left in a snit after she told the judge to stuff himself during the poise and presentation competition. She figured she couldn't win after that, and she was right. The Sue Warrior, who dresses like a lawyer and strips to her briefs for her talent competition, left after her boy friend punched her in the face and broke her nose. No way those bruises could be mistaken for war paint."

Jimbo had been taking pictures, but Ralph and I hadn't been paying much attention to the stage. Now, we sat up and noticed. Chocolate Suicide appeared, and it was like the room had a jolt of electricity. The audience was cheering and chanting, "Chocolate! Chocolate! Sweet baby girl!"

Semisweet, actually. Six studs in black leather carried her out in a sedan chair. She stepped out on their heads, then dismissed them with the flick of a whip. The music started, Tina Turner at her wildest. Chocolate was at her wildest, too, all fire and energy. Her rhinestones shimmered, her feathers shook. So did the rest of her. She strutted and high-stepped and practically turned herself inside out as she danced. The crowd cheered and showered her with money. She wiped her sweating face with a handful of bills. No doubt about it. She had style.

She was the last act in the talent section. Now it was time for the worst test a man can face: the evening gown competition. Wobbly high heels and heavy beaded gowns have dethroned many an aspiring drag queen. The judges were merciless. Careers were ruined by the slightest slip.

"You have to be able to walk naturally," Ralph

said. "The winners will be dragged around to all the talk shows. These are our movie stars, our society. They raise money for charity." Also, for themselves. I couldn't forget the ten- and twenty-dollar bills shoved at the contestants for tips. Tipping is an innovation female beauty queens should consider. The retiring queen and the new title holder parade on the runway, while the audience hands them money. Serious money. At this pageant, a winner might make one thousand dollars in tips, plus five thousand in prize money.

Who would wear the nine-inch-tall rhinestone crown this year?

It was down to three contestants, and just as in female beauty pageants, they were all Southerners. The judges made their choices, and I thought they were good ones. The bland, tuxedoed announcer called them out:

"Miss Florida!" She wore a stunning green sequin number that showed off her sleek, dark red hair. She was a sensational Third Place.

"Miss Lou-ee-zee-ana!" Her gown shimmered in gold. With her blond hair, it was a blinding combination.

"She'll probably get the crown next year," whispered Ralph.

But it was clear who the winner was: "Miss Texas!"

It was Chocolate Suicide, in a cocoa-brown gown to die for. I knew it looked like money, but I didn't know how much. Ralph did. "I heard

that gown cost thirteen thousand dollars," he
said.

The crowd chanted her name: "Chocolate Suicide! Chocolate Suicide!" and pressed forward to
give her money. I saw men waving tens and
twenties, crawling over each other to hand her
the money. They were practically rioting to
make her rich. Trust men to add this moneymak-
ing innovation to a pageant. It sure beat Bert
Parks singing "Here she comes, Miss America."

Chocolate graciously grabbed it all. "Get used
to this, girl," said the announcer. "It's going to be
like this for the next twelve months."

More cheers. The pageant was over. It was after midnight.

Jimbo the photographer packed up to go
home to the burbs. I told him I couldn't wait to
see his photos tomorrow.

Ralph wanted to talk a bit more. "Let's go to
Burt's Bar for a nightcap," he said. "It's on the
way home."

That was the beauty of Burt's Bar, and one of
the keys to its popularity. It was on the way to
everyone's home. Right on the edge of downtown, a few blocks from three major highways,
I-55, I-44, and I-64. The other key was Burt himself. He was the perfect old-fashioned bartender.
His martinis had zing. His beer was cold and his
glasses were chilled. Burt was a vigorous seventy. He always wore a starched white shirt,
striped tie, and clean white apron. His mahogany bar top was polished. There were no ashes

in the glass ashtrays on the shiny black-and-chrome tables. The bottles and glasses gleamed on the back bar. He ruled over this clean and pleasant place. No one, but no one, was allowed to say a four-letter word or harass a woman in Burt's Bar. Burt's wife Dolores did the cooking in the spotless stainless steel kitchen.

I thought Burt's Bar was a fine example of a city saloon. My readers agreed. Six years ago, when I ran a contest to find the Best St. Louis Saloon, they voted it Number One. Burt was so proud when he won. He gave the first prize—an engraved beer mug—its own shelf over the bar. He framed my column and hung it over the ice machine.

For years, Burt's was a neighborhood bar. Then he was discovered by the city's movers and shakers. Now you could spot them after midnight, hanging around the watering hole and trying to figure out why X was with Y and what it meant in their ugly little jungle. Burt gave me the credit for his late-life success, but I never thought I'd done much. If I hadn't written about Burt's, someone else would have. It's no great feat for a journalist to find a saloon.

It was crowded at Burt's, but we found a table. Instead of Sally, the waitress, Burt himself came over to take our drinks order—a high honor on a busy night. "Francesca," he said, a big smile lighting up his face. "You haven't been in here for months. I thought you forgot about me."

"Never, Burt. You're looking good these days."

"Awww, I'm just a hardheaded old Dutch-man," said Burt, blushing like a boy. "We never change."

"I hope not," I said.

Burt quickly got down to business. "What can I get you?" We ordered our drinks. Burt brought them and disappeared back behind the bar. He had too many customers to chat with me for long.

Ralph talked for a while about the female impersonators. I asked him what would happen to the contest's losers and dropouts. "Some are headed for trouble, like the Shady Lady. Rumor has it she's doing too many drugs. Sue Warrior will probably get her act together if she bounces her boy friend. I hear Maria Callous has a steady sweetie and may settle down for a while."

But I could tell his mind was elsewhere. He was restless and worried, and that made him wheeze. He took a hit on his inhaler. He wanted to tell me something, and eventually he'd get around to it. Finally he did.

"I had to cash in a lot of favors to get you into that pageant," he said. "You can write anything you want about us. We're different, but we have feelings. We get hurt. Please don't make us look like freaks."

I patted his hand. I was a freak, too. It just didn't show as much.

"I'll be careful, Ralph," I said.

I left some money on the table, and waved to

Burt as I walked out the door. It was near closing, and he was busy cleaning up behind the bar. I didn't stop to say good-bye. I didn't know it was the last time I'd see Burt alive.

3

The next day, I woke up early and energetic. The morning matched my mood—sunny. I dressed for work and decided to fix myself breakfast instead of eating a bagel in the car. I rummaged in the fridge, found a poppy-seed bagel that wasn't too stale, and toasted it. Then I fried an egg. Perfect. It was sunnyside-up, the yolk slightly runny, just the way I like it.

I plopped the egg on the toasted bagel and took a bite. The yolk broke, slid through the bagel hole, and ran down my suit. The rest of the day was going to slide down a hole, too. I just didn't know it yet.

I got dressed again and drove to work, still convinced that it was a good day. It had to be. It was fifty degrees in February, and I swore I could smell spring—along with the city blend of smog and freshly brewed beer.

I found my desktop piled high with mail from readers. Another sign things were going right. I

love my mail. There's always something to make
me laugh. Today, a seventy-seven-year-old
woman had sent me a photo of her cat watching
Wheel of Fortune. A group of outdoorsy guys invited me once again to go on their annual February float trip to the Ozarks. They know my idea
of roughing it is a hotel with no room service.

I was in such a good mood, I even laughed at
a letter addressed to "Francesca Vierling, Whore
of the *CG*" on my desk. Jeez, I always thought I
was fairly discreet. The envelope had my name
printed in black letters with SS lightning bolts.
The inside wasn't quite so funny. The lined notebook paper was covered with homemade lightning bolts and shaky swastikas. The writing was
more black printing, underlined with three colors. All sure signs of a nutcase. Yep. The letter
was signed by the "Aryan Avenger." It began for-
mally. "Dear Whore of the *CG*: You liberal
bitches are all alike. . . ." I didn't bother to read
the rest.

I wrote my column on the female impers.on-
ators and liked it so much I called my friend and
mentor, Georgia T. George. Georgia was fifty-
five, a small, smart, elfin blonde who wore the
ugliest, boxiest gray suits money could buy. At a
successful paper, she'd be managing editor. But
the Gazette papers had never had a woman ME,
and I didn't think they ever would. Not without a
lawsuit. The *St. Louis City Gazette* was one paper
in a chain of mediocre multimedia money-mak-
ers owned by a Boston family. The publisher
kept a mansion in St. Louis for his rare visits

here, but lived in the East. Decisions came out of corporate headquarters in Boston.

Corporate headquarters made Hadley the managing editor. He belonged to the right clubs, wore the right clothes, could talk culture with the Harvard-educated publisher—when he condescended to come to town—hold his coat and tell him what he wanted to hear. Hadley was no leader. The paper was hemorrhaging circulation. Morale was poor. The staff sniped at each other instead of working together. The *Gazette* was hated in its own community as aloof and arrogant. But Hadley was a genius for two reasons: First, he convinced the snobbish publisher that these problems were the fault of the stupid readers, not the stupid editors. Second, he kept profits high by cutting expenses and staff and hiring inexperienced young reporters and copy editors. Then he overworked them. They made a lot of mistakes, but it cost nothing to run a correction.

Georgia tried to explain to the publisher that this way of operating hurt quality, and ultimately, profits. Her career suffered for her candor. She could have transferred to another paper or a TV station in the giant Gazette chain, but she stayed in St. Louis because she loved the easy, comfortable life here, and the fourteen-room penthouse overlooking Forest Park for the price of a one-bedroom co-op in New York. At the paper, she was equally comfortable. As assistant managing editor for features, Georgia rated an office on Rotten Row, the string of private offices for newsroom execs. Each one was the size of a shower stall and had about as much charm. But in an overcrowded open newsroom, privacy was a coveted perk. I didn't want to be seen running into her office too often, so at work we usually talked on the phone.

She answered her phone with a sharp bark. "Georgia George."

"Got a minute? Call up my column for Tuesday and let me know what you think," I said.

"What are you trying to slip by Charlie now?" she asked warily.

Georgia is the only person at the paper I trust to tell me when a column is lousy or a joke doesn't work. Georgia was unflinchingly honest, even when I didn't want her to be.

She called me back ten minutes later. "I love it," she said. "But you better have a backup. You know, Miz Condom on the Grapefruit, that Hadley is on one of his morality kicks."

"But I ran the idea past Charlie and he said to go for it," I said.

"I've also told you what Charlie means when he says that. Grab your ass and kiss it good-bye," she said.

Like many newswomen, Georgia could be coarse. Newsmen generally kept their maidenly modesty, and rarely uttered a vulgar word. Newswomen showed they were tough by talking tough. In Georgia's case, she was genuinely tough. I knew she'd faced down a high-powered lawyer with a shady client who threatened her with a career-busting lawsuit. The *Gazette* had exposed his crooked client. Sometimes, even when the *Gazette* was right, its wimpy lawyers would settle out of court because they thought some lawsuits were too expensive to defend. Georgia stood her ground, the lawyer with the exposed client blinked, and the *Gazette*'s honor and her career were saved.

Georgia had saved my career, too. She was the one who'd opened my eyes to good-time Charlie. Ten years ago, when I had just started writing my column, I used to think that Charlie was my friend and mentor. He was always advising me on how to deal with Hadley. He told me I had to take a firm line with the managing editor. He urged me to go into Hadley's office and confront him. So I did. I didn't get anywhere, but I felt a lot better after I screamed at him. And it made me a hero to the staff. I was the brave woman who talked back to Hadley Harris the Third.

Charlie's advice advanced me all right. He almost advanced me right out of the newsroom. I probably never would have figured out what Charlie was up to if Georgia T. George hadn't taken me under her wing. In those days I knew her only as a distant figure, one of the *Gazette*'s rare women editors. She was frighteningly smart. She existed on another plane, far above Charlie's crowd. We said hello in the hall, but that was about it. Then I wrote my notorious Chicken Plucker column. It never made the paper, but the entire newsroom surreptitiously called it up on their computer screens and read it.

I wrote about the Rialto, an exclusive St. Louis men's club, which refused to admit women members because the men liked to swim nude in the club's penthouse pool.

I wrote, "The Rialto is supposed to be the club for the city's movers and shakers. Most of them are shakers, or at least tremblers. The average age of a Rialto member is a frisky seventy-five. The Rialto refuses to admit women to the club because it says it will have to discontinue its nude swimming. The club spokesman who told me this was a scrawny old gentleman. Without his exquisitely tailored suit, he would look rather like a plucked chicken. So would most of the other club members. The thought of all those old pluckers naked in that pool is enough to make a woman take the veil."

Hadley was a member of the Rialto (and a scrawny old plucker to boot). When he saw that column on the "Family" page proof, he killed it instantly.

Charlie said he would back me all the way on this one. He advised me to go in and yell at Hadley. "Shouting is the only way to make an impression on that guy," Charlie said. "It takes guts, but he'll respect you. Go in there and do it now. I'll back you to the hilt." After Charlie's pep talk, I was ready. I was stalking across the newsroom to give Hadley what-for when I was intercepted by Georgia T. George.

"Can I see you in my office?" she said sternly. Everyone standing nearby assumed she had been delegated to chew me out. That's what I thought, too. She looked so small and fierce. I followed her into her office. She shut the door, another sign trouble was brewing. "Let me guess," she said. "You are on your way to Hadley's office to give him a piece of your mind."

"Yes," I said. "He killed my column. He needs to be confronted."

"And Charlie told you to do that?" she asked.

"Yes, Charlie's very good about advising me on how to deal with Hadley. He's one of my best friends at the paper. He said he'd back me to the hilt."

"Would you like to see what your friend Charlie wrote about you?" she said. "I'll show you." Georgia had a high security clearance, so she could read the memos on the HADLEY desk in the computer system. This was where the upper editors sent reports they could look at, but the deckhands couldn't see.

Charlie wrote this memo to Hadley: "I am very concerned about Francesca's hysterical mood swings. She has become verbally abusive to some of the men on the staff. I believe she has taken a dislike to mature males. She told me she was 'going to give that old goat Hadley a piece of my mind.' I tried to stop her, but if she comes into your office screaming and violent, I recommend she be severely disciplined. These outbursts must be stopped."

For a minute, I didn't say anything. I felt numb. I could hear a strange blank sound in my head like running water.

"He backed me to the hilt all right," I said,

bitterly. "He put the knife right in my back, the self-righteous little sneak. Let me take that sawed-off snake out on the back lot and beat the tar out of him."

"You will do nothing of the kind," Georgia said, and she sounded like Sister Mary Grace, the principal at my grade school. "That is simply another version of what he wants—a show of violence on your part. You are not going to star in the scene Charlie has written for you. You will not touch him. You will not say a word in anger. Do not let him know you have found out about his double-dealing. Now get your coat, get outside, and cool off. Go do some interviews. I do not want to see you in this office the rest of the day."

It was the first of a lot of good advice from my new mentor. But today I was feeling cocky enough with the female impersonator column to discount Georgia's advice. Especially when she wanted to cut my favorite line. "I suggest that you can any mention of Maria, the Ass with Class," she said. "That's the first thing that's going to be cut. It may set off Hadley."

"You know my theory," I said. "I deliberately put in something that he can take out in the first three paragraphs. Then he leaves in the stuff I want."

Nine times out of ten my theory works. This was time Number Ten. Georgia warned me, but I didn't listen. After all, it was a good day. I even finished writing early. I sent the column to Charlie's computer desk at two o'clock, four hours ahead of my deadline. Thirty minutes later, Hadley's secretary, Nelson (Hadley believed male secretaries were classier than females), was at my desk. That meant Hadley was requesting an audience.

"Mr. Harris and Charlie would like to see you in Mr. Harris's office," Nelson said.

"How serious is it?" I asked. If things weren't too bad, Nelson would joke with me. This time he said nothing. Uh-oh.

It was a short trip across the newsroom to Hadley's office. Like walking the plank. Hadley's office looked like a newspaper museum. There were framed front pages going back to World War I. A wooden California job case with my favorite typeface, classic Caslon, designed by Londoner William Caslon in the eighteenth century. Small tools ranging from a pica stick to an eye-gouging copy spike on an ornate green metal base. Hadley even had a Mergenthaler Linotype machine from the late 1890s in his office. The landmark typesetting machine was big as an upright piano. I bet it was a bitch to dust.

The real museum piece was Hadley himself. Hadley longed for the good old days of newspapers, when editors could ignore life's ambiguities. News was clearly defined: accidents, government scandals, crimes against white people, and fires, floods, and other natural disasters. The only sex was in court cases about divorces, contested wills, and paternity suits, and none of these scandals were about the publisher's friends. Women stayed on the women's page.

Women's issues were society parties, bridge clubs, fashion, children, and recipes. Rape, race, sex discrimination, syphilis, suicide, and child abuse were politely ignored, like a fart in church. As for men with tits like women's, you could snigger about them with the boys at the bar, but you didn't write about them in a newspaper.

Hadley was sitting behind his desk. He hadn't taken a chair in his conversation group by the Mergenthaler Linotype machine. Another bad sign. He did not want a friendly chat. Charlie stood alertly beside him. He was so short, his head barely came to the top of Hadley's tall leather chair.

Hadley did the talking. "You have done your best to undermine the management of this newspaper," he said, his face pink with anger.

I thought the editors did a good job of undermining themselves. But for once I didn't answer back.

"This is the second time this month you've tried to sneak smut into a family newspaper," he said, making it sound like I was corrupting little children. "It is bad enough that you write about perverts. But now you're insulting the African American community."

"I am?" I said, genuinely bewildered. "How?"

"Chocolate Suicide," said Charlie, helpfully. He was eager to elaborate. "We read your column and then looked at Jimbo's pictures. This Chocolate person is African American."

"Yes?" I still didn't get it.

Hadley said, "At a time when the leaders of the African American community are demanding that their people be portrayed with sensitivity and dignity, you have featured a sexual deviant. In my newspaper. I am sick of your sick mind."

His voice had grown higher, his face pinker. The guy really was a wimp. In two seconds he was going to start pounding his desk. It's the only trick he knows for looking strong. "I am sick of your smut, smut, smut," he said, pounding his desk until he sent an avalanche of papers to the floor. Naturally, Charlie bent over and picked them up.

"Chocolate Suicide is a self-created work of art, and a performer with great energy and style," I said. "I thought I treated her and the other female impersonators, black, white, and Asian, with dignity and sympathy. But if you're concerned, I can make whatever changes you suggest."

"I am making one change," snapped Hadley. His color turned from delicate pink to dangerous red, and his voice rose to a teakettle scream. "I am killing your disgusting column. Killing it, do you hear? Get another subject by six o'clock and make it a wholesome one. I'm putting you on notice now. I don't want you writing about perverts, smut, or sex. I want family values in my newspaper."

"I'll make sure, sir," said Charlie, and I could swear the little creep was smirking.

I left Hadley's office. The newsroom was

strangely quiet. People were pretending to type and to talk on the phone, but no one looked my way. That meant they heard every word Hadley screamed at me.

I sat down at my desk, dazed and furious. The phone rang. It was Georgia. "He killed your column, didn't he?" she said.

"Yes. You were right. Charlie used it as a chance to run into Hadley's office and start trouble. I know he's the one who got Hadley fired up. Tried a new tack this time—I'm guilty of writing smut AND insulting the African American community."

"That is a new one," said Georgia. "I'll have to watch the little insect. Offending the African American community is the newest newsroom witch-hunt. A few charges of racism and you're in trouble, whether they're true or not."

"I have three hours to come up with another column, and I'm too angry to think straight," I said. "What am I going to do?"

"Something will turn up," she said. "It always does."

She was right about that one, too. When I picked up the phone to make a call I heard the soft *boop boop* sound that means there's a message on my voice mail. It was Burt's wife, Dolores. I hadn't spoken to her in six months, but I remembered her as a salty, hearty woman who talked a blue streak. Now she formed each word slowly, as if she could hardly talk. Her normally cheerful voice was a dull croak. "Francesca. Dolores. It's Burt. He's dead. I hate to

bother you, but I need you to come to the bar.
There's TV people runnin' around all over here.
You know those people. You can talk to them.
Please? For Burt?"

No. Not Burt. The room slipped sideways. I
felt like I'd been kicked in the gut. I just saw him
last night, and he looked fine. I knew he was seventy years old, and a heart attack could happen
anytime at that age, but Burt looked so sturdy.
He never missed a day of work. He was always
there behind his bar, and as long as he was alive,
so was a little piece of my grandparents' neighborhood, the South Side, the world I grew up in.

I knew the old South Side was dying. Some
would say it was already dead. The tough old
Germans who'd lived there were gradually dying
off. The city called them the Scrubby Dutch, a
corruption of "Deutsch," the word for German,
for their maddening habit of cleaning everything. For the Scrubby Dutch, cleanliness wasn't
next to godliness. It was better.

They were hardheaded, hardworking people
with an earthy sense of humor. They staffed City
Hall and ran the shops and saloons. They lived
in small brick houses with neat zoysia grass
lawns. They had character. They *were* charac-
ters. They were my people and I never felt at
home around anyone else. Now the last of them
were Burt's age or better. They were dying or
retiring to Florida or moving into the Altenheim
nursing home. Their children had left for the
suburbs years ago. Their South Side houses
were being bought by people never seen before

on the South Side—young married rehabbers,
gay couples, Asian immigrants, and middle-class
blacks. Those people gave the South Side a new
richness and variety. But some of the newcom-
ers weren't an improvement. They bought South
Side houses and flats cheap, and turned them
into rundown investment properties. These
greedy landlords rented to drug dealers, mug-
gers, and hookers, male and female. The safe,
solid German neighborhoods were disappearing,
especially in the area where Burt and Dolores
lived. Dolores had been after him to move his
bar to the suburbs, but Burt wouldn't leave his
beloved city, no matter how much it changed.

"I was born here, and I'll die here," he'd say.
And so he did. The stubborn South Siders generally did what they wanted, no matter what it cost
them or the people who loved them. I sighed. It
didn't matter that I saw Burt maybe twice a year.
I was crazy about the obstinate old guy. They
didn't make them like Burt anymore.

I had to park two blocks away, there were so
many vehicles in front of Burt's Bar: at least four
police patrol cars parked at odd angles, six unmarked cars, a white police evidence van, an or-
ange-and-white EMS ambulance, and three TV
trucks. They must have picked up the news from
the police scanner. Actually, the TV reporters
and camera people were behaving very well,
considering this was the murder of a news-
worthy figure. They were shooting stand-ups and
footage of the building and interviewing pas-
sersby. Plainclothes officers were doing door-to-

door interviews. Scene commanders—uniformed officers in blinding white shirts—were giving television interviews.

All the cameras swung to the front of the building as the door opened. They were taking Burt out of his bar as I walked up to the brick building. The man who loomed so large in life made a pitifully small bundle in the white body bag. I felt strangely numb watching them take him away. The blackness began closing in on me in an odd honeycomb effect, with red around the edges. Just before I slid down the brick wall to the sidewalk, I heard a voice call me from far away: "Francesca, are you okay?"

That brought me back. The blackness cleared away, and I saw that Homicide Detective Sergeant Mark Mayhew had me by the arm. An old-style homicide detective who looked like his wife bought his clothes on sale at JCPenney in 1977—just before she left him. Mayhew belonged to the new breed. He looked like an artsy monochrome ad in *GQ:* steel-gray cashmere jacket, a pearl-gray sweater so soft you wanted to pet it, perfectly cut charcoal pants. Dynamite tailoring. Decent guy, too.

"I'm a little dizzy. I didn't eat any lunch," I said.

We both knew why I had almost passed out. But Mayhew was a good man, so he didn't remind me. As for me, I would think about it later. Right now, I had to see Dolores. "For some reason, Dolores called me," I said. "She said she needed help with the TV people, but they don't seem to be a problem."

"She probably didn't want to be alone with strangers. It will take a while for her son to get here from way out in Chesterfield," said Mark. "But you know these old krauts—too proud to ask for help straight out."

Mark steered me around the yellow Police Line tape, and inside the bar. I recognized the homey smell of chicken and dumplings, the day's special, still chalked on the board by the cash register. Dolores was sitting in one of the back booths, but the big, robust woman I knew wasn't there. She seemed to have shrunk. Her jolly round body looked flabby. Her face seemed to sag and run, like melting wax.

"I told him and I told him this neighborhood wasn't safe," Dolores said to the two uniformed officers sitting with her. I could tell she'd been repeating this story, like a continuously running tape.

"But he wouldn't listen. He sent me home at one thirty when we stopped serving lunch, we only live a block away, you know, and he said he'd close up. Lunch is over at two and it takes ten minutes to close up. He should have been home by two fifteen. He always is. We reopen at four. He needs his rest in the afternoon, he's not so young anymore. When I didn't hear from him by two thirty I called over here and there was no answer. He could have been on his way home, but I just had a funny feeling, so I called 911 and came running. I found him in the kitchen with my own butcher knife in his back. The stubborn old son of a buck." She began to cry and the cops looked uncomfortable. Then she would wipe her eyes and blow her nose and start the tape again. "I told him and I told him this neighborhood wasn't safe. . . ."

I looked over toward Dolores's domain, her spotless stainless steel kitchen, and the first thing I thought was that the place was a mess and she was going to be really mad. There was a puddle of blood on the waxed floor, and long streaks on the counter and the cream-colored wall. It didn't look like movie blood. It was the wrong color, too red and too bright. Besides the blood there was black fingerprint powder on everything, yellow Police Line tape blocking the entrance to the kitchen, a paper silhouette of a body on the floor, and footprints tracked all over Dolores's shiny clean tile.

Then I realized something else. Burt didn't die of a heart attack. He was murdered. Stabbed in the back, it sounded like, if my dull wits were working.

"How did he die?" I asked Mayhew.

"Stabbed. Several times in the back. With a butcher knife. My guess is the killer got the aorta. If you're pissed off, you can stab anyone and kill them. Whoever did this got a lucky hit along the left side of the backbone. At least Burt died quick."

"Shouldn't there be more blood?" I thought if I kept talking, I might keep from thinking about another murder, a long time ago. There was a lot of blood then, on the walls and the floor and even the ceiling, and some of it dripped off a light fixture. In my dreams, I didn't see the two bodies. I saw that drip.

"Most of the blood's inside the body, in the chest cavity."

"Why would anyone want to kill Burt?" I kept rattling on, hardly taking it in.

"Money. They cleaned out the cash register. It was right after lunch, and the whole neighborhood knew he closed at 2:00 P.M. The killer didn't get that much, either. Took the cash and change in the register—Dolores thinks it was maybe two hundred dollars—but didn't look under the money drawer, where Burt kept the big bills. Missed about seven hundred dollars that way."

"How did they miss that much money?" I didn't think much of the local criminal class, but one thing they wouldn't miss was cash. Even I knew Burt stashed most of his tens, twenties, and fifties under the cash drawer. The local boys would, too.

"Probably got scared off," Mayhew said.

I didn't think someone who would knife Burt in broad daylight would pass up a pile of dead presidents just because they heard a noise.

Also, Burt was a city bartender. That meant he was cautious. When he let out the last lunch customer, he'd lock the door, and he'd never open up for the tough-looking kids in baggy gang clothes who slouched down the street. And if he did, he'd never turn his back on them so he could be stabbed with Dolores's own butcher knife.

Before I could say this, I heard Dolores call my name. "Francesca, honey, is that you?" She'd stopped the tape long enough to notice me. I went over to her table.

"I'm so sorry," I said. "Burt was a good man." I wanted to say something else, something profound or something that could ease her pain. But there was no comfort for Dolores, and there wouldn't be. "He wouldn't listen," Dolores said. "I told him and I told him. . . ." The tape started again.

The two young, sad-faced cops turned her over to me. I sat with her in the booth and held her hand and patted her shoulder and listened to her say the same things over and over until her son Harry arrived from his accounting office in Chesterfield. Dolores and Burt had worked hard to give their kids the best, and all six of them had turned out well. They had nice families and good homes and solid businesses in the safest suburbs. The other grown children would be coming in now, one by one. I handed Dolores over to her son Harry, and she began to cry, hard, harsh sobs that sounded like parts of her were being ripped out. He held her. He knew what to do.

I did, too. I left. I wanted to give Burt one last gift—the obituary he deserved. I wanted to send him off in style. I wanted everyone to know that he was a fine man, and to understand that a well-run bar took diplomacy, discipline, and hard work.

I didn't go back to the newsroom to write the column. I only had two hours until deadline, and I needed quiet. I sat down at my home computer, and I began to remember all the stories about Burt. Hadley would be happy with this column. Burt's life was as wholesome as you could get. He dropped out of high school to go to work in his family's saloon at age sixteen. He fought for his country in World War II. Heck, Burt was such a gung ho patriot, he'd lied about his age and gone into the Navy at age seventeen. He came back with a fistful of medals and married his grade-school sweetheart, and they worked together every day for the next fifty-one years, except for the one-week vacation Dolores made Burt take every August.

I think my favorite Burt story was something that happened two years ago. That was after Burt's Bar became fashionable, and all the local celebrities and politicians started hanging around his bar. Burt had a whole paragraph in *USA Today* as one of the nation's top ten bars. The *Chicago Tribune*, *The Washington Post*, and *People* magazine wrote about him. The BBC interviewed him for a series called *All-American Pubs*.

It didn't seem as though Burt changed a bit once he became famous. Until he told me he'd bought a hot tub. I didn't believe him. So he took me home to his plain brick two-family flat. We walked up that dark old stairway, past the brown three-piece living room suite he bought at the Fair-Mercantile furniture store thirty years ago, through the kitchen with the South Side National Bank calendar, and out to the sunporch.

The sunporch had the usual South Side plants: red geraniums and tall, skinny mother-in-law tongues growing in red Folgers coffee cans, scraggly philodendrons, and a fat new Boston fern that was obviously a Mother's Day present from one of the kids. But instead of the usual sagging slipcovered couches or wicker furniture you find on most city sunporches, there was this giant redwood hot tub. There was a silver wine bucket on a stand next to it, and a thick cushiony rug on the floor.

I couldn't get over it. Somehow, that sybaritic scene didn't go with Burt's stern Scrubby Dutch upbringing. I couldn't imagine Burt and Dolores bobbing around in the steaming tub, sipping white wine. I told him so.

"There's a lot you can't imagine about us," he said, and winked. "You young folks are so stodgy. Think you invented sex. She's still the only woman for me after almost fifty years, and we still have fun, more fun now that the kids have moved out. Besides, the hot tub makes my feet feel good after a day at the bar."

I loved that story. I thought about Dolores, alone now after fifty-one years. I started to cry, but decided to save it for later. Right now, I had work to do. I owed him a good good-bye.

Besides, if I wrote about Burt, I wouldn't have

to think about the other murder. The one that took place when I was nine. I wouldn't have to remember all that blood, dripping, dripping, dripping.

4

I guess I should tell you what half the city knows anyway. It's the reason I started to pass out at Burt's Bar. Burt wasn't the first murder victim I've seen. My mother murdered my father, then shot herself. This happened twenty-eight years ago. I was nine.

It was a big scandal because my parents were supposed to be such fine, upstanding church people. They lived in a suburb called Crestwood, in a split-level house with a carport and, in the front yard, a concrete statue of the Virgin Mary. Dad was a pillar of our parish church, and Mom did a lot of charity work.

The media acted as if Harriet had offed Ozzie. If you were living in St. Louis then, it was all over the newspapers and TV, and was talked about on KMOX radio for almost a week. There was a famous photo of me at their graveside, wearing white gloves and a little blue coat and staring into space. To most people, it is the picture of heartbreak.

If anyone had asked me, I would have told them my parents weren't quite the perfect young churchgoing couple the press painted them to be. Oh, they were religious all right. At least, they spent a lot of time at church. But they both drank too much. Nobody caught them at it, because they were weekend boozers. This brand of drunk can carry on for a lot longer than your ordinary get-smashed-every-night type. Mom and Dad got through the week with a few beers before dinner, and a few drinks when they went out in the evening. But I remember them with a beer or whiskey sour in their hands from Friday night through Sunday, when the hangover hit them like a truck full of bricks. They went to bed early on Sunday night. By the time Monday rolled around, Dad was sitting soberly in his office, and Mom was busily doing good.

They also fought all the time, but they were smart enough to keep the fights at home. They had loud, screaming battles where Mom broke things and Dad cursed and Mom cried and I hid in my room. I was an only child, so I had a room to myself. My mother did it up in pink and ruffles, because I was a girl. Actually, I hated pink AND ruffles. I also hated being a girl.

Everyone thought Mom and Dad were madly in love. In public, she called him Babydoll and he couldn't keep his hands off her. He was always patting her ass and petting her arm and squeezing her shoulders. Wives used to ask their husbands, "Why don't you pay attention to me like that?"

The trouble was Dad couldn't keep his hands off any woman. He played around. I think that's probably what drove her over the edge—his fooling around, plus the drinking. I figured out about his lady friends at age five, when Dee, the divorced redhead (well, orangehead, actually, but the color looked sexy on her) who lived down the street started inviting me to come over and play at her house. Even at age five, I suspected that ladies who wore gold ankle bracelets and that much perfume weren't interested in little girls who asked a lot of questions. Dee bought me a beautiful purple tea set made of real china and let me play with it in her basement rec room, which was a cool turquoise and gray. After I played awhile, pouring tap water into the pot and then into the cups and then serving several pretend friends, Dad would come over to Dee's and take me home. One day I came up out of the rec room early to get more tea water and saw him kissing Dee in a way he never kissed Mom, and I knew Dee didn't give me the tea set because she liked me. I went back downstairs to the rec room and broke every piece in the tea set.

There were other women besides Dee, and they all lived in the neighborhood. All but Dee were married. I usually could tell when one was having an affair with Dad, because she would play up to me, telling me how smart or cute I was, or offering to fix my hair. It made me real

suspicious about women. Men, too. I didn't like
how Dad used me for cover with his ladies. I
never said anything to Mom, because we didn't
get along. I was tall and skinny, and she thought
I was ugly and told me so. Often. I felt kind of
sorry for her. I thought she might have been
happier if she'd had my cousin Linda for a
daughter. Linda had blond hair that went into
soft natural curls. She was graceful and not too
tall. She took ballet lessons and wore pretty
dresses and never got them dirty. She put doll
dresses on kittens. She joined the Girl Scouts
and earned so many merit badges she hardly
had room to sew them all on her sash. Linda was
two years older than me, but I used to fantasize
that maybe our moms got us mixed up on a visit
and my mom took the wrong girl home. Mom
used to dress me in Linda's castoff clothes, but I
never looked as good in them as Linda did.

I never knew how much Mom knew about
Dad's lady friends. Mom was angry a lot. Maybe
she was hungover or maybe she suspected what
Dad was up to with the women. One story will
give you an idea of what she was like, and I'll tell
it because it kinda has a happy ending. I don't
talk about Mom much. I'm not looking for sympathy. It's over. Anyway, I was nine and she'd
been trying to brush my hair for church and it
didn't look the way she wanted and she
screamed, "You're hopeless, I can't do a thing
with you," and she hit me in the face with the
hairbrush, which left a red mark. I got out of

going to church that Sunday. That was the good part. I liked church even less than I liked Mom.

It was shortly after the hairbrush incident that she found Dad in a clinch with Marcy, her best friend, at a New Year's party. Mom and Dad had a huge, screaming fight right in front of thirty people at the party. Those people all told the police about it after the shooting. Mom and Dad had a bunch of fights at home after that. Every time Mom saw Dad, she'd scream insults at him. Once, she called him a lousy lay. I didn't know what it meant then, but it made him mad. He never walked out, though. They stayed together, fighting and drinking. I hid out in my room and tried to stay out of their way.

The next weekend after the party, Marcy's husband Tom put their house up for sale, and the weekend after that they were gone. I heard they moved to California. I thought things would calm down.

The Monday after Marcy and Tom left town, I came home from school and found the kitchen door was open. Mom always kept the side entrance to the house locked. Dad's car was in the driveway. That was strange, too. He rarely came home before five o'clock. The house seemed unnaturally quiet, except for this odd drip, drip sound, like a leaking faucet. There was no one downstairs. I went upstairs. The drip sound came from their bedroom. It was blood dripping off the light fixture. Dad's, I think. He was shot with the old shotgun he kept in the upstairs hall closet, and part of his head was gone. Some of it was on the wall over the bed, by the crucifix with the Palm Sunday palm stuck in it.

I couldn't figure out what happened. Later, the police said that Mom shot Dad, then turned the gun on herself. There was a huge hole in her chest, so it looked like she was wearing a red blouse and lying on a red bedspread, although both were really white. She and Dad looked gray green. People in funeral parlors aren't that color. I saw there was blood all over, but I never got a good look at things because I started screaming and I ran out of the house and Mrs. Marshall, the nosy neighbor lady, caught me as I ran into the street. I think she called the police.

Suicide is a mortal sin in the Catholic Church, and so is murder, so there was a debate in the parish about whether my mother could be buried in consecrated ground with two mortal sins on her soul. But the Church didn't want any more scandal, especially after the *Life* magazine story called "The Pillar Cracks: Wife-Swapping at a Suburban Church." I didn't think Dad was swapping. He just borrowed the wives for a while, and some of them, like Dee the Divorcee, weren't even Catholic. He didn't swap Mom with anybody.

Finally, the priest said no one could know what was in Mom's mind at the time of her death and it was possible she made a valid Act of Contrition at the last moment and was genuinely sorry, so the Church let her be buried next to Dad. I wondered what Mom and Dad thought about that, lying side by side. I used to wonder if their ghosts were screaming at each other when I heard the wind howl on cold nights. Or maybe, now that he couldn't chase other women, they were happy together.

After the double funeral, I went to live with my grandparents in the city. My father was an orphan. These were my mother's parents. Mom was kind of ashamed of them, because they were fat and poor and never got past the fourth grade, and my mother had a diploma from a secretarial college. Grandma and Grandpa had a confectionery on the South Side near Arsenal Street. They sold cold cuts and comic books and penny candy and things people ran out of at the last minute like Campbell's tomato soup for a meat loaf recipe, or milk and bread. They worked six days a week, twelve hours a day and didn't make much money. Everyone felt sorry for me because I went from living in this nice new suburban split-level in Crestwood to a rundown apartment over an old store in the city.

I couldn't tell anyone, but I was happier than I'd ever been in my life. My grandparents liked me. Grandma didn't think I was ugly. She and Grandpa called me Angel. They never hit me, even once. Grandpa bought me glasses and that made me more graceful. I could see where I was going and I quit falling over things. Grandma got new clothes just for me, and I quit wearing Cousin Linda's old things. I started putting on weight and didn't look so gawky, because Grandma liked to fix food for me—pancakes for breakfast, pork chops and fried chicken and gravy for dinner. She made biscuits and peach cobbler and blackberry pie. . . .

"Are you going to eat, or just stare into space?" asked Lyle, calling me back to the present. Lyle Donnegan is the man I love and wish I could live with. I called Lyle after I finished my story on Burt. He liked Burt, so I knew he'd feel bad. He did, too.

"The poor bastard," Lyle said. "That's awful, baby. He was a real gentleman. Are you okay? Come on over."

I could see him there in his wing chair, sipping single-malt Scotch. Women take one look at him and get this dreamy look in their eyes. Guys don't get it. They can't figure out what we see in Lyle. Part of it is the way he moves, as if he knows what he's doing. Part of it is his beautiful clothes. I especially like his navy blazer, made for him by Kilgore, French and Stanbury, the London tailor that sounds like an American law firm. The rest is that Lyle is genuinely interested when he's talking to you, and few women can resist that kind of attention.

He was waiting for me at the door of his house in the Central West End. He had warmed up some tenderloin in the oven. He has this special recipe. It includes fresh ground pepper, but no salt, because he believes salting meat before you cook it makes it tough. He slow-cooks the meat in the oven and it's incredibly tender. I hate kitchens, so I'm a sucker for a man who can cook. Lyle sat me down at his dining room table, and made sure I ate one of his tenderloin sandwiches on rye with hot English mustard before we talked about Burt.

"You and my grandmother have one thing in common," I told him. "You both feed me when I'm upset."

"We try to, but you're not eating. You keep taking that sandwich apart and putting it back together. Are you thinking about Burt?"

"No, I was thinking about my parents' deaths, and how much better my life was after they were gone."

A lesser man would have looked shocked, but Lyle let me talk. I picked up the sandwich, and took a bite to please him. Then I said, "My grandparents had that confectionery, I told you that. I had to help out in the store, but I liked that. After school, a lot of neighborhood kids would come in to buy penny candy. I was a big shot because I got to hand them the paper bag filled with ten cents' worth of Mary Janes, or red licorice whips or candy buttons on paper strips. I also read the comic books first when they came into the shop, before anyone else saw them. I met a lot of interesting people, too."

I could see the customers coming into my grandparents' store. I could hear the bell on the door that announced their entrance:

Mrs. Pennington, who talked about her eight children, except for the one boy who was in juvenile detention for car theft. Everyone *else* talked about him. Mrs. Pennington was always out of bread and milk, no matter how much she bought at the supermarket.

Mrs. Maloney, whose husband drank, and who came in with a black eye every couple of months. She was a tiny, pale woman with feathery hair, like a newly hatched bird. "She always looked scared," I told Lyle. I was warming to the subject. I was warming to the tenderloin, too. Between bites I said, "And poor Mrs. Ritter, who got thinner and thinner, and then one day we read her funeral notice.

"Then there was Old Mr. Brackenseck, who was always looking for something soft to eat because his false teeth hurt. He married the Widow Montini, and lived on her homemade spaghetti—we didn't call it pasta back then—happily ever after. He had this money clip. I'd never seen one before. It was gold, with a dollar sign. He'd slowly peel out each dollar with great ceremony. He kept his change in a coin purse, all wrapped with rubber bands."

"You didn't realize it, but those were your early columns," said Lyle. "You really noticed those people."

"I finally had time to notice. Life was so much calmer. Grandma and Grandpa didn't have screaming fights, although they did argue sometimes. She would call him a stubborn old fool and slam the bathroom door, and then later they'd make up. They didn't drink much, just a beer before dinner. Most nights, their place was very quiet. I liked that.

"The only bad thing about my new life was the way people acted around me. Whenever I went out with my grandparents, there would be this sort of whispery buzz, and I knew people were saying, 'That's the little girl whose mother shot her father and then killed herself. Poor little thing.'

"That's what the nice ones said. The mean ones said this would make me not right in the head and no man would marry me, because there was insanity and suicide in the family. After a while I got used to the buzz, and it died down a bit, too."

"Now there's a buzz that follows you around when you go in a place," said Lyle. "But it's because of your column. Everyone in St. Louis knows you."

That was Lyle. He always put the best interpretation on everything. He was never jealous of my success. I took another bite of the sandwich. I didn't mention the other bad thing—the dreams. Some nights I would dream of that drip, drip, drip sound, but the blood would be dripping on their coffins. On real bad nights, it would be dripping on mine, and I would wake up screaming.

After a few years the drip, drip, drip dreams faded. Now I only get them when things are very bad. I knew I'd get one tonight, because of Burt's murder.

"Hello," said Lyle, "anyone home?"

I realized I was holding the sandwich in midair.

"Francesca, I know you liked Burt, but you only saw him maybe twice a year. His murder reminds you of your parents' deaths, doesn't it?

That's why you're so upset. You aren't here. You're back in Crestwood."

Lyle was right. I'd been wandering around in the past to keep from talking about the present. "Burt wasn't quite a friend, but he was more than a source," I said. "He worked hard all his life, and he never asked for anything."

"Just like your grandparents," said Lyle.

"He did remind me of my grandfather in some ways, I guess. I admired him so much."

"Burt? Or your grandfather?" asked Lyle.

"Both. Oh, Lyle, it was just awful at Burt's Bar." And then I told him about the body bag, the bloody kitchen, and the weeping Dolores. Once again he listened. "Any leads on who did it?" he said.

"The police say it's a holdup gone wrong, but I think it's more than that. I can't imagine why Burt would have let in his killer or turned his back on him."

"Or her," Lyle said. He was always reminding me that sexism swings both ways. "Maybe Burt just made a mistake. We all do, and he was getting old. He got careless."

"Burt was Scrubby Dutch like me," I said. "We're very clean and very good at doing the same thing over and over again. That's why Germans make such good beer. It takes both those qualities."

Talking about Burt's death took away some of the horror. I was glad to have Lyle to talk to. We usually talked on the phone daily. I'd tell him about a column or something interesting I saw and he'd talk about the university. He taught English and did a little freelance writing—but he refused to work for the *Gazette*. Lyle had enough money so he didn't have to work and he said the *CG* delighted in making people miserable. I felt better when we started talking. We were good at that. We were good at loving, too. We did most things well together. Lyle was funny, he was sexy, he could wiggle both ears at once. Sometimes I spent weeks at a time at his town house on Laclede. I liked to tease him that it looked like a men's club, but I liked the marble fireplace, the stained glass, the cozy wing chairs and even the pictures of his rich dead relatives. I think he bought it only because of the huge mahogany wet bar. Then I'd get restless and run home for a few days to my grandparents' place over the store.

Lyle wanted to get married. I didn't. I couldn't marry him. I didn't see anyone else. I couldn't live without him. But sometimes I wanted to be by myself and sleep alone in my bed. Not often, but I could do it if I wasn't married and had a place of my own.

Lyle said I was afraid. That wasn't the reason. I couldn't say the marriage vows. Love and honor didn't bother me. I'd stand by Lyle in sickness and in health and for richer or poorer. It was those other five words that got me: "Till death do us part." When you had my parents, they have special meaning.

"Stay with me," he said, kissing my forehead and my eyelids.

"Not tonight," I said, kissing him back. His beard was nicely scratchy and the blond hair on the back of his neck was soft and fine. Part of me wanted to stay. But even as I kissed him I said, "I need to be alone."

I'm kind of funny that way. When I'm really upset, I like to be alone. I don't like to be touched. I knew that Lyle would try to hold me and love me and he never understands why I freeze up and don't want to be touched when things go bad. He won't say so, but I think it hurts him. I don't mean for it to. So I stay at my place. It's not really my place. I live there, but it's my grandparents' apartment. They died twelve years ago, within a few months of each other. I haven't changed anything.

One of my friends, who is now a decorator in New York, told me their place was a perfect example of Midwest kitsch and ought to be in a museum. I guess that's one way to look at it. I like it because I liked their good, ordinary life. So I kept the beige Naugahyde recliner, the picture of Christ with the eyes that follow you hanging over the Magnavox console TV, the davenport with the flowered slipcover, and my grandfather's bowling trophies. The bathroom has plaster fish blowing three gold bubbles. The kitchen still has the same gas refrigerator with the glass icebox dishes, a gray Formica-and-chrome kitchen set, and my grandmother's Aunt Jemima doll with the Sunbeam toaster under her skirt.

To me, it's home. The only change I made was

to set up my computer and laser printer on the dining room table. But I left on the table pads, to protect the finish. I also killed Grandma's African violets. It was an accident, of course. I forgot to water them when I was with Lyle for two weeks. I was secretly glad when the whole brass cartful died. There's something squishy and hairy about African violets. Grandma's other plants survived, but then philodendrons are the closest thing in nature to plastic.

Lyle put his arms around me, but he could feel me stiffen. Death makes some people feel sexy. They have this mad urge to make love. Not me. I wanted to be left alone. I put my plate in the dishwasher, found my purse, and kissed Lyle one last time. "Please stay," he said, but this time his kiss was cooler as if he already knew my answer. I didn't even have to think about it. "Not tonight." I said. "I need to be alone." Lyle didn't press me, and I appreciated his tact.

After I got home from Lyle's, I stretched out in the beige recliner, pulled my grandmother's brown-and-yellow knitted afghan over me for comfort, as I do sometimes when I have to make a hard phone call, and then I got up the courage to call Ralph. I didn't want him to hear about Burt on the evening news. Ralph was a big fan of Burt's. In fact, he was the one who first introduced me to Burt's Bar. If he was working in the area, he always ate there. Ralph was shocked by the news. I knew how upset he was because he started wheezing and had to use his inhaler while we talked on the phone. We made a date to meet at the wake.

The next day, I checked the *City Gazette* for the funeral notices. Burt would be laid out Monday and Tuesday and buried Wednesday at noon from St. Philomena Catholic Church, a lovely old nineteenth-century city church that looked like a small cathedral.

St. Louis Catholic funerals go on forever. Lyle, who grew up in the North, thinks they are barbaric and lack the simple dignity of a funeral in his Iowa hometown. I think those are indecently quick. After the drama of a St. Louis sendoff, they seem as cold and barren as a northern winter. I got a close-up look when Lyle's mother Vera died and I went to Marshalltown, Iowa, with him. Vera had the funeral she wanted and his aunts insisted upon: a rosary at the funeral home the night before, a funeral service at her parish church the next day, and stingy ham sandwiches and sheet cake in the church basement afterward. There were no flowers but ours. Vera's friends donated money to her favorite missionary society. She had a closed casket at her request. St. Louisans like to get a look at you, and a closed casket usually means something horrible. Like your mother shooting your father, and then herself.

I much prefer the three-day ordeal of a St. Louis funeral. It lets you get used to the idea the person is dead. By the time you finally get to the burial, you're happy to shovel the dear one into the ground and go on living. After the funeral, everyone comes back to your house and there's baked ham or roast beef and hearty heavy food like casseroles and mostaccioli, potato salad and chips, and lots of beer and wine. Then you sit around and talk about the dead person and all the funny things and kind things she did, and for an hour or two she lives again, and you know that she will live in everyone's memories.

Unless your mother shoots your father. Then everyone murmurs something sad and polite, pats your hand, and disappears.

Burt had a rousing sendoff at the old Grand Funeral Home on South Grand, which looks like a twenties movie star's home, all white stucco and red roof tile. The place was packed. They had to open the big double parlor, and there was still a line out to the lobby. All the bigwigs who drank at Burt's Bar sent big expensive rubbery-looking flowers. None of them bothered to come except for Burt's alderman and the Mayor's aide, a fat red-nosed Irishman who ceremonially ate and drank and shook hands everywhere the Mayor couldn't.

The people who turned out were Burt's friends and regulars. Everyone had a Burt story. I found out he lent money to folks in trouble and fed people who were out of work, and had one family eating his chicken and dumplings on the tab for six months straight until the father found work again. It was almost like a party, until the line moved up and I had to approach the casket.

Standing between her two grown-up daughters, Pat and Rachel, was Dolores, in a badly fit-

ting black dress. Dolores never wore black. She
looked like a stand-in who had been hired to
play her. She went through the motions, shaking
hands or standing still for a hug, but she hardly
seemed to recognize anyone.

Her oldest daughter, Pat, steered me to the
massive bronze casket covered with a huge spray
of red roses and white pompons. A red ribbon
said *Beloved Husband* in gold script. Burt was
lying in there, his head on a white satin and lace
pillow, wearing Pan-Cake makeup. My first
thought was that he wouldn't be caught alive
looking like this. His hair was combed funny
and a rosary was wrapped around his strong
hands. He didn't look like he was asleep. Not unless he slept with his glasses on. For some reason, the undertaker laid Burt out wearing his
gold-rim glasses, and they looked ridiculous because his eyes were closed. I kept staring and
staring at him the way I always stare at dead
people in their caskets, trying to get a fix on
them. It looked like Burt, and then it didn't and
then it did again, sort of. It was almost like he
was out of focus.

There was an old woman with frizzy pink hair
and a navy-blue dress with rhinestone buttons
kneeling by the casket. She said to me, "He looks
so young." But he didn't. To me, Burt looked so
dead. As I peered down into the casket, I saw a
bottle of Bud tucked in there, just above his elbow, with a Burt's Bar opener and a bag of Rold
Gold pretzels. One of his kids must have done
that. That's when I began to cry. I tried to stop,

because I wasn't family and I didn't want to make a scene.

I did notice that Burt was smiling, and it looked fairly natural for a dead person. I knew why he was smiling, too. Burt bought the Grand Funeral Plan Special back in 1956, when he was a thirty-year-old man with a young family. The plan was two hundred dollars, or two dollars a week for almost two years. Then Burt had the ultimate revenge. He proceeded to live for another forty years, until two hundred dollars hardly paid the light bill for his wake. It was the final triumph for a frugal South Sider like Burt.

I got up from the kneeler and saw Ralph come into the room. He was late, but he was dressed in his most subdued outfit—clean rehabber duds. He wore jeans and a jeans jacket and a fresh white T-shirt. There was a folding ruler sticking out of his back pocket and an inhaler in his front pocket. He looked sick and sweaty and paler than Burt.

"You look awful," I said, tactfully.

Ralph sounded worse. He started in with a hacking cough that ended with a wheeze.

"Are you going to the doctor?"

"It's just a cold," he gasped, as he reached for his inhaler.

Why do guys hate doctors? I knew it was hopeless to argue with any man about going to one, but Ralph sounded really sick. "Please say you're staying home tomorrow."

"I can't," he said. "I'm trying to finish a house on Utah Place by March first."

I was worried about Ralph. I knew he was taking out the ceilings at the Utah house. Breathing plaster dust was bad for him, even when he wore a face mask.

"At least let me get you a square meal," I said.

"Just a drink to cut the dust," he said.

We couldn't go to Burt's, his favorite hangout. Burt's was closed for the funeral, a black wreath on the door. Instead we went to the Cat's Meow, a little neighborhood tavern. The Cat's Meow was famous for its collection of cats. The bar had hundreds of cat statues: in plaster, plastic, and china. There was a big tiger with a real dried fish in its mouth on the back bar, a cat clock on the wall, and the bar's centerpiece: a painting on velvet of the Pink Panther sitting on the pot. The jukebox was playing something loud and just a little bit country-sad, but customers were laughing and talking. We found two stools at the far end of the bar. Gladys came over to take our order. "You two look like a load of old coal," she said. "Where you been?"

We told her we'd been to Burt's wake. "A darn shame," she said. "Burt was a good man. I'm sorry, too. Drinks are on me." We both wimped it with club sodas.

We didn't stay long. Poor Ralph was sick and wheezy and needed his sleep. He kept reaching for his inhaler. I gave him the bad news about our story on the female impersonators. "Hadley killed it," I told him.

"Why?"

"Hadley claimed it would offend the black community because of Chocolate Suicide."

Ralph rolled his eyes. He'd heard all my Hadley stories. He read a printout of the unpublished column while he played with the straw in his club soda. In four places, he laughed when he read it. I kept count. "You did a good job," he said when he finished the last page. "Your story was funny, but you took the girls seriously. It's the *Gazette*'s loss."

It was our loss, too. But there was no point in saying so. Ralph left. I followed him outside, and drove home in the dreary midnight cold. As I unlocked the door to my place, I heard the phone ringing, then the answering machine catch it. By the time I dropped my purse and flipped on the light, my voice stopped apologizing because I wasn't able to come to the phone, and I heard the caller: "Francesca, it's me, Ralph. Listen, I forgot to ask you something tonight. Guess my brain's not working too well."

It wasn't. His message was long and rambling. Ralph, who had been so tired and quiet in the bar, had gotten his second wind. Now he wanted to talk. His message droned on: "I know for sure you know this guy 'cause you work with him, except work doesn't really describe what he does, does it? At least that's what you always say, ha-ha. Anyway, I'm pretty sure you can tell me if I should do this. Come on, Francesca, pick up. I know you're there."

I was. But it was after midnight. I didn't want to talk. I wanted to sleep. I'd track down Ralph tomorrow, after Burt's funeral. I went to bed and slept with the light on all night. It didn't keep the dreams away. I still heard the dripping, dripping, dripping.

Burt's funeral was the next day. It was chilly and rainy, but I couldn't feel any more miserable than I already did. At the funeral Mass, Burt's six children and fourteen grandchildren sat in the front pews. They were an impressive achievement. His friends filled the church, all the way to the back pews. Burt had had a rich life.

I sat through the Mass in a kind of trance, until I heard the priest say, "The Mass is ended, go in peace." The congregation began to sing:

May the angels lead you into paradise;
May the martyrs come to welcome you
And take you to the holy city. . . .
May the choir of angels welcome you.
Where Lazarus is poor no longer,
May you have eternal rest.

I tried to imagine Burt, in a clean apron and a white shirt and tie, being led into heaven by angels. I wondered if eternal rest would suit him. Burt always enjoyed working.

At the grave site, it was cold and damp, but the rain stopped for a little while. The family sat on folding chairs under a white canopy. The rest of us stood behind them. The priest said some prayers. The service seemed so dignified and comforting, I wished I could believe it. The final prayer seemed a warning to people like me:

"By dying you opened the gates of life for

those who believe in you. Do not let our brother
be parted from you, but by your glorious power
give him light, joy, and peace in heaven, where
you live forever and ever."

Amen. The prayer was full of hope, but I was
thinking of another funeral. There was no hope
at that one. No one knew what to say or do, or
how to feel. Very few of my parents' friends were
at the graveside. The ones who were looked sick
and shell-shocked. It was mostly strangers, reporters and photographers, trying to get a look
at the two caskets and at me.

Burt's funeral was different. I saw real sorrow
on people's faces. They would miss Burt. I knew
I would. The rain had started up again while the
priest was praying. I could hear it on the canopy
overhead. Dripping, dripping, dripping.

5

I woke up from a nightmare I couldn't quite remember. My mouth felt dusty as an old doormat and someone had wiped their feet on my tongue. I'd had another bad night after Burt's funeral. I was tired, but I didn't sleep much. When I finally did fall asleep, I had bloody dreams mixed with real images of Burt's body bag and blood-puddled kitchen. At 7:00 A.M. I finally gave up and got up, took a shower and went to my office. I'm not talking about the *City Gazette*. I have a desk and a phone at the newspaper. I stop by regularly to pick up my mail and irritate my editor, Charlie. Sometimes, I even write a column on the paper's computer. But it's not really a place to work—not the kind of work I do.

My real office is Uncle Bob's Pancake House. I have breakfast there five or six days a week. My readers know that's where to look for me. They come by to tell me stories or leave messages or packages. I love the big old brown booths and the yellow paper place mats that double as menus.

I tried to keep my readers away from the *Gazette*. God forbid if they should try to get through the miserable *CG* phone system—I lost a lot of good stories until I finally paid for and put in my own answering machine at the *Gazette*. And bad things happened to good people who actually talked to a *CG* reporter or editor. Most were rude, and proud of it. I still remember Jasper, a vile-tempered city desk reporter, barking on the phone at a hapless reader, "Lady, I don't give a damn about your so-called hot tip. What are you calling me for?" She hung up in tears. He bragged about it.

My editor Charlie begrudged the time I spent at Uncle Bob's. No matter how many stories I brought back from there, he still thought I was goofing off. He didn't mind if the male reporters spent the afternoon at a bar. But Charlie didn't think big-city columnists should hang around pancake houses. He called my time there "schmoozing." He didn't understand how much work it took to get people to relax and talk—or how hard it was for me to be charming, or sometimes just civil, to the constant parade of strangers who stopped at my table with their stories, comments, criticisms, and complaints. There were mornings when I felt surly and impatient and I had to work hard to hide it. You don't get columns by being snippy and difficult.

Because Uncle Bob's was my office, I kept it

separate from my home life. I almost never brought Lyle here, though he loved the Uncle Bob's omelets smothered with ketchup and onions. Besides, we never got through a meal at Uncle Bob's without someone stopping by to talk with me.

If you write a city column, Uncle Bob's is the perfect place to keep an unofficial office. For one thing, a lot of City Hall types eat there: lawyers from the Prosecutor's office, aides from the Mayor's office, aldermen, city workers, clerks. You can hear some interesting things going on in the next booth. I got one of my best columns because I heard a street department worker complaining that during the snowstorms they had orders to shovel the Mayor's street first, before they cleared anything else.

For another thing, Uncle Bob's always had an interesting mix of city life. Some of the clientele wore tattoos that didn't wash off. Members of local crime families cut deals in the window booths, while the waitresses poured coffee and tried not to listen. There were cops and the people they arrested, salespeople, theater people, church people, and anyone else who needed a grease fix.

You did not go to Uncle Bob's for high-fiber, low-fat food. Uncle Bob's served pancakes any way you could think of, and a few ways you couldn't, like pancake-and-egg sandwiches. But some time ago I started ordering one egg scrambled and one piece of wheat toast. That became my usual, although the cooks hated it. Especially

Tom, a handsome man the color of his own coffee. "You eat like an old lady," Tom chided me, and tried to tempt me with a plate of Belgian waffles or his special fluffy three-egg omelet. But I stuck to my guns, and my usual.

For regulars, Uncle Bob's followed the routine of the best Midwest coffee shops. When my car pulled into the lot, Tom the Cook waved hello out the kitchen window, then dropped my egg on the griddle. By the time I had my coat off and was sitting down at the booth, Marlene had the plate in front of me. Uncle Bob's waitresses were not named Nedra or Heather and they were not waitressing to get through grad school or acting classes. They were pros, quick with the coffeepot and the snappy comeback.

Marlene was a generous woman—she was made along generous lines and she was generous to her friends and customers. She was strong, too. She never used a tray. She could balance six full platters on her arms, an accomplishment that fascinated me. She also managed another balancing act: she could balance a job, night school, and the duties of a single parent. Her ex walked out years ago and left her with a two-year-old girl. When her daughter was eight, Marlene felt she could leave the child with her grandmother three nights a week. She went back to school, and now she was finishing her junior year—with honors. I didn't know how she did any of it, but I admired her.

When Marlene and I first met, we regarded each other warily. We weren't sure we liked each

other. After six months, we discovered we had
the same slightly warped sense of humor, although hers was a lot quicker in the morning
than mine. I am not a morning person. She raz-
zes me about this all the time. Even at seven
thirty her complexion looked rosy and her black
curls looked crisp.

"Your usual," Marlene said, pouring me a cup
of decaf coffee and setting my scrawny egg down
in front of me. "Yum, yum," she said sarcastically. "I don't know why you bother to order
something like that. Any idiot could make it at
home."

"Not this idiot," I said. "I come here because I
like the way the staff treats me. At any other restaurant they fawn all over me, which is bad for
my character. Anyone looking for me?"

"Yeah, Roberta left a message that she'd stop
by this morning. She has a story for you. And
speaking of sucking up, are you going to order
any real food after you eat that scrawny egg, or
are you just going to sit there and suck up coffee?"

"I'll suck coffee," I said.

I might even get to finish breakfast before
Roberta arrived. I did a lot of interviewing at
Uncle Bob's. I wrote a column that either was
funny or spilled some city secret, and for either
kind, people needed to feel comfortable. At Uncle Bob's, the booths were as soothing as a
grandmother's lap. The food was comfortable,
too. Diners never had to ask "What's that?" at
Uncle Bob's. This was homey food, either sugary

or fried, or both. Besides, the prices were so cheap I could afford to pick up the tab even with my stingy *CG* expense account.

I was still staring at my cooling coffee when Roberta came in. I waved to her to join me. "I'd hoped you'd be here," she said, sliding in the seat.

"Her body is," said Marlene, pouring more coffee. "I can't vouch for her mind."

Roberta had given me several stories at Uncle Bob's. She looked like an ordinary woman with home-permed hair, an unstylish blue wool coat, and a knobby knit cap. You could find a dozen like her at Hampton Village Shopping Center. But to me, Roberta was one in a million. I thought she was one of the bravest women I knew. Three years ago, Roberta was a home-maker. Jim, her muscular, balding husband, worked in construction. She enjoyed staying home with their two young children, a three-year-old boy and a girl in grade school. She liked the PTA and her volunteer work. She sewed, worked in the garden, and made crafts. I used to tease her that she was a throwback to 1956, but her contentment was obvious.

Then one night Roberta came home from a PTA meeting to find her husband of twelve years packing his suitcases. Jim said he wanted a divorce. He was leaving her for another woman. Roberta had no idea that Jim was seeing someone else. Jim said his wife-elect wanted children and he really couldn't afford child support for their two if he started a new family. He was leav-

ing Roberta the house and two thousand dollars
in the bank. That was it. Jim walked out.
Roberta was dismissed. Fired from their marriage. Their children didn't exist.

The waitresses at Uncle Bob's found Roberta
a good lawyer—the same one they'd used for
their divorces. He pursued Jim for two years,
from state to state and court date to court date,
until Jim understood he had some responsibility
to his first family. Jim paid his child support
sporadically, and not until the judge placed him
in contempt. But he paid. Meanwhile, Roberta
got a job working at a discount store. If she
made twelve thousand dollars a year, I'd be surprised. But she kept the house spotless and her
children beautifully dressed. Roberta haunted
the garage sales and resale shops to buy them
the same brands their classmates wore.

She was never bitter. She never bored you
with nasty stories about her ex. She set about
methodically building a new life. The effort took
its toll. She gained eighty pounds. She weighed
close to two hundred now. Roberta was sensitive
about her weight. She didn't buy herself pretty
things or go out. Her friends thought it was
some sort of self-imposed mourning for her ex-
husband. They also thought he wasn't worth it.

Finally two Uncle Bob's waitresses, Jean and
Sue, persuaded Roberta to go out with them.
Saturday, they'd gone to McGurk's, an Irish bar
in Soulard. That was an old redbrick neighborhood deep in the city, known for its restaurants
and bars.

"I haven't been out much since Jim left," Roberta told me. "I had quite a night. I'll tell you my story if you won't use my name."

I agreed. Roberta ordered blueberry pancakes and ham, and Marlene took my plate. While Roberta talked, I took notes on the back of my Uncle Bob's place mat.

"I didn't feel like going out," she said. "I never do. But Jean and Sue wanted me to hear the Irish band. I got my mother to watch the kids. When we got to McGurk's and I heard the music and saw the Saturday-night crowd, I started feeling pretty good. Maybe my friends were right—I shut myself in the house too much.

"While I was listening to the band, my friends wandered off. Jean went to the bathroom. Sue went to the bar to get our drinks. I was standing there by myself having a good time. Then this big, fat redneck walked up to me and said, 'You know, if you dropped a little of that weight, you'd be able to get you a man.'"

I looked at Roberta. I couldn't believe anyone would be so rude. Her face stayed blank. "What did you say?" I asked.

"Nothing," Roberta said. "I could have kicked myself. I should have kicked him. But instead I just let myself be insulted. I know I'm heavy, but this guy was no Chippendale. He had a huge beer belly. His stomach hung out the front of his jeans. His underwear hung out the back."

"A skink!" I said. "That's what we used to call guys whose underwear showed."

Roberta grinned, and speared another piece

of ham. "I could see this guy's crack when he turned around and he's making remarks about MY appearance. But I was too stunned to say anything, so he kept talking. He said, 'You have a pretty face. It's a real shame you don't have a body to go with it.'

"I should have said I cultivate my weight to keep people like him away. But I couldn't say anything. I just stood there. I couldn't speak or move. It was like he turned me to stone. Then I felt an arm go around me. A muscular man's arm. And what a man. God, he was gorgeous. Like a movie actor. Six feet five at least, with dark curly hair and a deep voice. He even smelled nice.

"He said to Beer Belly, 'Are you talking to my wife?'

"Beer Belly said, 'Irk!'

" 'Well, don't,' said the gorgeous man.

"Beer Belly disappeared into the crowd. He was gone, like a bad smell after you open the window. The gorgeous man smiled at me and said, 'Don't buy in to that.' Then he was gone, too."

Roberta still looked a little dreamy after her encounter. "I think I've seen an angel," she said.

"I think you've seen a real man," I said. "There are some around."

"That's what my friends tell me," said Roberta, as if maybe she was starting to believe them. She put on her ugly knit cap, designed to ward off any man, good or bad. She slipped on her coat and went off to work.

Her story was a haunting one, and would make a good column. I kept thinking about her "real man." I knew one of them, too. It was now 8:30 A.M. I drove over to Lyle's house. I could tell he was awake. The front curtains were open to let in the morning sun. I had a key, but I rang the doorbell to give him some warning. I could smell fresh-brewed coffee. Lyle came into the hall freshly showered, wearing his big fluffy white robe.

"Hi," I said. "I missed you."

"I missed you, too," he said. He didn't say anything else, and I didn't want him to. He began kissing me. His lips were soft and warm and slightly rough and tasted of strong coffee. We kissed all the way up the stairs to his bedroom.

Afterward, I fell into a deep restful sleep, with no bloody dreams. When I woke up at 11:00 A.M., Lyle wasn't in bed. I could hear him in his office, typing on his old IBM PC-XT. The keys on the ten-year-old computer made an odd hollow *thock thock* sound. I felt good, except my left arm was numb. That's because Lyle's twelve-pound gray tomcat, Montana, was sleeping on it. I moved the cat. Monty purred and stretched. So did I. Then I showered, picked up my clothes off the floor, kissed Lyle good-bye and went to the office. It was a good day after all. I had a man who loved me. I had a column before noon. What more could I want?

Well, asbestos gloves for my mail, for starters. There was another letter from the Aryan Avenger, and this time I didn't laugh it off. Okay,

I did sort of snicker when I read the envelope. This one was for "Francesca Whore, *City Gazette* Toilet Paper." The mailroom had not marked it "Addressee Unknown," but sent it on to me. Thanks a lot, fellas.

Inside was a poem, and it was nasty:

> *Heard your bartender Burt*
> *Got himself hurt.*
> *The knife was red.*
> *The JewBurt was dead.*

Where did the Aryan Avenger get the idea that Burt was Jewish? He was buried from St. Philomena Catholic Church. Must be his last name. Burt was named Meyer. A lot of German Jewish people have that name, but so do lots of German Christians. The phone rang, and I set the letter down on my desk to study it later.

Once the phone started ringing, it wouldn't quit. The minute I finished one call, it rang again. The calls got weirder and weirder. It had to be a full moon. The first call was from an anguished-sounding woman. I couldn't tell anything about her except she seemed older and fairly educated.

"Pleeeeze, you must help me," she said, and began crying.

"What's the matter, ma'am?"

"I am the victim of a government conspiracy. The government is holding my daughter hostage. I will give you the whole story."

When you hear those words, you know it's not Deep Throat on the line with your Pulitzer prize.

Some poor soul hasn't been taking her lithium. "Can you tell me what's happening?" I said, cautiously.

"You won't turn me in? You won't give them my name?" Now she sounded frightened.

"No, ma'am."

"My daughter is being held captive by government scientists at Southern Illinois University."

Yep, definitely low on lithium. SIU is a staid commuter college. "I don't think SIU would be involved in something like that, ma'am."

"Please, help me. She's being held captive and forced to have sex with German shepherds."

"How old is your daughter?" I asked.

"Forty-five," she said.

"Listen, there's a lot to be said for a German shepherd. He won't leave the seat up or drop his socks by the bed. And shepherds rarely come home drunk."

I was sorry the minute I said it. The woman's problem may have been imaginary, but her pain was real. I had no right to make light of it. She didn't get angry at me. She sounded hurt, and that made me feel worse. "Please, can't you help me?" she said. She was begging.

"I'm sorry, ma'am. It's not the kind of story I do."

"Can you give me the name of someone who would do the story?"

I disliked several people enough to sic this woman on them, beginning with Charlie. But it wasn't fair to her. Charlie may have deserved her, but she didn't deserve him. "No, ma'am, I don't. I'm sorry. Maybe you could put your story in a letter and send it to the city editor."

"Pleeeze," she began wailing. "Pleeeeze. Help me."

I couldn't. I was sorry, and I said so. Then I quietly hung up. I automatically reached for my coffee cup and took a swig. Ugh. It tasted like old tennis shoes boiled in liquid shoe polish. It was left over from yesterday. The only thing worse than newsroom coffee is old cold newsroom coffee. Before I could get some fresh, the phone rang again. This time it was a man. He sounded angry.

"I want to talk to you about that stupid fucking column you wrote," he said.

"Er, which column was that, sir?"

"The one you did August eighth," he said. "You got your facts wrong." August? This was February. Surely there should be a statute of limitations on raging readers.

"What was the column about, sir?" I try to handle people with complaints, no matter how crazy, before they call Hadley. If the guy was a major advertiser, or related to one, Hadley might make me apologize, even if nothing was wrong. When I finally calmed the guy down, I discovered my error—I didn't mention his product. He'd invented a new pool toy, and I'd done a story about some of the wackier things floating around local pools.

"You mentioned all those out-of-town guys and said nothing about a local person, nothing!" he fumed. "I've invested thirty thousand dollars in this goddamned invention. It's the new pet rock, but not one store will carry it. It's all your fault." I thought he should spend a few hundred on charm school lessons. Instead I told him to send me some information about his invention.

"Fuck you, it's too late now. It's February," he screamed, and hung up on me.

I put down the receiver cautiously. I checked to see if the phone was glowing or something. Maybe someone put my number by the pay phones at the state mental home on Arsenal Street. Maybe I should just hang it up, phonewise, and not pick it up anymore. Let voice mail catch the next call.

The phone rang again. "Third time's a charm," I told myself stupidly, and picked it up.

It was another upset person, but I couldn't understand this man enough to find out if he was angry or anguished. He was crying and talking at the same time, and the sounds came out as a series of gulps, squeaks, and sobs. Finally, he was calm enough to talk slowly. "Francesca, it's Jamie," he said.

Jamie was Ralph the Rehabber's friend. They used to be lovers, but after a few years their romance mellowed into a deep friendship. Jamie found a nice young doctor to live with. Ralph found a nasty old drag queen. But Ralph and Jamie still cared for each other, and kept in touch. If Jamie was calling, something must be wrong with Ralph.

"He's sick," I said before Jamie could say anything else. "I knew he shouldn't be taking out plaster ceilings with that cold. He was hacking and wheezing. He has pneumonia, doesn't he? He had an asthma attack and you had to take him to the hospital. He's in intensive care."

I was describing the most benign of the possible disasters, so Jamie wouldn't tell me the worst. I knew the worst. I could hear it in Jamie's voice. But it wouldn't be true until he said it. That's why I kept talking.

Finally, he interrupted me. "Francesca," he said gently, "Ralph's dead." His voice wobbled, but he went on. "He had an asthma attack in the house he was rehabbing. No one was around to help him. The police think he died sometime yesterday morning. His mother didn't hear from him last night and got worried, because she knew he was sick and he'd promised to call her. She called me early this morning and asked me to check on him. I didn't find him at home, so I went to the house on Utah Place. I . . . I found him."

Jamie's carefully controlled composure fell away, and he began sobbing, harsh rusty sobs. I find men's tears more terrible than women's, because many men aren't used to crying.

"It was horrible," Jamie said. "I went around to the backyard. Ralph usually kept the kitchen door open, so he could run back and forth to his truck. I could hear the radio on upstairs— K-SHE blasting 'Stairway to Heaven.' But I didn't hear Ralph banging on the ceiling with his crowbar, bashing out chunks of old plaster in time with the music. He loved doing that. Called it Ralph's Greatest Hits. Said it was the best part of the job."

I laughed. There is still a lot of little boy in Ralph. Correction. There was.

"I went upstairs," Jamie said. "There were drop cloths down over the floors, and the staircase, woodwork, and floors were covered with thick gray plaster dust. Gravel-sized chunks of old plaster crumbled underfoot. I found Ralph in a room that had primrose wallpaper. He was lying on his back on the floor near his ladder, with hunks of plaster and drifts of dust all around him. There was a bloody cut over one eye. Ralph was slate-gray, almost blue. I knew he was dead, just by that color. He didn't go peacefully. He'd ripped off his face mask and clawed at his chest for air."

I shuddered to think of Ralph, who looked so cool and aristocratic, fighting frantically to breathe. He was so scared in December when the asthma attack sent him to the hospital. I remembered he never went anywhere without his inhaler after that.

"Didn't his inhaler work?"

If I asked calm, reporter-type questions, I would think calm, reporter-type thoughts, instead of picturing my friend gasping like a fish flopped out of an aquarium.

"He didn't have it in his pocket."

"Ralph always had his inhaler. Always. He never forgot that asthma attack last winter. He said it felt like a big rock was crushing his chest.

He kept inhalers everywhere. He even had one hanging on his ladder. What about that one?"

"It wasn't there."

"Something's wrong, Jamie. Ralph always had inhalers around."

"Nothing's wrong," Jamie said. "Ralph was sick and used them all up. He didn't have time to go to Walgreens for more."

"For that, Ralph would make time."

Jamie stayed silent, which is how he gets when he disagrees with you but doesn't want to fight. He was right. There was no point in arguing. A debate wouldn't bring Ralph back.

"What can I do to help?"

"Can you get Lucy and bring her over to his mother's house? She's parked on McDonald, in back of the Utah Place job."

"Sure." Lucy was Ralph's red truck, named for his favorite redheaded actress, Lucille Ball. The truck definitely had personality.

After a few more words I can't remember, we hung up. I did remember Ralph's message on my answering machine. The one I'd forgotten to return yesterday. Ralph had a question for me the night of Burt's wake, but I wouldn't pick up my phone. I was too tired to talk to my friend. I told myself I'd get back to him the next day, but I didn't. I was distracted by Burt's funeral and the column I had to write. I didn't have time to call Ralph back. Wouldn't have to worry about that now, would I? He would never bother me again. Well, I wasn't going to cry a bunch of useless tears. I was going to help him the one way I could. I called Lyle so he could follow me when I drove Ralph's truck to his mother's. Lyle said, "Hello?"

I burst into tears.

Now I sounded like Jamie: I was sobbing and gulping and trying to tell Lyle about Ralph's awful end. Finally, I pulled myself together enough to make Lyle understand that I needed to deliver Ralph's truck to his mother's house.

"Wait there," Lyle said. "I'll come by the paper and pick you up. You're in no shape to drive right now anyway."

I dried my eyes with an old Kleenex I found at the bottom of my purse and looked around my department. It was two o'clock, and the neighboring desks were empty. The staff was still at lunch. Nobody had seen me crying. Good. It was bad for my image. Now if they saw my red eyes, they'd think I was hungover or just plain surly. Much better. I reached for my briefcase, and knocked over the dregs of the day-old coffee on my desk. It ran all over the letter from the Aryan Avenger. The black letters smeared over the SS lightning bolts. The phone started ringing. I left it all—the coffee-soaked papers and the crazy ringing phone—and went outside to wait for Lyle.

He picked me up in front of the building in Sherman, his gigantic '67 gold Chrysler. The car was as big as a living room. The first time I drove Sherm I thought there was something wrong with the gas gauge. It kept going down. Sherman was a gasaholic. He was also a magnificent vintage car. When he rumbled down the street, smaller vehicles got out of his way, and larger ones looked at him with respect. But the best thing about Sherman was his bench seats. I don't know why they quit making car seats so you could snuggle up with the driver. I slid all the way over and kissed Lyle on the ear. He had the softest ears, like suede.

"How are you?" he said, and one look told him I was taking my loss hard.

"Poor Ralph," Lyle said. "Poor you. This is awful."

It was. I knew it was bad, because I didn't feel anything. Just an odd floating sensation, like I was watching myself outside myself, behind a glass wall.

I told Lyle what I knew about Ralph's death. By that time, we had turned onto Utah Place. I think Utah is one of the prettiest streets in the city. Handsome old houses line a wide grassy center parkway planted with graceful trees and gardens. The houses were built around 1904, the time of the St. Louis World's Fair, when the city was at its zenith. There was talk about moving the nation's capital out of that dismal swamp, Washington, D.C., to a successful city like St. Louis.

The houses here were built for the city's prosperous Germans—doctors, lawyers, and businessmen—and the brick-and-stone homes were as solid as their owners. European craftsmen had lavished their talents on the interiors. Some houses had hand-carved staircases and ten-foot stained-glass windows. The one Ralph was working on had rich dark woodwork like black satin. He delighted in the home's odd luxuries: a built-in dining room cabinet with art-glass side panels, a bedroom fireplace with dark green glazed tiles.

"Ralph worked on that house," I said, pointing to a big redbrick with a white stone porch.

"Where's his truck? Why isn't it parked out front?" asked Lyle.

"One of the neighbors got snippy about him parking it on Utah. She said it lowered property values."

"Why didn't he tell her to go to hell?"

"He thought she might hire him to rehab her place."

We turned the corner at Spring and headed for McDonald. It was a pleasant street, but nowhere near as grand. It was lined with plain brick homes and no-nonsense flats. I spotted Lucy, Ralph's truck, immediately. I used to call Lucy his running joke. She did run, too, no matter how hot or cold the weather. But Lucy looked like a refugee from the wrecker. The paint was faded red dotted with gray primer patches. The radio antenna was a bent coat hanger. There was a crack in the windshield and a deep dent in the passenger door. The dented door didn't shut properly, so Ralph had looped a rope around the handle.

Now there seemed to be something else wrong. Lyle saw it first. "What's with the window on the driver's side?" he said. He parked Sherman and we walked over for a closer look. Someone had broken Lucy's window. Ice-chips of glass glittered on the front seat.

"Damn. They broke into Ralph's truck," I said. "That's low, robbing a dead man."

"They didn't get much," said Lyle. "His radio is still there. Did he keep any money in the truck?"

"Never. He wouldn't even leave his tools in the truck."

It was hard to tell if the truck had been ransacked. I saw papers scattered all over, but Ralph wasn't too neat. He used Lucy as his office, and kept her filled with order forms, contracts, and receipts that slid off the seat every time he slammed on the brakes. He also used the truck as his Dumpster. In with the office papers were old White Castle hamburger wrappers, Coke cans, and Lee's fried chicken bags. Ralph's truck was a rolling landfill.

An older neighbor was peeping through her blinds at us. I went over and knocked on her door. When she heard what was wrong, she called the police. A squad car arrived quickly, but the two officers were clearly bored. One was fat and black and had a face like a wrinkled brown bag. The other cop was white, and young enough to still have peach fuzz. His radio made staticky sounds until he turned it down. I told them that the truck belonged to a dead man, but they weren't too interested. Ralph had died of asthma. I said I'd check with his mother, but nothing seemed to be missing, not even the ra-

dio. The cops filed a report and told me there
was no point in checking for fingerprints—the
damp, dirty surfaces wouldn't take them. I didn't
know if that was true or they were lazy, but I did
know they weren't going to bother. They left. I
began brushing glass off the seat.

Lyle spread a large red towel on the seat.
"That should protect you from the smaller
pieces," he said. "It's an old gym towel I found in
Sherman's trunk." Sherman's trunk was like a
magician's hat—Lyle could pull the most amazing things out of it. I wouldn't have been surprised if he'd also produced six colored silk
scarves, a white rabbit, and a pair of doves.

I drove the truck, and Lyle followed in Sherman. I was glad he was there. Lucy bucked and
shimmied all the way, and twice died at red
lights. I knew Ralph's death meant the end of his
beloved red truck, too. Only he could make Lucy
respond.

Ralph's father took off years ago, but his
mother, Billie, lived in an elfin brick house near
Hampton. It looked like a Black Forest hide-
away: a neat square of yard with a freshly
painted white birdbath, a dark door with a
rounded top and a little white stone gable. Inside, all four rooms were crammed with friends
and family. Some were weeping and hugging,
some were laughing and talking, some drinking
and arguing.

Ralph's mother sat dazed and dry-eyed at the
kitchen table, which was covered with casserole
dishes and coffee cakes. I could smell coffee

perking, but most people were drinking cans of Busch or wine coolers, iced in a big metal tub in the kitchen.

A woman with her gray hair in a bun and a neat gray dress stood protectively near Billie like a bodyguard. I'd always thought Ralph's mother looked slender and years younger than her actual age of fifty-nine. Now Billie's slenderness seemed shriveled. Her silky blond hair was like straw and the light was gone from her gray eyes. She had become an old woman overnight.

"I'm so sorry," I said.

She patted me absently, as if I were the neighbor's dog.

"I hate to trouble you further," I said, "but someone broke into Ralph's truck."

"Serves 'em right," Billie said. "He never kept nothin' in there but papers and trash. He even got the radio from a junkyard for ten bucks. My boy was resourceful." Then she seemed to stare straight ahead, at some place I couldn't see and couldn't go. I left the keys on the table. Her gray bodyguard told me that Ralph would be laid out Saturday and Sunday and buried Monday. I made my way to the living room, where Lyle was in animated conversation with a guy who had a panther tattoo and a biker vest. They were talking about Harleys versus BMW bikes.

Suddenly, I was very tired. I could hardly keep my eyes open. Lyle walked me to Sherman, and I slept on his shoulder on the drive to his house. I wanted to be with him tonight. He helped me to his bed and kissed me on the forehead. "Sleep, baby," he said.

But I couldn't sleep. Now, in Lyle's comfortable bed, I was wide awake and was afraid of the dreams I would have. Lyle wrapped his arms around me protectively. He felt warm and solid, but it didn't help. I didn't feel safe. I kept the lights on, but the dreams came anyway when I finally fell asleep after three.

In my dream, I went up that dusty staircase. I could hear the plaster chunks crunching. I could see my friend Ralph lying on that filthy floor, his hair coated with gray plaster dust so he looked like the old man he'd never be. He was gasping, strangling, for air. His face was the color of slate. He clawed at his chest, as if he could tear it open and let the air in. Blood dripped into the dust from a cut on his forehead. He tried to breathe, but he couldn't. I could hear him wheezing as he fought for air. I could feel his panic and see his frantic, futile efforts.

I woke up, wet with sweat. It was a horrible nightmare. Then I realized this was Ralph's nightmare, too. For him, it had come true.

6

She slithered into the room wearing a black picture hat the size of a wagon wheel and a tight black sheath dress cut in a deep V front and back. Her lips were bee-stung. Her breasts were inflatable. She carried a single red rose and a black leather purse with a gold clasp like my aunt Martha used to have.

I couldn't figure out if she was Blanche Du-Bois in *A Streetcar Named Desire* or Norma Desmond in *Sunset Boulevard*, or some combination of the two. But I did know she was a he. By day, he was a certified public accountant who worked in an office tower in conservative Clayton. By night, he was a female impersonator. Norma Blanche was one of several drag queens who showed up in costume at Ralph's wake to pay tribute to their friend.

The drab little South Side funeral home had never seen such magnificence—or such makeup. I wished some of his friends had worked on

Ralph a bit. He looked awful, even for a dead
person. His long hair looked like it had been
moussed with Crisco. His slate-gray color
showed through too-pink makeup. To give Ralph
a more natural color, the funeral home had put
tall torch lights with pink bulbs alongside the
casket. The lights made Ralph the color of a veal
chop in a cheap butcher shop.

His mother, Billie, had tried to make her boy
look good for his last public appearance. She'd
given the funeral director his favorite outfit, the
white pirate shirt, and the black leather vest and
pants, and the chains. But whoever dressed him
didn't quite know where to hook the chains or
how to arrange the leather, and poor Ralph
looked uncomfortable instead of unconven-
tional. I hoped if the angels led him into Paradise they'd fix those chains first. It was the only
way he'd find eternal rest.

Speaking of uncomfortable, there was Ralph's
only other relative, his older brother. Jonathan
was a lawyer. He was a Brooks Brothers poster
boy—I swear even his stingy little ears were
button-down. The only leather on that boy was
his tasseled loafers. Jonathan stood next to his
wife, Rebecca, a dumpy wide-assed blonde who
wore a navy suit with a pussycat bow, a perfect
pageboy, and a look of perpetual constipation.
Worse, Rebecca had on short white gloves. I'd
bet the rent she didn't have them for fashion, but
for fear she might catch some disease from
Ralph's friends. She didn't have to worry. They
didn't want to get near her.

Jonathan and Rebecca stood on the opposite side of the casket, as far away from Billie and Ralph's flamboyant friends as they could get without moving to another viewing room. Jonathan and Rebecca radiated disapproval. This made Ralph's friends edgy, so some of them camped it up, which made Jonathan and Rebecca look down their bony noses even more. Jonathan never forgave Ralph for coming out. He was embarrassed to have a gay brother. He thought Ralph should have shut up and pretended he was straight. Cover-ups didn't bother Jonathan. He'd been pretending to be human for years.

The whole wake was a bad scene. Ralph's mother was so tranqued she could hardly talk. And Bambi, the three-hundred-pound drag queen Ralph loved, who was always conspicuous, was now conspicuous by her absence. She was the one person Ralph would have wanted there, weeping and throwing herself on his coffin. Instead, I suspected Bambi was throwing herself on her hunky muscle man, wearing one of the green outfits Ralph made for her.

A young person's funeral is always awful anyway. The grief is raw because a short life seems so unfinished. Burt's passing was sad, but he had accomplished so much in seventy years. Ralph was only twenty-seven, just getting started in his business. Some of his rehab customers were there, but his gay friends made them uneasy. Ralph's customers stood uncomfortably next to Jonathan and Rebecca and stared at the men in drag, the men holding hands, and the men with crewcuts and spike earrings.

I went over and stood with Ralph's friends. I didn't really belong, but I felt more at home with them than with Jonathan's button-down pin-stripes. That was my parents' world, and I knew it was killingly dull.

I thought the funeral would be just as grim, but it wasn't. The service was conducted at the funeral home. The minister was Gary, a friend of Ralph's. Gary, slender and elongated as a Goya saint, had been ordained by mail for a buck through the Universal Life Church, but he con-ducted a ceremony that was sweet and sensitive. Gary invited all Ralph's friends to come forward and talk about him. He gently moved us on if we talked too much, so we wouldn't get maudlin.

Jamie read Ralph's favorite passage from *Archy and Mehitabel*, the one where Mehitabel, the worldly old alley cat, tells Archy the cock-roach that she has no regrets because she gave her life to her art.

Norma Blanche, in a little black velvet coat-dress and a tiny veiled hat, shyly revealed that Ralph took her to the New Orleans Mardi Gras the year Sinéad O'Connor was on a tear about the Pope and tore up his picture. Ralph won a prize in a Bourbon Street bar for Best Costume. He dressed as the Pope, and tore up pictures of Sinéad O'Connor.

A young married couple, high school teachers from University City, got up and thanked Ralph for doing such a splendid job on their old house.

He fixed the dry-rotted windows, redid the kitchen, stripped their mahogany fireplace by hand, and charged them only what they could afford, which they later found out was well below the going rate.

Next, I got up and walked to the front. It seemed a long trip. I was afraid I'd break down, so I started out talking too fast. "Ralph restored some grand mansions, but he loved the city's small brick bungalows best," I began. "He always said he could spot a classic city house by these signs: The brick house had gutters and trim painted dark green or white. The bath had a claw-foot tub. The kitchen was the biggest room in the house, and it had a large pantry that smelled good. The husband had a workshop in the basement, where he puttered.

"Ralph had one final test for a classic city house," I said. "He always said you should step outside and take a deep breath. You should smell a brewery or a bakery. Unless you get the chemical plant first."

I'd quit in time, and left them laughing. Other friends talked, and a portrait of Ralph emerged, complex, crazy, charming, full of love and friendship. Only Jonathan and Rebecca had nothing to say.

There was a long procession of cars and rehabbers' pickups to the cemetery. At the grave site, Gary, the one-dollar minister, asked us to offer our own silent prayers. Then we sang the Rolling Stones song that has become a funeral favorite since *The Big Chill,* the one about how you can't always get what you want. Ralph got the send-off he deserved, thanks to Gary.

After the funeral, I went home to my grandparents' house. I was so sad I hurt. I felt like I'd been cut by a knife across my chest: two funerals in one week. Burt was a symbol of my grandparents' vanishing world. Ralph was a good friend. I valued Burt for his seasoned wisdom. I loved Ralph for his outrageousness. The two had one thing in common. They were craftsmen. Burt ran his bar with skill, kindness, and discipline. Ralph rehabbed his houses the same way. He had a real love for the city and a feel for its gently timeworn homes.

I knew I'd miss them for selfish reasons, too. Ralph and Burt were top-notch sources who gave me insider information about the city. Ralph haunted City Hall for his permits and inspections. He knew who was on the take, who did drugs, who did favors, and who honestly tried to help. Burt heard interesting things at his bar. The politicians who drank there treated him like wallpaper when they wanted to talk business. Once or twice a year he'd give me a tip, and it always paid off. I picked up some good scoops from both men. Their deaths were a double loss, personal and professional. And I couldn't get it out of my mind that their deaths were connected, and there was something wrong. I never believed that Burt had died in a robbery. He was too wily for that. And I didn't think Ralph would go anywhere without his inhaler, especially if he was working in plaster dust. He knew dust was dangerous for an asthmatic.

But I couldn't imagine who would take Ralph's inhaler, or why. No one benefitted by his death. He had less than five hundred dollars in his bank account, and no life insurance. His tight-assed brother Jonathan might have wished him dead, but he wouldn't kill him. It might mess up his suit. It wasn't necessary, anyway. Jonathan lived way out past Ellisville. He rarely saw Ralph.

None of it made sense, and that made me feel worse. I felt guilty as well as sad. I should have returned Ralph's call. Maybe I could have persuaded him to get his inhaler or see his doctor or stay home and rest. Maybe he'd still be alive if I had.

It didn't help that I was still getting letters from the Aryan Avenger. Usually I shrugged off nut mail as one of the hazards of having your picture in the paper. I read it and dropped it in my Weirdo file in the back of my desk drawer. I used to joke with Lyle that if anything happened to me, he should make sure the police checked that drawer. The Aryan Avenger and his lightning-jolted jingles had fattened up the file. He was still writing about Burt's death, and he still thought Burt was Jewish. His latest poem said:

> *Your JewBurt friend is a disgrace.*
> *His death improves the master race.*

If the Avenger was an example of the superior human being, I'd say the gene pool thinned when it got to his great height.

February drifted on. That lousy month never seemed to end. The days reflected the way I felt—cold, gloomy, and gray. Lyle called often. He sent a dozen red roses on Valentine's Day. We went to dinner. We made love. But I was restless and distracted. I would never stay the night at his place in the Central West End. No matter how late or how cold it was, I would get up and go home to my grandparents' place and brood.

Sometimes the hurt would go away for several hours, or even a whole day. Then I'd see Ralph walking by me in a store or Burt sipping coffee in a restaurant. And I'd be so happy, I'd start to go over to him. Then the person would turn my way, and I could see he looked nothing like Burt or he wasn't Ralph, and I'd realize they were gone for good and the hurt would start again.

My writing saved me from sliding into a deep depression. The first sign of recovery was when I did a story about the reopening of an old German restaurant, the Cuckoo Clock. The restaurant had closed in the eighties, and the building had been badly vandalized. For a while, it looked like the old landmark would be torn down for a new gas station. But a local family stepped in to save it. The new owners spent a year restoring the building. I wished them well. The place looked successful now.

I also had a feeling the story would irritate Hadley, although I didn't know why. Sure enough, he called me into his office the morning after it ran for a little talk. This was a friendlier chat than our last encounter, so I sat on the red velvet Victorian sofa by the Mergenthaler Linotype machine. The sofa felt like it was stuffed with billiard balls. Hadley staked out a carved rosewood side chair with extravagant looping arms. I noticed it had soft down cushions.

Hadley leaned forward, as if he didn't want to miss a word I had to say. His spotted bow tie perched on his collar like a big yellow butterfly. His thinning silver hair fell jauntily over one eye. His pink scalp was a warm rose-petal, so I figured he must be in a good mood. It only turns bright red when he's really angry. Hadley looked intelligent and sincere. He was good at faking both. "You do a good job of covering the city," Hadley told me. "You have a real feel for St. Louis."

"I like the city," I said, slurping up his praise. I could hate myself later for falling for his lines. I was going to enjoy them now.

"I can tell," he said, and showed some teeth. That passes for a Hadley smile. "But we must not forget that the downtown is St. Louis's front porch. We must remember where the people live. If we forget to cover the city's bedroom and living room, we're neglecting a vital part of our readership."

Why was Hadley giving me a metaphorical house tour? Before I could ask, he shook my hand and guided me out the door, still showing his teeth. Roberto, city editor and consummate suck, saw the flash of Hadley ivory and decided I must be in favor again. He almost leaped over his chair to get to me.

"Terrific column Sunday," he said, pumping my hand in front of the whole newsroom. I surreptitiously wiped my hand on my skirt. It felt slimy. Roberto didn't know who I was when Hadley was angry with me.

I knew there was a veiled warning in what Hadley was saying, but I couldn't figure out what it was. I risked a visit to Georgia T. George. I rarely talked with my mentor at the office, but I was seriously puzzled by Hadley's not-so-friendly friendly talk. Georgia was on the phone, so I settled into an old leather club chair by her comfortable paper-strewn desk. On the wall behind her desk, Georgia had a framed copy of my favorite poster of the Gateway Arch. It was made to look like a blueprint, and it revealed that the Arch was one half of a giant coat hanger, buried deep in the ground. Georgia was wearing a rumpled gray suit with a mustard-yellow silk blouse that I knew cost two hundred dollars. It made her look like a wealthy jaundice victim.

"What does it mean when Hadley compliments me on how I cover the city, then says downtown is the area's front porch and I shouldn't forget the bedroom and living room? He was friendly on the surface, but it sounded like he was giving me a warning."

"He was," Georgia said. "He wants you to write more about the nice white folks in the suburbs."

Now I was really confused. "I write about them," I said. "But my column has always had a city focus. Besides, suburban people are interested in the city, too. They come here for the ball games and Shaw's Garden and the zoo and—"

Georgia held up her hand. "I know that. Hear me out. I'm trying to tell you what Hadley is saying. He's telling you that your city columns may be entertaining, but you write too much about blacks, bikers, poor people, and other types who don't interest major advertisers. Many of the folks you feature would be followed around by store security, and the rest couldn't afford to buy anything. I realize those are some of your best columns. But Hadley is telling you in code to tone it down."

"Why?"

"The advertisers want you to write cute—a dash of sex, a hint of humor, but nothing that's going to upset anyone."

"What's upsetting about an old landmark restaurant reopening in the city?"

"These people prefer to believe the city is failing," Georgia said. "They want their newspapers to tell them that the city is full of crime and poverty and whites and blacks who hate each other. Stories that say city neighborhoods can be successfully integrated and rehabbed upset that image."

"But Hadley's wrong," I said. "The downtown isn't the city's front porch, it's the foundation, and if we don't take care of our foundation, St. Louis will crack apart."

"Hadley is the managing editor," Georgia said, sternly. "That may be how you see it, but it isn't the way he does. He knows the big ad money is in the suburbs, and that's where he thinks you should be, too. He can't actually come out and say it, but that's what he wants. Back off. Write a few suburban stories and get him off your back." She stood up and grabbed a leather-bound notepad. "Now, if you'll excuse me, I have to go to the ten-thirty meeting."

"What happens there?"

"We discuss what we did at the nine o'clock meeting," Georgia said.

Hmmm. That yellow blouse was giving her a jaundiced view.

My mentor's interpretation of Hadley's remarks was confirmed when Charlie, my weaselly editor, sauntered over to my desk after lunch. "Keep up those city columns," Charlie said. "Good gritty stuff. I loved the one about Diana the Dumpster Diva. Imagine making your living that way."

Yeah, Charlie, I thought. Imagine it. It might be less revolting than what you do.

Charlie oozed on. "I had a talk with Hadley. He says he wants to see you write more about the city, especially disadvantaged persons."

Typical Charlie. This was the exact opposite of what Hadley had just told me. It was also the reason why I counted my fingers when I shook hands with the sawed-off shrimp.

"I appreciate you telling me this, Charlie," I said. I did, too. It confirmed that Georgia was right. I'd get on those suburban stories. Hadley would see a couple, then have other worries and forget about me. I wrote two columns. Then I went back to my grandparents' house. I decided I needed serious comfort. I ordered a fourteen-inch St. Louis thin-crust pizza. St. Louis pizzas do not come with cilantro, goat cheese, or roast chicken with lime. They are the perfection of grease, and the crust is the key. None of that thick crust stuff, like bad French bread smeared with tomato sauce. A true St. Louis pizza has a thin crust, not much thicker than a cracker. It's topped with provolone cheese, which bubbles up and turns bright orange when heated. It has only the traditional fat-filled ingredients: pepperoni, bacon, or sausage. The only vegetables are onion, green pepper, and mushrooms. And the mushrooms better not be an exotic variety like shiitake or portobello. They come out of a can.

My pepperoni-and-mushroom pizza was delivered in thirty minutes. I settled into the beige recliner for a pig-out, wrapped in my grandmother's brown-and-yellow afghan. I channel-surfed until I found *Gilligan's Island*. I always thought it was an underrated show, along with the TV versions of *The Addams Family* and *The Munsters*. Lyle voted for *The Wild Wild West* and *Get Smart* as most underappreciated. We'd debate the merits of our favorites endlessly. I fell asleep in the recliner with the TV on.

I woke up about 8:00 A.M., but I didn't hear the usual morning traffic noises outside. The city streets sounded strangely silent. I got up, step-

ping on the grease-spotted pizza box, and looked
out the window. Sometime during the night,
about twelve inches of snow had been dumped
on the city. Twelve inches was enough to leave
St. Louis semiparalyzed, with only the main
snow routes open. It looked like I'd have to write
my column from home, rather than fight the un-
plowed side streets. St. Louis's attitude toward
snow is "God put it there and God can take it
away."

I went down the back steps to my grandparents' store. It was now run by Mrs. Indelicato, a
widow with a good head for business. "Can I buy
some eggs?" I asked her.

"I can only sell you half a dozen," she said.
"It's all I have left. There's been a run on everything with this snow."

"What's selling fastest?"

"Toilet paper and milk," said Mrs. I. "The minute the weatherman starts predicting snow,
they're in here buying toilet paper and milk, like
war has been declared and there's going to be a
month-long siege. Milk I can understand. But
toilet paper? Do they think snow causes diar-
rhea?"

"Maybe they should lay off the milk," I said.

I took the eggs upstairs and fried up two. I
plopped them on a piece of toast, and peppered
them lightly. They looked pretty good. I carried
my plate and a cup of tea into the living room
and looked out the window. My neighbors were
industriously digging their parking spots out of
the deep snow. Cleared spots were marked with

trash cans, sawhorses, and old kitchen chairs. One guy held his place with a camper shell. Mr. Stewart put out two lawn chairs with busted yellow webbing. Taped in between them was a cardboard sign with a homemade skull and crossbones.

City people have an emotional attachment to their parking spaces. It's hard for suburbanites, spoiled by driveways, garages, and carports, to understand what that rectangle means in front of our home. Never mind what the law says. City people believe they own that parking spot. Some have defended it to the death—literally. There have been shootings over parking spaces. The lucky ones get their cars shot. Even in good weather, people get touchy about their parking spaces. Last summer I heard about a newcomer who ignored the local custom and parked anywhere he wanted on his street. He said he could. It was his legal right. His neighbors warned him repeatedly to stay in his place, but he ignored them, and inconvenienced everybody. One day, he came out and found his back tire shot out— with arrows. I thought that was sporting.

I also knew a guy who was a wood-carver. He made a replica of a city fire hydrant, painted it the proper colors, and put it in front of his house while he was at work. When he came home, he put the fake hydrant in his trunk and claimed his spot.

Another South Sider was having trouble with a new neighbor taking his spot. He solved the problem with psychology. To understand this

story, you have to know two things: The South
Sider had a beautiful daughter who dated a
handsome dark-haired young man, and there's a
local crime family I'm going to call the
Samuelses, because that's not their name. The
Samuelses were involved in a series of car-
bombings. Anyway, the South Sider put up with
the parking-spot stealer for weeks. He tried to
set the guy straight, but nothing worked. The
newcomer stubbornly parked in the South
Sider's spot. Finally, the South Sider had
enough. He went over to the guy's house and
said, "Look, you can park where you want. It's
your right. I just wanted to let you know my
daughter is dating a Samuels." After that, the
spot was untouched.

When the weather turns nasty, the parking
wars grow fiercer, and the spots become more
precious. That's why people were digging out
their parking places and marking them with
skulls and crossbones. I looked outside and saw
my neighbor Janet, bundled up in a down coat
and a heap of knit scarves. She'd been shoveling
the spot in front of her house for two hours, ever
since her husband Kevin left for work. Forget
Romeo and Juliet. When a woman shovels snow
for her man, that's true love.

As I watched, Janet finished the job, salted the
spot and went up to the porch to get the two
folding chairs she was going to use to mark her
place. That's when I saw a woman pull right into
Janet's freshly cleared parking place, just like
she owned it. It was Melanie, who lived in the

superrich suburb of Ladue, where people have servants and snow removal services. We'd all been watching her romance with Jim, a down-market South Sider, and this was the second time this week her little red Miata had been parked in front of Janet's house. Obviously, Jim hadn't spent the time clueing her in on local customs. Melanie didn't realize she was claim-jumping. Or maybe she did and didn't care. After all, Janet was standing right there. I thought Janet was going to hit her with the shovel. Janet yelled, but Melanie ignored her, and sailed into Jim's house, twitching her little fox-fur-covered tail. Janet rang Jim's doorbell. Melanie came to the door. They had some kind of conversation. I could tell it was angry, because Janet was waving the shovel. But Melanie shut the door firmly. She did not move her car.

Janet, still angry, gathered up her shovel, her folding chairs, and her bag of salt and went inside. I knew Janet too well to expect her to accept this defeat. She was going to do something. I had to know what it was. Every half hour or so, I'd pass by the front window and check out Melanie's Miata.

Two hours later, Janet was back outside with her green garden hose. She hooked it up to the spigot by the front porch and turned on the water. Then she stood out by Melanie's car and began watering her yard. The fight over the parking spot must have driven Janet out of her mind. Was she crazy?

Like a fox. The water splashed all over Melanie's car. Janet kept watering her yard, until the Miata was thoroughly wet. Water was dripping off everything on the car, from the door handles to the bumpers. Some of it was already turning to ice. The windshield had frosted up quick. Then Janet turned off the water, rolled up her hose, and went back to the house. I called Janet the minute she was inside. "I've been watching this drama all morning," I said. "It's better than a soap opera. Give me the latest chapter."

"You saw me shoveling out a spot for Kevin when he comes home," Janet said.

"I did. I was touched. I'm not sure I'd do that for Lyle."

"Then you must have seen that rich bitch pull into my spot like I'd been shoveling it for her. I was standing right there. She refused to move the car."

"Didn't tip you, either." I took a chance with a joke, but Janet kept talking.

"I followed her to Jim's house and said, 'You are going to move.' She said, 'I'll try,' in that baby voice of hers.

"I said, 'My husband gets home at five and you will be out of there.' She said, 'I'll try,' in that soft, infuriating way. I told her she had two hours to move. She didn't. So I called the police. I wanted her arrested for stealing. The officer explained that the police couldn't do anything. 'There is no law protecting your spot,' he said.

"Then the officer said, 'There is also no law that says you can't water your lawn in February. If her car happens to be in the way, that's too bad. You'd be surprised what that water does. It freezes doors and locks. It freezes wipers to the windshield and tires to the ground.'

"I said, 'But won't the police arrest me?'

"The officer said, 'For what?'

"I took his name, just to be on the safe side, and then you saw what I did."

"You watered your lawn."

"Yep. Too bad her car was right there. I'd say she has an inch of ice all over."

About four o'clock that afternoon, Melanie flounced out to her Miata, wearing her fox fur coat. By that time, her car looked like a Sno-Kone. The street around it was a skating rink. She skated up to the car and tried to open the door, but it wouldn't budge. She yanked the handle hard, slipped, and went down right on her butt. Couldn't happen to a nicer person.

Melanie went back inside. When she came out again, she was wearing one of Jim's old winter coats. She had a can of deicer, a knife, and three scrapers. She set to work chipping the ice off her little red car, but it was slow going. It took thirty minutes to free her windshield wipers. I could see Janet peeking through her miniblinds on the second floor. I started giggling. Then I was laughing, hard, for the first time since Burt and Ralph died. God, I loved this city. It was a theater, just for my entertainment. When Kevin came home at five, Melanie was working on the driver's door. And I was working on my Snow Wars column. I felt alive again.

7

wo days later, the temperature shot up to fifty-five degrees. Only rags and patches of snow remained. People packed up their parking-place markers, the broken lawn chairs and death's head signs. They put away their anger, too. Janet even smiled at Melanie, but the Ladue-ite ignored her, preferring to nurse her grudge. Maybe Melanie would make a good city woman after all.

My own sadness was also going, melting like the snow. But something about Ralph's death bothered me, nagging at me like a name I couldn't quite remember. I figured if I didn't try to force it, whatever it was would come to me.

That night, I had the dream again about Ralph dying in the plaster-covered room. I saw his dusty hair. I saw his ladder. And when I woke up, I knew what I didn't see and nobody mentioned: Where was Ralph's inhaler? Even if it was empty, it would still be around somewhere. Ralph didn't take out the trash—he drove it.

When Ralph rehabbed a house, he dumped his burger bags, chicken boxes, and soda cups in the room where he was working. When he cleaned up the room and literally shoveled out the old broken plaster, the trash went out with it. I was sure he'd toss his old inhalers in with the mess, too. And an orange-and-yellow Proventil inhaler would be easy to spot, even in that gray dust.

I went by Ralph's mother's house to ask if an inhaler had turned up in his effects. Billie did not answer the door at her little gnome's house. Instead, her gray guard, wearing the same gray dress, came to the round-topped wooden door. She was still on duty, protecting Billie from any more pain. It turned out that she was Billie's sister Dorothy from Minneapolis.

"Billie is finally asleep after a bad night," she said in a half whisper. "I don't want to wake her up unless it's important."

"That's all right. I don't want to bother her. I just have a question and you can probably answer it. Did any of Ralph's inhalers turn up in his things?"

Dorothy didn't ask why I wanted to know.

"No," she said. "We got his wallet and some things back, but there was nothing like that."

"Can I check Lucy?"

She smiled at the truck's name, then looked sad, as if remembering the man who named Lucy was dead. "Sure," she said. "Lucy is still parked where you left her. She's not locked. I've been meaning to go out and tape up that broken window."

I took the hint and offered to do it for her. Dorothy sent me out armed with a roll of silver duct tape and a dark plastic garbage bag. Poor Lucy looked more forlorn and faded than ever. Along with her broken window, the front bumper seemed to have developed a definite droop on the driver's side.

I opened the door. Yeech. Even with the ventilation from the broken window, the truck smelled like old White Castles. They're good going down, but the leftovers can smell like sweaty armpits. There was a greasy bag on the seat, with a half-eaten Castle, an empty fry box, and a pile of wrappers and pickles. Next to it was an empty Big Gulp. I scooted across the seat, careful to avoid any glass chips.

God, Ralph was a slob. How could he do such exquisite work and live in the bottom of a trash barrel? Under the White Castle bag was a fragrant pile of order forms, estimate sheets, and envelopes. Stuck inside one envelope was a spiral notebook Ralph evidently used as an appointment book. I flipped through it and found some notes in pencil for the last days of his life. The whole year, fifty-two weeks, was neatly marked out by hand with a ruler. His handwriting was clear and readable, another surprise.

I saw these appointments:

"L. estimate. Tue. noon"

"Meet F. at Gr. Tues. nite." That was Burt's wake at the Grand Funeral Home.

"Utah—Meet Ed Wed. ten A.M."

Who was Ralph meeting Wednesday morning at the Utah Place job? Who was Ed? There was no clue, not even an initial for a last name, and he didn't mention anything to me. I thought guiltily about Ralph's question that I never answered. I didn't have a clue, except that it was about someone Ralph thought I worked with, and I didn't work with anyone named Ed.

I came across a Walgreens receipt for a Proventil inhaler dated the Friday before he died. But no inhaler. I did unearth a fried chicken receipt dated September 27, 1995. That's how long Ralph kept junk around. I should have found an inhaler, but there was nothing, not even a used one. I even checked the glove compartment. Ralph may have been the only person on earth who actually kept gloves in there—two pair, one wool knit and the other brown leather driving gloves.

That afternoon, I called Jamie. "I know you said Ralph didn't have an inhaler in his pocket when you found him at the Utah Place house. Was there one anywhere around, maybe on the floor or with his tools?"

"No, but I wasn't looking for one," Jamie said. "All I saw was Ralph, lying there. Then I called 911."

"Who owns that house?"

"A young woman lawyer, an EEOC expert. Just won that big judgment for race discrimination. Her name is Sandra." Jamie gave me Sandra's office number.

I had one more question. "Did you know Ralph had an appointment Wednesday morning at the Utah job with someone named Ed? Did he ever mention an Ed to you?"

"No," said Jamie. "But we weren't close enough to trade that kind of information anymore." He sounded sad when he said that. "Gary gave Ralph a good funeral, didn't he?"

"Yes, he did," I said.

"I miss him," said Jamie, and hung up before I could answer.

Sandra the lawyer returned my call at home that evening. She missed Ralph, too, for different reasons. She couldn't find anyone she trusted to finish the job on her Utah Place house. "The last contractor I talked to told me I should drop the twelve-foot ceilings and tear out that old molding," she said. "He didn't care about my house the way Ralph did. Now I don't know what I'm going to do. I wanted to move in at the end of March, when my apartment lease is up."

I gave Sandra a couple of rehabbers' names, then asked if she'd let me look around the house for his family, to see if he'd left anything behind.

Like an inhaler.

"Sure. You'd do me a favor if you packed up his things," Sandra said. "There's a toolbox and a radio and some other odds and ends. I feel guilty. I should have taken them to his mother by now."

It wasn't often I was invited to snoop. Now

Sandra regarded my nosiness as a public service. We aim to please. "How do I get in your house?"

"There's a key on a nail by the garage door," Sandra said. "It opens the kitchen door. Have a look around, and don't forget to turn off the lights."

I got to Utah Place about ten the next morning, and parked my Jag out front. None of the neighbors complained, even though I was wearing my oldest jeans. I knew this was going to be a dirty job. I walked around back to the garage. The garage door was not locked. There was no reason. It was empty except for a stack of rusty window screens, a garden hose, and a slab of grayish marble like you find in bathrooms in old public buildings. The key was right where Sandra said it would be.

I walked through the backyard and opened the kitchen door. The work on the first floor was finished, except for the final cleanup. I don't know much about kitchens. My favorite appliance is the phone, and I can tell you every restaurant that delivers in thirty minutes. But Sandra's kitchen was a knockout. The counter was covered with deep blue Mexican tiles. The stove looked like something you'd find in a five-star restaurant. I wondered what my scrambled egg would taste like if I cooked it on that baby. I liked the double sink, too. It looked big enough to hold a week's unwashed dishes. Everything—the counter, the stove, and the floor—was covered with a gray film of plaster dust. It's insidious, fine as face powder but gritty as sand.

I walked through a dining room paneled in dark wood and a living room painted all white. The front hall was the size of my first apartment. It was the only room on the first floor that showed the signs of Ralph's trauma. The grit on the hardwood floor was trampled with dozens of frantic footprints. Long stripes in the dust from the stretcher wheels went across the hall and up the wide, carved staircase. There were raw scrapes in the wood of the steps and a nasty gouge in the plaster on the landing where the EMS crew had swung the stretcher around the corner. Too bad they had no reason to hurry. Ralph was already dead when they arrived.

The floor of the upstairs hall and the room with the primrose paper were covered with plastic drop cloths. The wide sliding doors were open, and I could see more plastic taped over the fireplace. The plaster had crumbled into bits about the size of gravel in a driveway. It crunched when I walked. I followed the footprints and wheel marks to the room where Ralph had died. At first, I couldn't bring myself to look at the six-foot-square area by the ladder where the plaster was tracked over and pounded down. That's where Ralph had died. Instead, I looked up at the work he'd been doing. He'd knocked out almost the whole ceiling, except for about three square feet in the far corner.

Plaster is tricky. It can crack and fall on your head in the night when you're asleep. But even old, bulging ceilings can be tenacious when you try to take them down. Ralph had to beat the stuff with a crowbar. I saw the crowbar he used, dropped on the floor. Nearby was a dented metal thermos and his battered old boom box, dusty and spattered with paint. I saw a grimy three-foot pile of Big Gulps, foam coffee cups, and White Castle bags. I saw a blue dust mask, the elastic band broken. I saw everything but an orange-and-yellow Proventil inhaler.

I began searching the room systematically. I started in the corner closest to the fireplace, sifting through the dust and debris, moving the larger chunks of plaster with the crowbar. I found Ralph's almost new red toolbox under a tarp, his tools neatly placed inside, with compartments for the duct tape, nails, screws, and washers. He was a fanatic about caring for his tools. If only he'd taken care of himself so well. I found his jeans jacket, folded next to the toolbox. I found a bag of petrified jelly doughnuts and more empty coffee cups, a can of Spackle and a Red Devil putty knife. But no inhaler.

I packed up the tools, thermos, jacket, and radio to take to his mother. Then I took a look at the aluminum stepladder. Like everything else in the room, it was coated with plaster dust. A dusty red bandanna hung on one step. A half-empty Big Gulp was on the top step. The inhaler should have been somewhere around there, too. He kept it in a pouch tied about halfway down on the ladder. Ralph had showed it to me once. "That's my medical insurance," he said. "Right within reach, in case of emergency."

His insurance had been canceled. The inhaler

wasn't there. But I did see the string that held the pouch. It had been cut. It was time to have a talk with my favorite homicide detective, Mark Mayhew. I waited till three o'clock that afternoon. I could usually find Mayhew in his office then, doing paperwork and drinking even worse coffee than the swill at the *City Gazette*. I called and he picked up on the first ring. "Mayhew," he answered the phone.

"It's me, Francesca," I said.

"Of course it's you, Francesca. I'd recognize that voice anywhere. You give great phone." Mayhew was fun to talk to, but he never hit on me. He liked women. He loved his wife. If he fooled around, I didn't know about it. He was a lot more discreet than some of the cops, who brought their girl friends into Uncle Bob's.

"How about if I give great lunch? I have something I want to run past you. Money's no object, up to ten dollars or so. You want to go to Uncle Bob's?"

"Jeez, Francesca, don't you ever eat anywhere else? You're in such a rut."

"I like the food."

"Everything tastes like a pancake there. Even the coffee."

"I like Uncle Bob's atmosphere. But if you want to go somewhere different, name it."

"Crown Candy Kitchen," he said.

"Crown makes Uncle Bob's look like a health food restaurant," I said.

"You don't want to go there?"

"Of course I do. Sugar is one of the four food

groups, along with alcohol, grease, and chocolate."

Crown was an old-fashioned city soda fountain, one of the last places where you could get a real chocolate malted and a handmade shake. Crown mixed them in tall metal cups, poured half into a footed fountain glass, and brought the rest in the metal cup to your table along with a shaker of nutmeg. It was a time warp, the sort of place where Archie and Veronica would hang out, lost in a tough city neighborhood. Crown even had those little jukebox selectors on the wall in each booth.

For some reason, a lot of cops went there. They ate their ice cream like gunfighters in a Wild West saloon. The cops always took a corner table, and sat with their backs to the wall, so they could see the whole room and watch who came in the door. Once, just for fun, I took that seat and left Mark with his back to the door. He was so uncomfortable he could hardly concentrate on the conversation. I finally took pity and switched seats with him. This time, since I wanted a favor, I let him sit where he'd be comfortable, with his back to the wall. Mark had on a scrumptious outfit, like something on the menu at Crown: a butterscotch-brown corduroy sport coat and a rich-looking sweater the color of French vanilla ice cream. It set off the bulge of his shoulder holster nicely.

Maybe eating ice cream helped him keep that choirboy face after what he'd seen. His skin was so clean and pink it looked like his mother had scrubbed him with her handkerchief before she let him out of the family car.

"I'll have a bowl of chili and a chocolate shake," Mark told the waitress. Chili with a white sweater? I'd heard homicide detectives had a foolhardy streak.

"I'll skip the first course," I said. "Just bring the shake."

She did. All the food showed up at once. The shakes were cold and magnificent concoctions that reduced us both to silence while we shoveled them in. These were shakes so thick you could eat them with a fork, but we used a spoon and a straw. Mark's chili remained untouched. I figured he'd have it for dessert. But he was thinking about the fresh-made candy in the glass case by the front door. Maybe that's why he took that seat, so he could watch the chocolate.

"They have almond clusters," he said. "My favorite."

"I'm waiting for the Easter candy," I said. "Did you ever see the chocolate crosses? I wonder how you eat them. You know, with chocolate rabbits, you eat the ears first. What do you do with a chocolate cross? Bite off the arms first? Or the top part?"

Mark looked at the ceiling. "We're going to get struck by lightning." He said it as a joke, but I could tell I was making him uneasy. Cop humor is as tasteless as reporter jokes, but Mark didn't like joking with civilians. I switched the subject to something less sacrilegious.

"How's it going with Burt? Did you get any-where?"

"Nothing," he said. "There's an office building right across the street. We questioned everyone. No one saw anything unusual. None of the in-digenous local population"—his phrase for the tough black gang kids—"were seen in the vicin-ity between two and two-thirty, the approximate time of death. The only person seen leaving the building after two o'clock was a white male. He could have been any age between forty and sixty. He was wearing a beige all-weather coat and a beige hat."

"That only describes about half a million busi-nessmen," I said.

"Nobody noticed anything unusual about him. The two people who saw him were on the upper floors of the building. They said he wasn't real tall, but he didn't seem real short, and he didn't seem overweight or very thin, but it was hard to tell. They weren't sure if his hair was light brown, dark blond, or gray. One said he looked 'kinda average.' The other said he looked like a lunch customer going back to work. He wasn't running or doing anything suspicious. They didn't know if Burt let him out, or if he opened the door himself."

I'd been sucking up the last of my shake with a straw and it made a loud slurp. I felt about twelve. I tried to recover by asking a grown-up question. "What about his car?"

"Nobody saw it," Mayhew said. "He turned right at the corner and walked up the hill. Must have been parked on a side street. I had some hope for the back of the building. A rooming house with a lot of retirees overlooks the back parking lot. Retirees are alert to anything unusual in their neighborhood."

"That's for sure," I said. "People used to complain about the nosy South Siders. Now, when the neighborhoods are changing, nosy neighbors are a built-in security system. If I had my choice between a pit bull and a retiree who watched everything, I'd take the retired person every time. Pit bulls won't dial 911 when they see something suspicious."

"This time no one saw anything," Mayhew said. "I think they would have noticed if someone was creeping around back there. Those teenagers make them nervous to begin with, and I don't blame them. Some of those kids are more dangerous than the grownups. They don't hesitate to kill. Did you see where that thirteen-year-old shot and killed that guy at the gas station on Tucker? The old people are always calling us if they see kids in gang clothes loitering near a car or a basement window. Besides, the old people in that building all liked Burt. He let a lot of them eat lunch on the tab until their monthly Social Security checks came in."

"So nobody saw anything."

"Yeah, that's about it," Mark said. He slurped his shake, too, so I didn't feel so bad. I wondered if Clint Eastwood would consider a scene at a soda fountain with dueling straws. Mark put his empty shake glass aside, and reached for a package of crackers. He tore it open and crumbled the whole thing into his chili. The man's stomach belonged in a medical museum.

"What about fingerprints?"

"Millions of those," Mayhew said. "It's a bar. But there were none on the weapon—it was wiped. Only Burt's and Dolores's fingerprints were on the cash register. The killer could have put prints all over the rest of the bar and it wouldn't help us. There were too many."

"Any word on the street? Anyone bragging?"

"Nothing there, either. Nothing anywhere. But that doesn't mean we're not going to get 'em."

"What if it wasn't a kid? What if it wasn't a robbery? What if Burt was killed for some other reason besides money?"

"Like what?" said Mark. "Who'd want to kill Burt?"

"Maybe he knew something," I said.

"He knew lots of things. But he was careful, he never talked."

"He talked to me," I said.

"Francesca, I don't want to bust your bubble. I know you admired Burt, but he wasn't quite the cute old guy you thought he was. He was using you. He talked to you when he had a reason to."

I started to protest, but he held up his chili spoon. "Hear me out. Then you can argue with me. You were right about a lot of things. Burt was honest. He worked hard and he never stole anything. He didn't take money, either. And he did help people, although generally he helped them so they'd give him information later. That's what he traded in. Those scoops he gave you were things his pals in City Hall wanted leaked to the paper, to help nail someone they didn't like. Remember when he told you about that black clerk who'd been embezzling parking ticket money?"

"The clerk was guilty," I said.

"So he was," said Mark. "But there are a lot of sticky-fingered clerks in City Hall, and most of them are still helping themselves. But that one was a threat to the white alderman in his increasingly black ward. The black clerk was getting ready to run against the white alderman in the next election, and there were now enough blacks in that ward so that he had a good chance of winning. The white alderman wanted him out of the way. So Burt planted that little tidbit with you, and you went after him."

I felt sick. I hated being used. "But the clerk was guilty," I said. "The courts said he'd taken more than a hundred thousand dollars."

"I never said he wasn't. You got him, fair and square. You deserved the awards your story won. The clerk deserved to go to jail. That's why I never said anything. I am saying this: Burt steered you to that particular clerk, and you never knew the reason. You wanted a kindly old grandfather so bad, you made Burt into one."

"How do you know Burt did that to me?"

"I spent a lot of time in Burt's Bar, sitting back by the ice machine. Nobody liked that booth. Too noisy and too close to the kitchen.

Burt let me sit there and drink coffee because I was cheap security. He thought I'd scare off anyone thinking about holding up the place when it wasn't crowded. It helped me, too. That corner was a natural listening booth. I could hear everything that was said at the bar. If the voices dropped to a whisper, I could hear even better. I've got ears like a bat anyway. I can tell you this. Burt was a shrewd old guy. I used to like to watch him. Some of his regulars would bring their wives in one night and their girl friends the next, and Burt never blinked an eye. He'd listen to the city politicians talk about who they were going to screw next and never say a word. He only told you what they wanted you to have passed on. I know for a fact he kept his mouth shut about some sleazy deals, because I heard them, too."

"Maybe one of those pols killed him."

"Give me a reason why."

"Burt knew something and this time he wouldn't keep quiet."

"I doubt it. If you can tell me what it was, I might take you seriously. But right now, you're just throwing out excuses."

I was getting mad. I didn't want to believe his cynical appraisal of Burt. I wouldn't believe it. "Burt was a good man," I said.

"I never said he wasn't," said Mark. "But he wasn't naive."

"No, he wasn't. My point exactly. He'd never let in some gang kid to hold him up. He was too sharp for that. I can't believe Burt was killed in a robbery gone wrong. Besides, if it was a gang kid, someone would have seen him running from the building. You said Burt's Bar was watched front and back, and no one saw anyone suspicious."

"They could have missed him," Mayhew said. "It wasn't watched by the Secret Service."

"Old people are better than the Secret Service," I said.

Mark was at his most irritating. He'd slipped into the cop attitude I hated most, the patronizing "you're just a civilian who can't understand us professionals."

"Francesca, the old people could have been at lunch. They could have been taking a nap. The office workers could have been on the phone or in a meeting. Burt was killed in a holdup. I can give you a motive—money. Give me a better one and I'll believe you."

I didn't have a better one. I just knew there had to be one. I also knew I wasn't going to get anywhere with Mark. Now he was trying to jolly me along. "Come on," he said, smiling. "I could have told you this on the phone. Why did you ask me to lunch? It's not just for my baby-brown eyes." He waggled his eyebrows at me, Groucho style, but I was still ticked off. It's a cop habit, accusing everyone else of being unworldly. And I didn't like Mark's picture of Burt as a schemer— or me as a gull. It was time to change the subject, before I lost my temper and a good source.

"You know Ralph the Rehabber?"

"I know a lot of rehabbers, but not one named Ralph."

"This one died of an asthma attack in a house on Utah. He was a friend of mine. Listen, there was something funny about his death. I think Ralph was murdered."

"What makes you think that?" said Mark, suddenly looking more interested. He was even leaning a little bit forward.

"His inhaler was gone. He had really bad asthma and he never went anywhere without an inhaler. But there wasn't one on his body, with his things, or in his truck. I searched the room. I searched his truck. I looked at his ladder. He kept a spare inhaler tied in a pouch on his ladder, but when I checked it out, the string was cut, and his inhaler was missing."

"So, he used it."

"No, he called that inhaler his medical insurance. He'd never do that. He'd replace it right away."

"Francesca, if this Ralph was like all the other rehabbers I know, he'd work with plaster dust and fast food bags and crap all around. Pardon my French, but how could you tell anything was missing? Those inhalers are pretty small. How can you be sure you didn't overlook it?"

"I searched the room pretty well. I know what the inhaler looks like. It's bright yellow, so people can find it in a hurry. Here's something else. Ralph's truck was broken into."

"Where was the truck parked?"

"McDonald, near Spring."

"He's lucky the truck was still there at all."

"He's not lucky. He's dead," I said flatly. "It was a strange break-in, too. His radio was untouched, but papers were scattered all over the truck."

"Was anything missing?"

"Didn't seem to be," I admitted.

"Neighborhood must be getting better," he said.

"You're not taking me seriously."

"No. I'm not. There's nothing to take seriously. Burt was an old man with a bar in a neighborhood going bad. His wife and kids wanted him to retire, or at least move to a safe suburb, but Burt refused. He died in a stupid small-time robbery."

"But the killer left the big money under the cash drawer," I said.

"Maybe Burt wouldn't tell him where he kept the big cash, and that's why he got stabbed. Maybe the killer thought he had it all. It's a small bar. We don't know. These are animals. They'd kill for a pair of shoes or a leather jacket.

"As for your friend Ralph, he was taking out plaster ceilings and he had asthma. You know dust can trigger an asthma attack. He didn't have an inhaler at hand, and it killed him. Period. No big plot. He was sick and he was working and the work was dangerous for his condition." Mark was pounding the table with the handle of his chili spoon as he made each point.

"Someone took his inhaler," I said.

"Who? Who? I hate sounding like an owl, Francesca, but name one person who would want to kill a guy like Ralph."

"Well, he was gay. He hung out with drag queens."

"This doesn't sound like a homosexual killing," Mark said, sounding a little impatient. "It sounds like he was pushing to get his work done on that ceiling, didn't take the right precautions, and died. Face it. The man was a slob. He couldn't find his inhaler when he needed it."

"No. That's not true. He was terrified of dying like that. He kept an inhaler with him, no matter what. He had another one tied to his ladder, because he knew dust was dangerous. Someone took his inhaler and that killed him. He was murdered, just as sure as if he'd been stabbed like Burt."

Mark stopped for a moment, as if he were carefully organizing his thoughts. "Look," he said. "We both know that you have an ugly murder in your past. But that doesn't mean the death of everyone you know is murder. Burt and Ralph both died close together. It's bound to affect you. Learn to accept your grief and your loss. Let them go. Stop making these useless inquiries. You can't keep Burt and Ralph alive. They're dead, Francesca."

I didn't need pop psychology from a cop who'd taken a night course at a community college. It was time to go. I left some money on the table.

"Thank you Dr. Freud," I said.

"I didn't mean to hurt you," Mark said. He looked contrite. "I'm just trying to give you some free advice."

"Yeah, well, you know what they say about free advice," I said. "You get what you pay for."

I walked out of the Crown Candy Kitchen with as much dignity as I could muster. I was angry. I knew Burt and Ralph were both murdered. And I was going to prove it, if it was the last thing I did.

It very nearly was.

8

"DUNRIGHT DONE WRONG IN DOWNTOWN HOTEL: CAUGHT WITH PANTS DOWN— LITERALLY!"

I saw the gleeful *Gazette* headline as I passed the red newspaper coin box outside Uncle Bob's Pancake House. My, my. Either Hadley's smut ban went down with Dunright's pants, or this story was so good it was beyond Mr. Morality's restrictions. I bought a paper and took it to a booth. No doubt about it. This was too juicy for any editor, no matter how moral, to pass up.

David Dunright was a city official, the license manager. Normally, the LM was a cushy job for some friend of the mayor's. All he did was supervise six clerks who'd been there for thirty years. The clerks did the work, issuing licenses for everything from tavern jukeboxes to restaurant refrigerators, from boardinghouses to hospitals. LMs made a salary of sixty thousand dollars a year. Some greedy LMs collected a little extra in graft on the side. The honest and/or ambitious ones went after businesses that avoided getting licenses and made them cough up their fees. A city official could get a lot of headlines that way. By the time the next election rolled around, an LM could be considered a serious crusader—and contender.

Dunright was the most ambitious license manager yet. He'd discovered a section in the city ordinance that said licenses could not be issued to "immoral businesses." That was the nineteenth-century way of ensuring that whorehouses couldn't be licensed. Dunright put a twentieth-century spin on it. He interpreted "immoral businesses" to mean video stores selling risqué tapes. He began raiding any store selling X-rated tapes. He busted them under the city porn laws and then revoked their licenses. Soon Dunright was all over TV, radio, and the *CG*, spouting about how city stores were not going to rent pornography to children. No store was ever busted for renting X-rated tapes to children, nor did any parent ever complain that their child came home with a rented porn tape. It didn't matter. It might happen. Dunright's simple-minded statements appealed to a certain kind of moral minority, the ones interested in your morals, not theirs. The *Gazette* managing editor, Hadley Harris, couldn't decide whether to come out for public morality or freedom of the press. In the end Hadley did remember that newspapers were supposed to support the Bill of Rights. It was close, though.

Any citizen who protested that Dunright was interfering in areas that were none of his business had to listen to a lecture about public morality. Dunright began giving TV interviews with this sound bite: "The city will not license licentiousness. With Dunright, it will be done right." Sounded like a campaign slogan to me.

Dunright kept up the raids on the video stores. He never arrested the owners. They were often corporate entities in distant cities, and their high-priced attorneys would never let Dunright haul them off before blazing TV cameras. Instead, he went after the hapless clerks on duty. His last raid was after an undercover agent rented *Goat Busters*. Dunright bagged a student working his way through Forest Park Community College and a single mother with two kids. Nice work, Dunright.

But now Dunright himself had been caught, and now he was evading the reporters' questions and avoiding the microphones and the glaring TV lights. Dunright had done wrong, indeed. At least for a man who set himself up to monitor everyone else's morals. He'd picked up a prostitute at a city hotel who turned out to be a vice squad officer. He'd been attracted to her magnificent endowment. It had been well wired, and I'm not talking about her WonderBra. Better yet, the money he'd offered her was alleged to come from city funds. Maybe Dunright could say he was doing undercover work. He was about to go under the covers when he got caught.

It wasn't often I got to feel morally superior to

anyone, since I was semi-living in sin with my significant other, but Dunright was so good—or bad—that even I could take a swipe at him. I began planning the column in my head, when Marlene came over with more coffee and an even better column. This is why I loved Uncle Bob's and made it my unofficial office. Things happened there. I knew a lot of city officials ate at the pancake place. So it wasn't much of a surprise when Marlene said, "Don't look now, but Dunright is in the back room."

"With or without his pants?"

"He's got his pants, but I think he's going to lose his shirt," she said, pouring coffee as she talked. She didn't spill a drop. "He's been meeting with the city attorney's office for the last two hours. They're sitting back there talking and taking phone calls on a portable phone." The city attorneys often used the back room for informal meetings. During the week, the back room was usually empty, so they could talk about sensitive matters without being overheard by gossips at their office. Of course, the waitresses picked up a few things while they poured and put down plates piled with waffles and eggs. Marlene certainly did.

She reported the scene with Dunright. "At first, everybody was real buddy-buddy. Sharky, the city attorney, sat down next to Dunright and advised him that if he'd keep his mouth shut, he'd probably get through this okay. The yuppie lawyers in Sharky's entourage were laughing and making jokes about it. Then the calls started

coming in. Sharky looked more and more serious each time he answered his briefcase. The
yuppie lawyers quit cracking jokes. Sharky took
his last call in the men's john ten minutes ago.
When he came back, he didn't sit next to
Dunright. He sat across from him. I couldn't
hear exactly what was said, but I heard 'resign'
and 'leave of absence' at least twice. There's supposed to be a press conference tomorrow afternoon. The yuppie lawyers wouldn't even look at
Dunright. I think Dunright is done for."

This was a tip worth checking out. I could
have hugged Marlene, but it would have caused
talk. Instead, I would leave an exorbitant tip,
which was easy to do when your breakfast was
three bucks. "Good," I said. "I'm glad they got
him. We've got drug dealers on the street corners, and he's wasting city money busting video
store clerks."

"Buying hookers with my tax dollars too,"
said Marlene. "That makes me real happy."

"Are they still back there?"

"Yep, but not for long. The guys asked for the
check and they're getting their coats."

"Fine. I'll give them an hour to settle into City
Hall, then give Sharky a call. Dunright's being
dumped—couldn't happen to a nicer guy."

Dunright's downfall didn't surprise me. But I
was glad to have the inside scoop. Marlene was
my always reliable source. She was a master at
picking up stray facts and interpreting body language and a shrewd judge of people. Once, I
praised her to a business owner who ate at Uncle

Bob's. He said, "If she's so smart, why isn't she rich?" I stared at the guy. At first, I thought he was joking. Then I realized he meant it. He really believed that rich people were smarter. And this was from a man who'd made one smart move in his life: He'd chosen the right parents. His mother and father were loaded, and had the decency to die when he was in his twenties. I'd like to see how smart he would be if he found himself in Marlene's white nurse's shoes. Her husband walked out on her when their daughter was a toddler, and she had no trust fund to keep her going.

Unfortunately, a lot of men had the same attitude about Marlene: If she's so smart, why isn't she rich? If she's hauling around plates and coffeepots, and I'm carrying a briefcase, then I don't have to take her seriously. So they didn't. They were rude to her because they could be. They didn't tip because they didn't think she was important. Which meant Marlene reported their more interesting conversations to me. Since none of these men ever noticed Marlene in the first place, they never figured out where my information came from. They'd turn the office upside down looking for the spy, and never realize they'd spilled the beans on themselves at breakfast.

"When's your break?" I asked Marlene.

"Ten minutes," she said.

"Got time to talk to me? I have something I want to run past you."

"Sure." Before she could say more, I heard a

loud voice yelling, "Marlene, get over here. This coffee tastes like crap!"

"Oh, God, is this week over yet?" said Marlene. She went to the Bunn coffee machine, poured a fresh cup, and hurried off to a table with two gray-haired men in suits. I watched her talking and laughing with them. Then she spent the next ten minutes hustling plates, taking orders, and pouring coffee. Finally, she poured herself a cup and sat down in my booth with a sigh. "I've had some weird ones lately," she said. "It happens every time we get a warm spell in late winter."

The temperature the last few days had shot up to seventy degrees. Some of the early spring flowers were starting to send up green shoots. Nobody was fooled except a couple of crocuses. When the wind blew, the winter cold was there, like shark fins slicing through a warm ocean. Winter would be back in a day or two. In the meantime, this premature taste of spring made us all a little crazy.

"I worked the late shift last night," Marlene said. "In comes one of my regulars, a quiet woman who always orders coffee and a double stack. She usually wears a nice pantsuit. Last night she came in wearing a red shortie nightie with a live boa constrictor around her neck."

"I thought boas were out of style," I said.

"You can laugh. You've never faced a snake with little beady eyes," Marlene said.

"I have too. I was in Hadley's office this week. What did you do with the Snake Woman?"

"I told her we couldn't serve snakes after midnight, and she left."

I laughed. Marlene could handle anything, including fights on the parking lot. "You had something you wanted to run past me," she said.

"I think my friend Ralph and Burt the bartender were murdered."

Marlene raised one eyebrow, and her cheerful face looked grave. I told her what I knew about Burt's death, and how Homicide Detective Mark Mayhew thought the motive was robbery, but I didn't. "The killer took about two hundred dollars, but left seven hundred dollars in the register, under the cash drawer. The police say it was probably one of the neighborhood gang kids who either got scared off and left the money or didn't know where to look for the rest of it."

"They know where to look," said Marlene flatly.

"Anyway, no kids were seen near the building at that time, and there were people in the rooming house behind it and the office across the street from Burt's Bar. The police also say Burt probably let his killer in, but Burt was always careful."

"Yeah," said Marlene, "but I know a lot of restaurant owners who were careful, and wound up dead anyway. Remember Preslee's?"

"Who doesn't? I still miss Preslee's steaks. You'd think a steakhouse next to a police station would be safe," I said.

"Preslee certainly did. He was the most careful restaurant owner I knew. He courted the cops," Marlene said. "Fed them royally. On steak, yet. You couldn't eat there without stumbling over two or three cops. Used to make me nervous, personally, surrounded by all those police officers. I always felt they could see that roach in the bottom of my purse. But they made Preslee feel safe. Still didn't help him. He died in his own restaurant, stabbed to death with a kitchen knife after he chastised a busboy for not cleaning off a table. It happened after hours, when all the steak-fed cops were gone."

"They did catch his killer quickly, though," I said. "I always wondered if the cops felt guilty."

"They had a steak in solving the murder," said Marlene.

I groaned.

"Okay, I see what you're getting at," I said. "But what about Ralph's death? Ralph was absolutely paranoid about being caught without his inhaler. He always carried one in his pocket. He even kept an inhaler in a pouch on his ladder. But when he died, they didn't find one in the room where he was working, and the one on his ladder was cut. So explain that one."

"Easy," Marlene said. "You said he was so sick and groggy, he could hardly talk. I could see him forgetting his inhaler, using the one on his ladder and then forgetting to replace it. You do dumb things when you're sick. And, Francesca, you said that man was sick."

"He was also afraid. He was afraid of dying just the way he did."

"There's a reason why people have those fears.

I've always believed they're slightly psychic. On some level, they know how they're going to die. I can give you several examples, but the most dramatic was Mrs. Ames. She was a regular customer who was afraid of flying. Went on and on about how she was going to die in a plane crash, every time she had to fly. I used to razz her. We all did. I even gave her a magazine article saying air travel is safer than car travel. Didn't convince Mrs. Ames. She said it didn't make any difference how good the statistics were—if you were on the wrong side of them, you were still dead. She died in that Florida crash. I thought her epitaph should have been 'I told you so.'"

I laughed. Marlene didn't believe me any more than Detective Mark Mayhew did, but at least she listened. She didn't try to psychoanalyze me. "You haven't said anything yet to convince me that their deaths were anything but what the cops said. Mark is in here all the time. He isn't just any cop. He's a good one. He's solved some big cases, like the murder of that little girl. He can be arrogant, but he has a good heart, a good head, and a cute tush."

"For shame, treating men as sex objects."

"Okay, I'll get serious," Marlene said. "You asked for my opinion, and this is it: People die of asthma all the time. Single people don't take care of themselves as well as married people, and they don't live as long. It's a fact. It's also a fact that bartenders get killed in holdups, and not just city bartenders. I can name you at least three I know who died, and one worked at a high-priced place in the county. But I promise you I'll keep my mind open. My eyes too."

"Good. You have a lot to see here. Everyone eats at Uncle Bob's, especially if they keep late hours."

"Tell me about it. Last night, besides the Snake Woman, we had the chief of police and the mayor's press assistant—but not together—two known drug dealers, three cops, and several lowlifes with homemade LOVE and HATE tattoos on their hands. Speaking of lowlifes, even some of the *Gazette* staff are starting to eat here, I mean besides you, and they are lousy tippers, especially your editor."

Figured. Hadley was better at hanging on to his money than his girl friends.

"Oh, God, look who just walked in," said Marlene.

It was the *Gazette* gossip columnist, Babe Currane, known as Babe because he greets everyone with "Hiya, babe, whatcha got for me?" Babe scanned the room for important people. His eyes flicked over Marlene. All he could see of me was the back of my head, and with any luck he couldn't see that. Babe sat two booths away, in back of a skinhead with a KISS T-shirt. He ordered blueberry pancakes with extra whipped cream.

"How come he eats like that and never gains an ounce?" said Marlene. "Babe is so skinny and sad, he looks like an undertaker."

"There's a reason he looks like an undertaker,"

I said. "He knows where all the bodies are buried."

"I wish he'd bury himself. He's never written one thing I know that's accurate."

"He gets it right often enough," I said. "I used to sit near him at the *CG*. It was an education in the art of negotiation. When people complained he had an item wrong, he'd say things like, 'Okay, sir, maybe I did have a small part incorrect. But I do know for a fact that you are having sex with your new sales associate.' Suddenly, the guy would drop the complaint."

"Speaking of associate, he used to be seen around town with a very handsome young man," Marlene said. "Babe said the guy was his driver."

"There's a lot of speculation whether Babe is gay," I said. "I think he gets off on getting information for his column. Sitting near him was like listening outside a bedroom door. It was embarrassing. Someone would call with a hot tip and Babe would be on the phone panting and begging for it. 'Tell me. You can tell me. Go ahead, tell me,' he'd say. That would be the seduction, and he'd be good at it. Soon the person would give in. While they were doing it, Babe would say, 'I love you. I love you. I love you.' He had a regular rhythm going. The I love you, I love yous would come harder and faster, until the person reached the climax. Then Babe would shout, 'Good, Good! Oh, God. Oh, God.'"

"Gross," said Marlene.

"I'm sorry to say that once Babe had them, he didn't respect them. He'd hustle the person off the phone, then slam it down and say, 'That stupid bitch! Who does she think she is?'"

"It's nice to know Babe is as attractive inside as outside," Marlene said. "Why does your newspaper let that slimeball do that to people?"

"Because Hadley, the managing editor, loves gossip, and Babe tells him everything. Knowledge is power. Babe makes himself useful at work too. He's a company spy. Anything you tell him, you might as well tell Hadley. Anything he sees or hears goes straight to Hadley. And, since it looks like Charlie's on his way up, he gives Charlie juicy tidbits too, to keep on his good side."

"Did you know they were both in here, Hadley and Charlie?" Marlene said.

"Together? Now, there's a scoop!"

"They didn't come in together, if that's what you mean. And they both had different girl friends. But I think Charlie passed off his date on Hadley. Hadley often comes here with his new squeeze. He thinks we're too dumb to know what he's up to, and, besides, even if we do know, we don't count," Marlene said sourly. "The one I saw him running around with early in February was a looker, by the way, a little blonde with more class than his latest fling."

"His latest fling is the comics editor," I said. "Hadley's taste is eclectic. If she says yes, he's in love. At least for three or four weeks."

We were interrupted by a lugubrious voice. "Oh, Babe, you don't want to say that. I know

Hadley and I have to tell you, I love him like a brother."

Oh, damn. It was Babe, blueberries on his breath, coming down the aisle to our booth. The *Gazette* gossip columnist looked thinner and more mournful than ever, like a codfish with a secret sorrow.

"Why, Babe, how nice to see you," I said, telling my first lie of the day before ten o'clock.

Marlene didn't bother to lie politely. She said, "I hope you enjoyed listening to our conversation. We tried to make it entertaining for you."

"Now, Babe," he said. "You shouldn't talk about people that way."

I hung my head. Had Babe heard me making fun of his phone sex routine?

"Come off it," Marlene said. "We were just doing what you do—gossiping. Except we don't have pro status. We don't get paid for it."

"I don't gossip," said Babe, looking like an offended codfish. "I present the news in its embryonic form."

"Ever think about an abortion?" said Marlene.

This was getting out of hand. It was fun to score off Babe now, but he would even up the game later. I should stop it. But I'd already screwed myself by yakking about the man's sex life. Might as well let Marlene have her fun. She was enjoying pinning Babe to the wall.

"If you're really presenting the news, why not write about your bosses? Charlie and Hadley bring their girl friends in here all the time, and I've seen them with some really strange chicks. I

guess boys will be boys. How come you don't
give your readers this scoop: Charlie, editor of
the Family section, rarely spends a night at
home with his own family. Hadley Harris, the
man who writes ad nauseam about the joys of
his darling daughters, regularly betrays his wife
and children. After all, this was the man who last
Sunday said in the *Gazette*, 'Family is the only
reality. Life is not real until you have children.
They fulfill you. When I see my girls play soccer,
I don't see two freckle-faced, skinned-kneed
imps at play, I see my future, I see my past.'

"Maybe if he really thought he'd see his past
in the paper, he wouldn't play around on his
wife and those two cute kids."

"Hadley really called those two brats 'imps'?" I
said, astounded. "They've been thrown out of
three schools."

Babe and Marlene ignored me and kept glaring at each other. I had to break it up. I tried
again. This time I said something diplomatic.
"I'm sure an important man like Hadley is used
to having his affairs discussed," I said. Oops. "Affairs" was a poor choice of words. So much for
my diplomacy.

"Maybe if he did, he wouldn't sneak around
on his family so much," said Marlene.

"Don't be so rough on Hadley," Babe said,
looking like a noble cod. "We can't understand
the pressures a great man faces. Sympathetic female companionship can help a man through
hard times." Marlene snorted, but Babe gave no
indication that he'd heard her. He continued his

history lesson. "Look at Jack Kennedy. Sure, he had a few affairs, but he was still a great president."

"He'd have been a greater president if he'd kept his pants zipped," said Marlene.

I kicked her under the table. That was no way for an Irish Democrat to talk. Maybe the kick woke up Marlene. She abruptly changed the subject. At first I thought she was pouring on the flattery like maple syrup. "Everyone was talking about your column this morning," she said. "Congratulations." They had been too. Customers pointed out three spelling errors, two wrong names and one error of fact—a record, even for a Babe column.

"What did they say?" asked Babe, hungry for praise.

"They said, '*Good* is not the word for Babe today.'"

Babe looked at her suspiciously, like a codfish that swallowed a bad worm. Babe was a lot of things, but he was not stupid. He knew when he was being shivvied. Marlene had declared war, and she was going to keep it up. She was fearless. "Look, if Hadley and Charlie didn't want us talking about their affairs, they wouldn't flaunt them in public," she said.

"They don't flaunt them. This isn't public," said Babe, his voice scornful. He looked around the room at the tables where South Siders were chowing down.

"You could have surprised me," Marlene said. "The place is packed."

"Nobody goes here," said Babe snidely. "It's too crowded." He stomped out the door.

Their voices must have gone up during the fight. The skinhead was obviously listening. He had turned his head slightly to get a better earful. I saw he had a cut on his bare dome. He must have cut himself shaving his skull. I wondered if men put toilet paper on a skull-shaving cut like they did when they shaved their face.

Babe left Marlene fuming. "Well, there's a little more room now that his swelled head is out of here," she said.

I groaned. "There's another reason he looks like an undertaker. He'll bury my career," I said. "He heard me make fun of his phone sex act. He'll report everything we said to Hadley and Charlie."

"He's doing that anyway," said Marlene. "You should hear some of the things he says behind your back. It's better to have an open enemy."

"Easy for you to say," I said.

"Yeah, what can he do to me?" she said. "I'm just a waitress."

I'd never heard her sound so bitter. "Guys like him make me sick," she said. "He comes in here like a big shot, hounds the customers, and mistreats the waitresses. Last week he had Diane, who's seven months pregnant, running back and forth waiting on him like he was some pasha. The worst was when that poor thing was loaded down with plates and coffeepots and he calls her over and says, 'Light my cigarette.' Light his cigarette! What does he think this is—the Four Seasons? Then, after all that, he complained about the blueberry pancakes, but not until he ate every bite. He refused to pay, and didn't tip Diane. What a pig! Hadley and Charlie aren't much better, one running the staff ragged and the other tipping fifty cents. If you ask me, the whole *City Gazette* bunch needs to be taken down a notch or two."

Marlene was angry. The laughing waitress who could handle anything was out to lunch, replaced by a furious and frustrated woman. Then the Marlene I knew came back, like the sun breaking through a cloud. "Break's over," she said, jumping up. "I'm going to have some fun. You see that skinhead who was sitting by Babe?"

"How can I miss him? If I didn't see the shaved head, there's the motorcycle boots trying to pass as jackboots and the KISS T-shirt with the SS lightning bolts."

"Yeah, him. You can't see his hands, but he has swastikas on his knuckles. They're not tattoos. Looks like he drew them himself with black ink."

"That way he can wash them off before he goes home to his mother."

"He's going to wash them off now," said Marlene. "I'd march his butt straight back to the men's room, but I don't want to make a martyr out of him. It would upset my older customers. Watch this." She went smiling to his booth. "Can I get you anything else, sir?" she said respectfully. I couldn't hear what Skinhead mumbled. But Marlene said, "Certainly. Another large milk coming up." She was back in two minutes with the milk. The glass seemed to slip right out of her hand. It landed on the table, splashed Skinhead's hands, and flowed into his lap. "Watch it," he screeched as the cold milk hit his crotch.

I knew Marlene wasn't that clumsy. She could carry six loaded platters on her arms. "Oh, sir, I'm so sorry," she said. "Let me get you another glass on the house. And the rest room is right over there." By the time Marlene had mopped up the milk, the skinhead was back at the table with a red face, wet pants, and scrubbed, swastika-free hands.

Marlene went to the Bunn coffee maker to make a fresh pot. I went into my other office, the one at the newspaper that I visited as little as possible. I called Sam Sharky, the city attorney who'd been at the table with Dunright. He was in. Amazing.

"Hi, Mr. Sharky," I said cheerfully. "I hear you're planning to dump Dunright at the press conference tomorrow."

"Where did you hear that?" said Sharky. For once, he sounded surprised.

"I can't reveal my sources," I said piously.

"It's Dunright," he said. "He went whining to the press after I told him to keep his mouth shut."

"I can't say, sir," I said. "But you've just confirmed that it's true."

"I won't confirm or deny," he said, which is governmentspeak for yes. I'd quote Sharky accu-

rately and really upset him. Now I had one
source, and I needed two for my story. I called
Dorreen, my low friend in high places. She was a
secretary in the mayor's press office, shoved off
behind a door and a file cabinet. She knew everything and everyone. "They're dumping Dunright, right?" I said.

"Just typed the press release," Dorreen said.
"Goes out tomorrow."

Marlene was right, but I already knew that. I
wrote the column at the CG offices for a change,
and smiled all the while I typed. I loved nailing
people like Dunright. His exit was literally a
back-room deal. Too bad word would get out in
my column before the big press conference. If
those lawyers had tipped waitresses like Marlene
a little more and treated them a little better, I
wouldn't find out so much. I finished the story
early and sent it off to Charlie.

He came back an hour later, while I was answering some letters. "Hadley is running your
column on the front page instead of in my section," he said. "Congratulations." He said the
word as if he were spitting out something sour.

Sorry, Charlie. You'll get the credit for having
a columnist who can get the big stories. But you
won't be happy. I know your secret. You don't
have the guts to do what I do.

Charlie used to be a good writer when he
started at the CG. But he'd sold out his craft to
become a corporate coat-holder. It was easier
for him to sit in meetings and write memos than
write stories. Charlie once told me he could do

the reporting, but he couldn't take what he called the three A.M.'s—those nagging doubts all writers have in the middle of the night: Did I spell her name right? Did I quote him right? Did I check that one last fact? We all knew the old saw: "Doctors bury their mistakes. Lawyers put theirs in jail. Reporters put theirs on the front page." Everyone knew when we screwed up.

"I couldn't stand second-guessing myself," Charlie confessed to me once, and then instantly regretted it. In his eyes, he thought he'd revealed a weakness. Now my success was a reproach to him. It increased the tension between us. Sometimes he tried to write a feature story, but his work was flat and lifeless. It lacked a point of view. He didn't have one anymore. Charlie looked like he had a lot of power, but he did as he was told.

And he'd been told to tell me I did a good job. So he swallowed his pride, and grudgingly gave me a verbal pat. I took it. "Does city desk have any questions?" I asked.

"You're fine," he said. "Go home." He wanted me out of his sight. I was glad to go. It was three in the afternoon. I went home early for the first time in months. Home for the last week or so had been Lyle's house. He was in the dark paneled living room, reading a Lawrence Block mystery and wearing my favorite blue sweater. He looked lean and relaxed.

I told him about my triumph, and then my failure—the fight with Babe. He thought the scene with Marlene and Babe was funny. "I'm not laughing," I said. "I was stupid. I shouldn't have said those things. I know Babe is a snake. He'll report everything that was said to Hadley and Charlie."

"Come on, you're too rough on Babe," Lyle said. "He's a pretty good guy. He'll cool off. He always does. And you didn't say anything derogatory about Hadley and Charlie, Marlene did. Besides, Babe's not going to go running to Hadley and Charlie over what a waitress at Uncle Bob's said about them. And even if he does, they have more important things to worry about."

"But I made fun of his phone sex routine," I said.

"So, he's a sexy writer. He'll be flattered. At least you didn't call him a closet queen, like most of the staff. Get your coat. It's too nice a day to sit around here and worry."

"Where are we going?"

"To the zoo," he said. "We haven't seen the bears yet this year."

He was right. St. Louis has a really world-class zoo. It's one of the last free zoos in the country. It was also one of the few zoos where I didn't feel sorry for the animals. These weren't cages full of listless creatures. They were lively. Well, some were. An enormous brown bear was spread-eagled by the pool in his outdoor area, soaking up the rays like a sunbather. His bearish neighbors two doors down had a better idea of how to spend the afternoon. They were humping away to the cheers of the crowd.

"Three times," said Lyle admiringly.

The male bear swatted the female playfully on the rump, and they ambled inside away from the curious humans. We went on to see the penguins.

"They're behaving in a far more dignified way," I said.

"Must be the tux," said Lyle.

We saw Rajah, the baby elephant, and the first elephant born at the zoo. The zoo was immensely proud of the little fellow. Then we strolled through the cast-iron outdoor birdcage, a graceful structure left over from the 1904 World's Fair. If you imagined a giant platter, the birdcage was shaped like its huge cover. The high, airy structure was big enough to house whole trees and flocks of birds. Walking through it was an exotic experience, provided you didn't take any direct hits from the flying residents. I was staring at the pink flamingos wading in the pool in the cage. They looked amazingly like the plastic ones on lawns, only not as smart.

"Hello," said Lyle. "Are you in there?" He put his arm around me and drew me close. He smelled good, like coffee and Crabtree & Evelyn sandalwood soap. "You've been lost in thought all afternoon," he said. "You're not still brooding about Babe, are you?"

"No," I said. "A little fresh air blew him out of my mind. I'm thinking about Ralph and Burt."

"You miss them," he said.

"I do. But that's not the only reason. I keep thinking there's something wrong with their deaths. I still believe they were murdered. You think I'm nuts on the subject, don't you?"

"Not necessarily. Why do you feel that way?"

"I don't know. There's nothing I can put my finger on. People I respect, like Mark and Marlene, give me good reasons why their deaths were what they appear to be: a stabbing during a robbery and an asthma attack."

"But you don't think they were," Lyle said.

"No. I don't. And I have nothing to go by but my feelings."

"Then follow your feelings," said Lyle.

"But all I have are some nagging doubts. Where do I go from here?"

"You're a reporter," Lyle said. "Start asking questions. When you get the answers you want, you'll have the facts to go with those feelings."

That was what I needed to do: treat their deaths like another story. Start interviewing the people involved: Burt's wife, Ralph's mother. I felt better now that I had a plan. I would find out who murdered them and why.

I smiled up at Lyle and picked a small bit of bird fluff off his blue sweater. "I love you," I said. "You're wonderful."

"I know," he said modestly.

9

The murderer confessed the next morning. It was the Aryan Avenger. I found the letter in the mail on my desk, along with a circular for the Opera Theatre of St. Louis. He claimed he'd killed Ralph and Burt both.

I'd always dismissed his mindless drivel. He sent me letter after letter after Burt died, and I'd tossed them all in my Weirdo file. His cretinous brain could only hold one thought: Burt was Jewish. It was so stupid and so wrong, I'd simply ignored his primitive poetry that oozed malice like an open sore. Not this time. Not after this letter.

It even looked lethal. The lame verses and limping meters seemed murderous. The swastikas were big and black and dripping blood. The SS lightning bolts slashed down the paper like saws. The block printing had degenerated into black spikes, driven into the blue-lined paper. For once I read every rambling word. The six suppurating lines were addressed to "Francesca, the Liberal Bitch":

> *What's better than two hundred dollars?*
> *Making the JewBurt holler.*
> *And my final solution for a filthy fag?*
> *Breathless death. Choke and gag.*
> *Beautiful to see. You'll thank me.*
> *Lightning white Justice makes the Christian free.*

Burt's killer took two hundred dollars from the register, but that number was never in the news. The police held back that information in their interviews with the press and I didn't print it. It could help identify Burt's killer. But the Aryan Avenger knew exactly how much had been taken. And that wasn't all he knew.

There were no newspaper stories about Ralph's death, just a brief obituary notice that didn't say how he died. So how did the Avenger know that Ralph had had a "breathless death," choking and gagging? Unless he'd been there to see it. Did he take Ralph's inhalers and watch him die? Did he stab Burt with Dolores's butcher knife? Did he kill two men for some crazy, bigoted reason? What else was in his letters?

I got out my Weirdo file and pawed through the folder for the Aryan Avenger letters. From the postmarks, they started right after Burt's death. They were easy to pick out. The envelopes were covered with lightning bolts and swastikas. Reading them caused major mind pollution. No wonder I tossed them in the file without finishing them. Most of the Avenger's verses were anti-Semitic insults with rhymes like "dirty Jew" and "hate you." T. S. Eliot needn't worry that this St. Louisan was after his poetry title. The Avenger also sprinkled his work liberally (no, that's the wrong word) with insults for other minority groups: gays, Asians, African Americans, and "women's libbers."

Otherwise, there was nothing to distinguish the Avenger from any other prejudiced pervert in the file. I looked through the stack. Most letters were block-printed and had a lot of underlinings. Some were in pencil. One was in orange crayon. My favorite nut letter was from the guy at the Hospital for the Criminally Insane. It began, "Dear Francesca: I saw you on TV and you're not too fat. I would like to marry you but the doctors say I can never touch another woman again." He planned to ignore his doctor's advice and marry me as soon as he got out. Then he sent me a poem he'd written—"Darkness and Blackness and Very Bad Smells"—that made me grab the phone and ask the hospital director if the nuptials were anytime soon.

"Oh, dear," said the director. "He's been writing letters during recreation again."

"Anything you can do to curtail his fun? This boy sounds scary," I said.

"Oh, don't worry," said the director. "He won't be getting out for a very long time. He writes letters to the President, too. The Secret Service watches him very closely."

I hoped he wouldn't get red Jell-O for dessert for a week after the letter he wrote me.

I knew I had at least one more Aryan Avenger letter in the file. Ah, there it was, stuck on the back of a "Dear Dumb Bitch" letter in black furry ink. The writing looked like a spider had crawled over the page. This was the coffee-stained Aryan Avenger poem from the day Ralph died. I'd never gotten past the snappy opening. It began:

"Dear Whore of the *CG:* You liberal bitches are all alike. . . ." The ink had smeared, but I could still read the rest of his epic:

> *Imagine a world with no more fags and*
> *   kikes.*
> *Won't it be Grand?*
> *No, it will be by Klocke!*

That poem made even less sense than the others. Was it just Nazi nonsense, or did "by Klocke" mean something? Maybe it was German for "by crackey." It nagged at me. Klocke sounded vaguely familiar, but I didn't know what it meant. For all my German heritage, I didn't speak a word of the language. Well, a few cusswords, but that's about it. I wasn't allowed to learn German. I wanted to take it in high school, but my grandparents believed in the melting pot. "You're an American, speak English," they said. "You don't need to know how they talk in the old country." In the sixties, German was still the language of the vanquished enemy, and there was no reason to speak it. Ethnicity, especially German ethnicity, was not particularly prized.

Marlene, the waitress at Uncle Bob's, knew a little German. One of her Irish uncles had married a second-generation German, and Aunt Gertrude taught her some of the language. I grabbed the letters and hit Uncle Bob's at eleven thirty, just before the lunchtime rush. I was going to have a scrambled egg twice in one day. There was no point in thinking about ordering anything else. Tom the Cook saw my car pull into the lot and dropped my egg on the grill. Marlene brought it out by the time I got to my booth.

"Couldn't stay away from us," said Marlene. "Nobody scrambles an egg like Uncle Bob's. McDonald's offered us a million dollars for our secret recipe, but we refused to give it up."

"I like the food," I said. "But I really come here for the conversation. When I need to be taken down a notch, I go to Uncle Bob's."

"Must need it a lot," said Marlene. "You're in here all the time."

I showed her the smeary, coffee-soaked Aryan Avenger letter. It was the color of a paper grocery bag. "Do you want me to boil this and pour it for you?" she said.

"I want you to read it and analyze it," I said. "What do you make of this letter?"

I told Marlene the story and said I was looking for some hint as to where I could find this anonymous Aryan Avenger. "This section here bothers me," I said. "Why does that K-word look familiar?"

Marlene studied the crude couplet:

> *Won't it be Grand?*
> *No, it will be by Klocke!*

"Klocke is a South St. Louis street," she said, pronouncing it "Clock-key."

"That's right. It is. A short street right off Grand Boulevard. Between Merb's Candy and Giuseppe's Restaurant."

No true St. Louisan gives an address when she can name a landmark. And maybe that's what that crazy phrase was: a way to locate Klocke Street, off Grand. I suspected the Aryan Avenger was a South St. Louisan. Klocke wasn't a street most people from any other neighborhood would ever find—or go looking for. You had to be there.

"It's a good place to start looking for the Aryan Avenger," I said.

"What if you find him?" Marlene said. "I've seen some of those neo-Nazis in the restaurant. They're scary looking. Remember the kid with the shaved head and the swastikas on his hands the day Babe was in here? Did you see his muscles? Did you notice his boots? What if he's your killer? Do you think you can go up against someone like that?"

"If it was a fashion showdown, a DKNY pantsuit beats an old kiss T-shirt any day," I said.

Marlene didn't seem impressed. "I think you should tell your cop friend, Mark Mayhew," she said. "The police keep tabs on those hate group guys."

"I'm not going to have Mark tell me I'm crazy again. If the Aryan Avenger turns out to be a harmless nutcase, I'll have wasted Mark's time and confirmed his suspicions about me. Besides, I haven't found the Avenger yet."

"What are you going to do? Walk down Klocke, listen for which house has Wagner blasting, and bust down the door?"

"You saw that movie, too," I said. "If it is the guy in the KISS T-shirt, I don't think I'll hear the 'Ride of the Valkyries' playing."

I went back to work and finished writing my column. It was three thirty by the time I hit the button and sent it into the oosphere. There was still time to check out Klocke Street. I grabbed my coat. The elevator doors opened just as I pressed the button. What luck. Uh-oh. The managing editor, Hadley Harris the Third, stepped into the elevator as the doors were closing. I always felt uncomfortable with that man. Being caged in an elevator with him was torture. Slow torture. *CG* elevators shuddered and bumped down every floor, as if they were lowered by a hand with a rope. If I was lucky, Hadley would be in a grumpy mood, give me a curt nod and ignore me. Unfortunately, today he was going for jovial. "Well, Francesca," he said, "are you sneaking out early, ha-ha?" He spoke with that phony-friendly headmaster's voice.

"I'm tracking down someone in deepest South St. Louis," I said. "On Klocke. A little street you've probably never heard of, but I hope it will be a good story and . . ." And I was babbling and the light indicated we had two more floors to go. At last, we landed. "Good-bye, Francesca," Hadley said.

"Have a nice day," I said—probably the dippiest good-bye in the language. The fact that I used it showed how rattled I was. Hadley smiled and went out the back door to his executive parking spot. I went out the front to the peons' lot. I took a deep breath. The smog, underlined with that faint beery smell, was a reviver. So was the sunny, chilly air. The unseasonably warm temperatures were gone, and the crisp cold weather made you want to go for a brisk walk. It was a good day to visit South St. Louis. I drove south on Grand. Klocke was a one-way street emptying out on Grand, and getting to it was tricky. I parked my car on Klocke and started walking. I had no idea what I would find. I just wanted to look.

The people who lived on Klocke were starting to come home from work. I saw tired-looking men in tan or blue coveralls and women in plain cloth coats made to last several seasons. This was not a street where lawyers and accountants stayed late at the office. There were no Beemers or Mercedeses in front of the houses, and nobody went out for sixty-dollar expense account lunches. People on Klocke worked hard at the plant or the office, paid their bills, and took one vacation a year, in the Ozarks.

The houses were mostly two-bedroom brick

bungalows, neat homes with small pointed-roofed porches and little slanted square lawns with steep concrete steps and metal-pipe hand-rails. The lawns had concrete ornaments and yellow plastic sunflowers. The trim was painted either white or green and most of the paint was fresh. So were the black SS lightning bolts next to the mailbox of the house just past the middle of the block.

Lightning bolts?

I stopped dead on the sidewalk and stared.

A long brass mailbox was bolted beside the front door, precisely even with the door knob. On either side of the box were black SS lightning bolts. They looked like the ones on the Aryan Avenger letters. I pulled the Avenger letters out of my purse and checked. The lightning bolts sure seemed similar, at least to me, standing down here on the street. I climbed the narrow concrete steps to the porch. Definitely the same lightning bolts.

The house was as well-kept as its neighbors. The back porch had a well-crafted wheelchair ramp, painted white. The front porch was white, too. So was the birdbath. The gutters were forest green. The steps were painted battleship gray. These were the classic South Side colors. A traditionalist lived here.

I rang the doorbell, and a man about forty-five answered it. He looked like he needed to sleep for a week. His black hair was thin. His hips were wide. His brown sweater was shapeless and pilled, and made his face look yellow. His shoul-

ders slumped, emphasizing a small round pot-
belly. His Hush Puppies looked like they should
have been put to sleep. I bet he didn't know they
were back in style. I felt tired and defeated just
looking at the guy.

"Yes?" he asked.

Might as well try the shock approach. "Hi. I'm
looking for the Aryan Avenger," I said brightly.
He backed up like I'd kicked him in the gut, then
turned pale and blurted, "It's not me."

"He's here," I said sternly, looking him in the
eye and willing him to obey. Francesca, She-
Wolf of the SS.

"No! N-nobody here," he stuttered, and tried
to shut the door. I must have been a vacuum
cleaner salesperson in a past life. I stuck my size
11 foot in the door, and the rest of me naturally
followed. I was six inches taller than this guy,
and he looked timid and out of shape. I found
myself standing in a tiny living room with a
huge brown plaid couch, a brown recliner, and a
boxy brown TV. The TV was on. The coffee table
was piled with magazines and paperbacks showing swastikas and guys in brown uniforms. I was
in the right place.

"Frank! Get in here!" said a man with a com-
manding voice. I followed the big voice down a
little hall. Frank ran after me, crying, "You can't
go in there!"

I went. The Aryan Avenger was in the room at
the end of the hall. The walls were decorated
with homemade swastikas and SS lightning
bolts and a faded Nazi flag that looked like some

GI's war souvenir. A portable toilet under the flag spoiled the effect.

The Aryan Avenger was sitting in a shiny metal wheelchair. He had to be at least eighty. His pale, papery skin was veined and speckled and hung from his arms and neck like old wrinkled rags. His bushy eyebrows were still mostly black, but his hair was yellowish white, like old pillow feathers. At one time, he must have been a big man, well over six feet tall. Now he was shrunken and stoop-shouldered. There was no way this guy could have killed Burt or Ralph. He could barely push himself around the room. He grasped the rubber-edged chair wheels and rolled over to me. "Who are you?" he demanded in a loud, angry voice.

"I'm Francesca. Why are you sending me those disgusting Aryan Avenger letters?"

"You got them?" He seemed pleased. Every author wants recognition.

"Yeah, I got them. What I don't understand is why you sent them."

"Why, to warn you, my dear," he said. His face took on a crafty look, like a sly parrot.

"About what?"

"The Jews. The Jews did this to me. They crippled me. People need to know." Yuck. The *p* in "people" set off a spray of spit at my belt level. I could see spit spots on my coat.

"What's that got to do with Ralph and Burt's deaths?"

"I read about JewBurt in your story in the paper," he said. "I didn't cry when JewBurt died."

"If you really read the paper, you'd know that Burt was buried out of St. Philomena's. Not many Jewish people are buried from a Catholic church."

He looked abashed. "Oh. I didn't read your article all the way to the end," he said. "It was kind of long."

Everyone's a critic.

"How did you know that two hundred dollars was taken from the till? That information wasn't published."

"Perfect poet inspiration," he said. The triple *p*'s turned on the shower. I was in danger of drowning from the Aryan Avenger.

"What's that supposed to mean?"

"I needed to find a rhyme for 'holler.' Holler—two hundred dollars. That's all."

"Oh, yeah? Then explain how you knew Ralph choked to death?"

"Who's Ralph?" he said, and suddenly looked lost, like I'd slipped in a question that wasn't supposed to be on the test.

"Ralph was my friend, and he had asthma and he couldn't breathe because someone took his inhalers and he died."

"But what's that got to do with me?" he whined. Then his eyes brightened with malice. "He's a fag, isn't he? I also warned you about fags in my letters, especially the last letter. But I didn't mean just *your* fag should choke and gag. I meant all fags. I had fag nurses in the hospital. Snippy, they were. I wanted them all to choke on . . . I can't say what exactly in front of a lady.

But I wanted them to choke because of the filthy things they do with their mouths."

"Nothing's filthier than your hate mail," I said. "And you didn't mind saying those things on paper. Why are you writing that disgusting stuff?"

"I have reason to hate the Jews. If it wasn't for them, I'd be walking. Dirty, filthy, stupid Jews did this to me. Look at that goddamned portable toilet. I can't even stand up like a man and take a piss!" Another P-word. Another spit shower. He got me again. Spit happens.

"I'm not too pleased with the sit-down plumbing problem myself," I said, hoping I got him back with a little spray. "But you have no reason to say those ugly things, or claim you killed Burt. You didn't. You couldn't."

"I know," he said. "I can't even leave the house. I can't even take a crap without being lifted out of this chair. I can't do anything anymore. I'm useless. Useless. Useless. I can't even die and I want to so bad." His rage turned to tears, then to harsh, racking sobs.

Frank, who'd been lurking slump-shouldered at the door, grabbed me by the arm and dragged me out of the room. He shut the door and started chewing me out in a harsh, low voice. "Now look what you've done," he said between clenched teeth. "You've upset him."

"I've upset *him*? Listen, Bud . . ."

"Frank," he hissed.

"Listen, Frank. Your father sent me that ugly antigay, anti-Semitic slop through the mail. He threatened me, too."

"You're strong," Frank whined, while he picked fuzzballs off his sweater. "You can stand it. You don't have to live with him, day in and day out. I have no life. All my money goes for a sitter to watch him when I'm at work. She leaves at three thirty, and I have to come straight home from the plant to stay with him. I don't sleep through the night because he calls me to help him every time he has to go to the john. Maybe the letters aren't very nice, but they keep him quiet for hours. He loves to write the poems and color in the drawings."

"Not very nice? They're evil, Frank. Evil. He's not some kindergartner drawing pictures of his puppy. Those are swastikas. And SS lightning bolts. A lot of people died because of those symbols. Take his pens and paper away."

"He's my father," he wailed. "I can't do that. The letters are the only thing that keep him occupied."

"Look, you're lucky he sent the letters to me first. What are you going to do if he sends those letters to a Jewish person? There are death camp survivors living in this city. This Nazi nut mail could drive them to suicide. You could be responsible for a death like that. Do you realize it's a federal offense to send hate mail? The FBI could be here next. What's the matter with you? What's the matter with him?"

Frank looked dazed, and kept picking at his sweater. Then he said, "He didn't used to be like this. He didn't used to hate people. It was the accident that did it. Before that, he was a self-reliant widower. Mom died ten years ago. It was hard on Dad. They were married forty-seven years. But he picked himself up and went on. He made a life for himself. He played cards with some other retirees from the plant. He had a garden and grew beefsteak tomatoes and gave them to the neighbors. He went to church and he danced every Saturday night at the VFW hall.

"Then about two years ago, he was driving to church on a Sunday. An old lady named Mrs. Cohen had a heart attack, drove through a stop sign, and broadsided Dad's car. Her big old Buick wiped out his Chevy Nova. Mrs. Cohen died. The accident left Dad paralyzed from the waist down. Some people can do fine in a wheelchair. Dad turned mean and bitter. Because the old lady's name was Cohen, he's hated Jewish people ever since. I think he throws in gays and blacks and everyone else for a little variety.

"You want to hear the funny part? They were so alike, Dad and Mrs. Cohen. She was eighty-three, and a little shaky behind the wheel. Her daughter should have taken her license away, but she didn't want to interfere with her mother's independence. The old lady didn't drive more than once or twice a week. Dad was eighty-one. His eyesight was going and his reflexes weren't so good. But he could still drive during the day and he only drove to church and the doctor's office, so I didn't do anything about his license, either.

"Well, we both have to live with that, Mrs. Cohen's daughter and me. Except sometimes I

think she got the best of it. Her mother is dead. I
have to live with Dad. It's awful. I hate it. I think
I hate him, too. I didn't used to. I admired the
old man because he was so independent. But
now he's wearing me down, and I promised him
I wouldn't put him in a home as long as the
money doesn't run out."

He looked down at the floor, ashamed, and
went back to picking at his sweater. I softened
my voice. "I'm sorry, Frank. I really am. But you
can't let him send those letters anymore."

"I know that. But what am I going to do with
him all day? When he's bored he gets so mean, I
know the sitter will quit again. It's hell finding
another one, and each new one wants more
money because he's such a difficult case. And I
don't have any more money. You don't understand."

I felt sick, sad, and sleazy for forcing my way
into this small-time tragedy. "Fraaaank!" the
Aryan Avenger called. "Get me some water, god-
dammit." Frank went back to wait on his father.
I let myself out the front door. So much for
Francesca and the Adventure of the Aryan
Avenger.

Maybe Detective Mark Mayhew was right.
Ralph died of natural causes. Burt was murdered in a holdup. One unknown murderer did
not kill both men for an unknown reason. I
should quit searching for someone who didn't
exist. I should mourn them and let them go. I
should grow up. The search on Klocke Street
was one of the low points of my life.

Mayhew said it, but I didn't hear him: Not everyone is murdered. Poor Burt died because he lived in a bad neighborhood. Poor Ralph died because he didn't take care of himself. I owed Mayhew a lunch and an apology. Boy, was I glad I didn't follow Marlene's advice and tell him about the Aryan Avenger. I didn't want to think about the razzing he'd give me.

I'd get it over with, tell Marlene I'd found the Avenger but he wasn't a killer. He wasn't anything but a sad old man. Oh, well. He did live on Klocke. At least some of my detecting skills were working. What time was it? I checked my watch. Not even four o'clock. My visit had taken less than half an hour. Uncle Bob's was a few minutes away. The place was usually half empty at this hour. The dinner rush didn't start for another thirty minutes. Marlene and I could have a quiet talk and I could have my third scrambled egg of the day.

I pulled into the lot and parked back by the alley. The lot was deserted, except for the staff cars parked by the side fence. I stepped carefully out of my car, because there was black ice on the back lot. I heard a car roaring down the alley. People drive too fast in that alley all the time, but I could tell this car was booking—moving faster than usual. I looked up and saw it swing into the lot. That car is heading straight for me, I thought, slowly. Too slowly. Why was I standing there?

Because I couldn't believe it. Someone was actually trying to run me down. On purpose. I also couldn't believe how big that sucker was. All I could see was the shiny bumper and grille, like an evil smile, coming straight for me. The car must have been six feet away when I finally had sense enough to jump back. The car swerved and missed me, then slammed on the brakes, backed up and went for me again. I looked around for help, but no one saw me. No Uncle Bob's cooks looking out the kitchen. No neighbors looking out their windows. No customers pulling into the lot. I might as well be in the middle of the desert, instead of the center of the city. Unless a customer drove into the lot, I was roadkill.

The car drove straight at me again. I ran between two staff cars, Marlene's blue Dodge and the cook's old tan tank. I hit a patch of ice, slipped, and grabbed on to a fender. The car backed up and went after me again. This time, it looked like he was going to ram into the staff cars and squash me between them, so I ran out of there and the driver veered away. I kicked off my heels for better traction. The ground was cold. I didn't realize I could run so fast. When your life depends on it, you can give Jackie Joyner-Kersee a run for her Olympic gold. I jumped the speed bump to the fried chicken place next door. That was a mistake. That lot had even more open space and no back windows. Now nobody could see me and the car had a straight shot at me. No staff cars and no Dumpster for me to hide behind.

I turned and ran back down the alley to Uncle Bob's lot. The car roared behind me like a hungry animal. The driver was going to catch me. I was out of breath. My coat was heavy and I was sweating. I was going to get run down. Suddenly, I saw a big red commercial laundry truck lumbering down the alley. At last! Help. It was turning into Uncle Bob's lot. The car couldn't chase me back to Uncle Bob's with that big old truck there, blocking the way.

I ducked behind the truck. I saw the white shed at the corner of Uncle Bob's lot. I had no idea what was in the shed, but if it wasn't locked I was about to find out. The shed looked strong enough to withstand a direct car hit. I grabbed the doorknob, threw myself in, and landed head-first in a cart full of dirty napkins. I just lay there in the cart in the dark, trying to catch my breath.

I realized I didn't get a license number for the car. I wasn't sure of the color, except it was beige or gray or dirty white, probably American, maybe ten years old. I couldn't tell you much about the driver because he was wearing a black-and-red ski mask, a beige coat, and gloves. I wasn't even sure the driver was a he, except there was something about the set of the shoulders that made me think it was a man. But if you told me it was a woman, I wouldn't argue with you. All I could say for sure was, somebody wanted to kill me.

Now that I thought about the chase, I did it all wrong. I should have headed toward the building and tried to get to the front door. But it happened so quick, all I could think about was getting away. I'd recovered enough to realize I was shivering, and the dirty napkins smelled like cold bacon grease and old eggs and were sticky with syrup. I was thinking about moving, when the laundry truck driver banged open the door and said, "I've told you guys about using my laundry shed as a sleeping area. This isn't a motel."

I started laughing. And laughing and laughing and laughing. I couldn't stop. I had tears in my eyes. The laundryman looked scared, and ran to the Deliveries Only door. Marlene came out and said, "Francesca, what the hell happened to you?"

Good question. My coat was ripped on the right sleeve and striped with black grease. My shoes were gone and my stockings were in shreds. But suddenly, I felt good. Very good. "Someone tried to kill me," I said cheerfully. "I didn't imagine it. Burt and Ralph were murdered, and I'm going to find out who did it."

10

The next day, I had no time to look at death. I had to deal with the facts of life. Elvis was getting married, and he wanted me at the wedding. He was waiting for me when I got in to work.

Louise, the "Family" department secretary, grabbed me as I passed the copy desk. "Do you know that guy?" she said, lowering her voice and pointing. I could see him sitting near my desk, his drink-sogged nose glowing. I thought I saw a woman sitting next to him.

"Sure. That's Elvis Fairmount, one of the South Side's most noted barflies."

"Looks like a drunk to me, too," said Louise. "He insists on seeing you. He's got a woman with him, but she looks okay. I gave them coffee and chairs."

"Good God. After that treatment, they're still here? Elvis must be desperate." The *Gazette*'s coffee looked and tasted like something that leaked out of your car. *Gazette* chairs were instruments of torture. I think the paper bought them used from jury rooms.

The minute I got to my desk, Elvis popped the question: "Edna here and I want to get hitched tomorrow. We want you to be our best man—or woman—or person, however you're supposed to say it. We need a witness. The guy who was supposed to do it had a heart attack last night. We got the license and everything. Edna's boss is going to be one, but we need two and we can't find no other witness on short notice. Unless you stand up for us tomorrow, we'll have to postpone our wedding until the guy recovers."

Elvis gave Edna a lovesick look. I'd have to be a hardhearted creature to ignore his plea. Fortunately, I was. "I'm sorry, Elvis, but you don't want me for your witness. I'm no great believer in marriage. I'm not even married."

"That's okay," Elvis said. "We aren't that crazy about it, either. But her daughter from California wants to visit us, and she's real religious, and she won't stay in a house where people are living in sin. So we decided to tie the knot. We love each other and we don't want to listen to her lecture us, and we thought maybe you could write about us if you wanted. We don't care what you say."

I said yes. This match was based on mutual need. They needed a witness in a hurry. I needed a quick column.

Elvis must have been in his sixties, and Edna looked ten years younger. Elvis was so skinny, I figured he kept rocks in the pockets of his brown polyester pants so he wouldn't blow away. Edna picked out his clothes, and she kept her man color-coordinated. Today Elvis was wearing a brown suit, yellow shirt and socks, and a brown-and-yellow striped tie. Edna, his bride, sat beside him. She looked so small, so pretty and pink-cheeked. She was a delicate woman with little pearl earrings and softly crimped hair. She looked like your favorite aunt. "What do you like most about Elvis?" I asked Auntie Edna.

"He's the home of the whopper," she said, giggling and patting his polyester knee. I nearly fell over. I'll never look at polyester pants the same way again. Now I knew what was weighing Elvis down.

Elvis popped the question to me Tuesday morning, and I said yes. Now it was 2:00 A.M. Wednesday, the day of the wedding. I didn't know how the bride and groom were feeling, but I was scared for them. This was serious. These two people were going to be tied together for life. It made you think. I switched on the nightstand light and sat up in our unblessed bed.

"What's wrong?" asked Lyle sleepily.

"I think I'm making a mistake," I said. "Why am I helping Elvis and Edna get married? They're living together now. If they have a fight and Edna wants to leave Elvis, or vice versa, she packs her suitcase and walks out the door. If they tie the knot, they can't get out unless they pay some lawyer thousands of dollars."

Lyle got up, wrapped his dressing gown

around himself, and sat next to me on the bed. Monty, his big gray cat, wrapped his tail around his paws and sat on the other side. Both were ready to listen. At that hour, Monty looked the smartest of the three of us. "Ever hear of palimony?" said Lyle. "Even singles don't always walk out now without paying lawyers."

"I don't think Edna and Elvis are rich enough for those problems," I said.

"How long have they been living together?" asked Lyle.

"Two years."

"Why are you worried? They're not kids. They love each other and want to be together permanently. Anyway, he might find it sexy to make love to a married woman. I'd like to try it some time," he said.

I didn't want to joke. I wanted to worry. "Lyle, what if things go wrong for Edna and Elvis? I know he drinks."

"She knows it, too. If she's living with him, there are no surprises after marriage."

"What if they have an argument some Saturday night and Edna shoots him? I'll be responsible. I was a witness. I helped make that wedding possible."

"She'll be responsible," he said. "She pulled the trigger. I've never seen a husband-wife murder story yet that mentions the witnesses at their wedding."

I didn't laugh. I didn't answer. I just sat there.

"Francesca, Edna is not your mother," he said, gathering me into his arms. "Some people do live happily ever after. Some marriages do work out. Theirs might. Ours would. Will you marry me?"

"No. I love you, but I can't marry you."

I kissed him and got out of bed. He looked sad but soon fell back asleep. Monty curled up at his feet and slept, too. I spent a restless night, wandering through the house like a ghost, wishing I had the courage to marry Lyle. I knew there was no other man for me. But every time I saw us standing before a minister, I saw myself standing at my parents' grave. They had not been parted in death, but they should have separated in life. They shouldn't have married at all, and I didn't want to make that mistake.

The night matched my mood. It was typical St. Louis weather. Another false spring day had turned suddenly cold by sundown. The temperature dropped forty degrees in a few hours. Lightning flashed. The wind moaned and lashed the tree branches outside Lyle's window. By morning there was snow, light, fluffy flakes like someone had cut open a feather pillow. The snow melted when it hit the streets, but it frosted the yards like icing on a wedding cake. By midmorning the sun was out. The snow sparkled. Elvis and Edna would have a fine day for marrying. I put on a suit and went off to their wedding.

Edna and Elvis wanted their ceremony at the Fit-Mor Footwear Factory, a depressing old red-brick building behind the railroad tracks. For Elvis and Edna, it was as romantic as the lily pond at Tower Grove Park. She was a secretary and he ran a forklift in the Fit-Mor warehouse. They met at the office copier, when he sneaked in to copy some receipts for his taxes. It was love at first sight. They wanted to marry at the place where they met. Edna's boss, Sadie, a sweet woman in her fifties, was delighted. Sadie was as romantic as a young girl, and she appointed herself mother of the bride. Today, Sadie was a valentine in bright red from her lips to her shoe tips. She opened the office door for me.

"Francesca, I'm just thrilled you're here," she said. "I recognize you from your picture in the paper. It's an honor. We're almost ready."

I could see frantic wedding preparations were going on. The whole Fit-Mor front office had chipped in to make this wedding work. Three women were hanging white paper bells and crepe paper streamers over the dusty metal desks. A fourth was taking all the risqué cartoons off the filing cabinets. Two men were unrolling a white runner down the main aisle, to cover the cracked and speckled tile. A woman arranged flowers on the file cabinets. Other office workers brought in Corning Ware bowls filled with bean dip, artichoke dip, taco salad, and mostaccioli for the buffet after the ceremony. Sadie had cooked and sliced a whole ham. Now a young guy came in toting a big bucket with four iced bottles of champagne. There were white ribbons on the handles.

I could see that Elvis was a bald-faced liar. Any one of these people would have stood up for that low-down lying groom. Wait till I saw him. I did see him, dipping into the bean dip at the buffet. Everyone else was occupied with chores at the moment. No one was near him. Good.

"Elvis, you awfully wedded weasel!" I hissed. "You lied to me. You didn't need me for a witness. You could have asked anyone in this office."

"Yeah, but I promised Edna I'd get her wedding announced in the paper, and I didn't want to pay the *City Gazette*'s hundred-dollar fee. I figured if I got you to stand up for us, you'd write about it, and I'd get a wedding announcement for free. Besides, you'd do a better job of writing it and more people would read it," he said, giving me his most sincere smile.

"It's too late for flattery, you four-flushing faker. You're starting your wedding with a lie."

"I am not," Elvis said, with surprising energy and indignation. "I love Edna and she loves me and I'm glad her daughter's visit gives us a reason to get married. We want to be together forever." He spoke with great dignity for a man waving a corn chip full of bean dip. "Besides, you'll get your story, and that's all you care about anyway."

I winced. That hit home. Maybe I couldn't marry Lyle because I was already married—to my work. I didn't want to argue with Elvis on his wedding day. "Peace, Elvis," I said. "I'm here. I might do the story anyway, if you give me decent quotes. And I wish you much happiness."

"Thanks," he said, and he did look happy. "She's terrific."

I caught a glimpse of the bride, carrying a clothing bag into a back office. Friends and family had begun arriving. They were standing around or sitting on desks, drinking white wine and looking happier than most people do in an office. Sadie announced that it was time for the wedding. Someone put the office phones on the answering machine. Someone else popped a tape of Elvis (the other Elvis) singing "Love Me Tender" into a boom box, and pretty Edna tottered down the aisle on powder-blue spike heels, wearing a powder-blue lace dress and a dyed-to-match corsage.

Elvis was also dyed-to-match in a powder-blue suit, dark blue shirt and socks, and blue striped tie. He was wearing a big grin, as Edna walked down the long rows of desks to the copier. Her Elvis took her hand.

It was the preacher's job to make sure the couple matched permanently. He wore a navy blue suit, set off with specks of dandruff, a bad haircut, and a pious look. Only the two witnesses broke the color scheme. Sadie was wearing red. And I realized, to my horror, that my suit was black. How festive.

The wedding party stood at the office high altar, the copying machine. It was decorated with white bows, candles, and flowers. "Ought to keep it this way all the time," whispered Edna. "Only time the damn thing's ever done what it's supposed to."

The phone nearest the copier rang twice, then

stopped. "Good," said Elvis. "That makes it a double-ring ceremony." Everyone laughed.

"This is a marriage that can't be duplicated," the preacher said. "Edna and Elvis wanted to have their marriage take place at the spot where they first fell in love. They also wanted you, their family, friends, and co-workers, to be with them today to celebrate their love.

"Do you, Edna, accept Elvis as your lawful husband?"

"I do," she said, and shyly took his hand.

Elvis also took Edna for his lawful wife. He said the beautiful old vows: "I, Elvis, take you, Edna, for my lawful spouse, to have and to hold, from this day forward . . ."

Edna recited her part: ". . . for better, for worse, for richer, for poorer, in sickness and in health, until death do us part."

Then the preacher weighed in with: "Having said that, in the presence of Edna and Elvis's family and friends, and these witnesses, Sadie and Francesca, and by the power vested in me, I now pronounce you husband and wife from this day forward. What therefore has been joined together, let no one put asunder.

"You may now kiss," he concluded.

Edna and Elvis did kiss, a dreamy kiss with their eyes closed, like teenagers on a date. They looked so happy, I envied them. The whole office applauded.

I stuck around while the minister did the paperwork and we witnesses signed some stuff. Then I shook some hands, stuck a few chips in the dips, congratulated the newlyweds, and left. I felt oddly lonely. I couldn't talk with Lyle. He was at the university. This was his late day. He had classes until nine thirty at night. I had nothing to do but find a murderer.

Fit-Mor was a few blocks from Billie's house. I might as well start with Ralph's mother. I drove down Hampton Avenue to Billie's house. This was one of my favorite sections of South St. Louis. Most cities put their workers in plain ugly boxes—a prelude to their long-term residence in a plain pine box. But St. Louis workers lived in houses made with style and imagination, brick bungalows with delightful details: a brick arch over a front door, a small stained-glass window, stone trim on the porch.

Billie's neighborhood always gave me the feeling I'd entered an enchanted forest. The steep peaked roofs of the small brick homes looked like they belonged in a German fairy tale. And Billie, who had seemed much too young to be Ralph's mother, was a blond enchantress who'd cast a spell so she wouldn't grow older.

The spell was broken at Ralph's death. The woman who came to the door of the enchanted brick bungalow could have been Billie's mother. Her small and shapely figure had shrunk so it looked like an empty sack. Billie didn't care anymore. She was suffering horribly after her son's death.

Billie's gray bodyguard, her sister Dorothy, had gone back home to Minneapolis. Billie was alone now. She looked like she'd been sleeping, and my knock on the door woke her up. "I was going to call you," she said, "but I just don't have the energy these days. I sleep all the time, but I never feel rested. Ah, well, you don't need to hear that. Can I get you some coffee or a beer?"

I said coffee was fine. We sat at the kitchen table, where South Siders feel most comfortable. I was pleased. The living room was for company, the kitchen for close friends. After we settled in with our coffee mugs, Billie said, "I have something for you from Ralph."

I must have looked startled because she said, "It wasn't a bequest. Ralph didn't leave anything but bills and that old truck and it cost me to have it hauled away. This was something he wanted to give you before he died. Ralph was going to drop it by your office, but he got distracted and left the envelope on my kitchen table. Before he could pick it up and take it to you, he died."

I looked at the envelope and smiled. Ralph had removed the postage and pasted a sticker with my name over the previous name. That was Ralph. He believed in recycling. "I'll read it later, unless you want a look now."

"No, take your time. He was always clipping newspaper articles and cartoons and crazy stuff for you. But I'm not sure I want to see it. I think I've cried all I can."

I could feel her sorrow. It sat in the room with us, as if it was another presence. I wanted to pour it a cup of coffee, it seemed so real. I put the envelope away for later. I had something I wanted to ask her, and I didn't want any distractions. "Did you ever wonder why there were no inhalers found near him? Do you think someone removed his inhaler and that's why he died?"

"I would love to believe someone killed Ralph," she said. "But I know my son too well. He killed himself with his carelessness. He'd get caught up in a job, and that's all he'd think about. He wouldn't stop to get an inhaler."

"But he was afraid of dying of asthma."

"He was afraid of dying of AIDS, too, but he chased after a drag queen who was unfaithful to him," Billie said.

I must have raised an eyebrow. I can't keep the unruly things down.

"I knew Ralph was gay," his mother said. "We talked about it. I asked him if he practiced safe sex, and he said safe sex was almost as bad as no sex at all. I lectured him, I really did, but he didn't listen. He told me the risk was what made it so exciting. He said he didn't want to die an old man. Well, he got his wish."

It sounded harsh when she said it. I wondered if under that sorrow, she was angry at her son.

"Ralph took risks," Billie said. "It was just the way he was. I've asked myself again and again how I could have brought him up differently, so he wouldn't take chances. But if I had, then he wouldn't have been Ralph.

"I guess I did the right thing. I let him live the life he wanted, and I didn't interfere. It is the biblical curse, you know, to outlive your child. If only he'd had some of his brother's caution."

His brother had plenty to spare. I remembered Jonathan, the Brooks Brothers poster child, and his boring wife, Rebecca, from the wake. They were so cautious they were lifeless. Ralph wasn't the only stiff in the room.

Billie stared into her coffee cup. The coffee was growing cold, but she hardly drank any of it. She went on as if she were talking to herself instead of to me. "Maybe I encouraged Ralph to be wild in reaction to my straight son. Maybe, maybe, maybe. I don't know. I love both my boys and they are so different.

"Did someone take Ralph's inhaler? No." As she said this, her gray eyes came alive and I saw a flash of the beautiful Billie of old. "But I'll tell you this much. I'd love to have someone else to blame, so I could quit blaming myself. But I don't think I will ever stop."

I could hardly look at her sorrow-ravaged face. I left her sitting at the kitchen table, and let myself out. I took the envelope with me and went home to Lyle's house. He wouldn't be home for hours yet, but I wanted to see what was in Ralph's envelope. I set it down on the couch, while I lit a fire in the fireplace. Might as well get comfortable. Big gray Monty sat down firmly on Ralph's envelope. I moved the cat's dozen pounds of muscle. He jumped down and began playing with my shoestrings. When I opened the envelope, Monty began batting something across the carpet, but I didn't pay much attention to him.

The first thing out of the envelope was a "Far

Side" cartoon. It showed a herd of dinosaurs smoking cigarettes. "Why the dinosaurs are extinct," it said. I laughed. Ralph and I were dinosaur buffs, and we'd been discussing the latest theories on what killed them. Trust Ralph to have the last word on the subject—or in this case, the last laugh.

There was also a souvenir program for the Miss American Gender Bender Pageant, the one we went to together, a thousand years ago. It was folded open to the page where the queens and pageant winners wish one another well in large ads. I thought again how girlish their congratulations looked—they could have come straight, if you'll pardon the word, from a Junior Miss program. Ralph had circled one full-page color ad. It said: "Good luck to the sweetest girls in the world. You're all winners, no matter how the pageant turns out." It was signed "Maria Callous, the Ass with Class—Last Year's Third Place Winner, Miss American Gender Bender Pageant."

The picture showed a petite, pretty blonde, surprisingly subdued for an impersonator. Maria didn't go in for the usual outrageous sequin outfits and dramatic makeup. In the photo, she was dressed like a young woman going to tea at her fiancé's family mansion for the first time. Maria was looking coyly over her shoulder. She wore a navy-blue suit with a little bow at the back, to set off the Ass, and I had to admit it had Class. She wore white gloves to give her hands class, too. Even her hair was classy. Instead of the usual wild mane of curly red, blond, or black hair, she had a silky blond wedge cut. Maria looked rather like Princess Di, as I remembered Ralph saying at the pageant. He'd also said Maria was a no-show. Ralph thought she dropped out of the pageant rather than risk her title.

Why had Ralph circled that ad in the program? Maybe her act was a little different, but under the suit was one more drag queen.

There was something else in Ralph's envelope. A *City Gazette* "Police Notes" column. The one Rita the Retiree read to me on the phone. Rita insisted there was a story in that item, and I'd told her no, because I really didn't want to go up against Hadley's current smut campaign.

Now it looked like Ralph agreed with Rita. He'd circled the same small item that fascinated the salty retiree. It began: "Police found the body of a prostitute in a Dumpster in the 700 block of Bedler St. An autopsy showed the person had been beaten and strangled and was undergoing a sex change. The victim was 22, and believed to be taking female hormones. The name has been withheld pending notification of the victim's family. . . ."

What made Ralph circle that item? And why did he have Maria's ad circled? I looked inside the envelope but there wasn't anything else. Then I noticed that Monty was batting a yellow Post-it note around on the floor. I grabbed it away from the cat when I recognized Ralph's neat, precise writing. The note said: "Francesca—Do you think this is Maria?"

Did I think what was Maria? Oh, did I think the dead hooker was Maria, and she got her classy ass dumped in a vacant lot? That might be another reason why she dropped out of the pageant without a word—she was murdered. Ralph was wired enough in to that world to pick up any rumors. He would have asked me to check them out.

I could, too. What time was it? Almost seven. Good. Not too late. Time to saddle up the Jag and head for the *Gazette*. I started to leave Lyle a note—"Off to the morgue. Won't need dinner."— but when I read it over I decided maybe it would be better if I didn't leave a note. I sounded like a member of the Addams Family. Maybe I'd call him from the paper.

By seven o'clock the first deadline on the paper was over. It was another half hour for the second edition. That's the edition for corrections and additions and late-breaking news stories. This was the newsroom at its most serious, when everything—and everyone—worked. The sniping and backstabbing were at a minimum at this time. People were too busy. They were on the phone correcting or chasing down stories. Editors were reading at their computers or checking proofs. Charlie was gone for the day, but I could see Hadley reading page proofs at his desk. The newsroom had a sense of purpose and a high energy level. It was exhilarating to be in the room then.

But I wasn't going to be working in the newsroom tonight. I headed to the morgue—the newspaper reference library. I always wondered if it was called the morgue because nothing is deader than old news. The *Gazette* morgue had newspaper clipping files dating back to the 1890s. For the last ten years, the newspaper stories were kept in the computer.

The people who work back there are not morgue attendants. They're reference librarians, and the *Gazette* had some good ones. Unfortunately, the paper, which suffered from chronic stinginess, cut back on its morgue staff when the reference library went on computer. The paper's money men reasoned that the news staff could do their own checking on the computer and save the cost of several reference librarians.

It was a nice theory, but most reporters were only so-so at the intricacies of the computer system. We made some colossal bloopers because we didn't know the fine points of searching the system. Once an error got into a story, and that story got into the reference system uncorrected, it stayed that way. The most famous example was a local politician with the name of Waavermann. Some reporter spelled his name the way it sounded—Waverman—which is the name Waavermann would have gone by if he'd had any decency or compassion for the press. Anyway, the wrong-way Waverman got into the computer system and became the rock that many a reporter crashed on. The last time I looked, Waavermann had his name misspelled at least eighteen times, more times than he had it spelled right. And unless you knew how to look for the correct spelling, a skill most reporters never mastered, you'd check the name Waverman in the reference computer, see that it had racked up an impressive number of hits, and assume it was the correct spelling.

I didn't rely on my computer skills when I worked on something important. I threw myself on the mercy of the reference librarian. Fred was on tonight, and he was good. He was also cute. His hair was permanently mussed from running his fingers through it, and he had freckles on his nose. He frowned at the "Police Notes" clip I showed him.

"Fred, was there a follow-up on this story on the murdered prostitute? Did the *Gazette* ever print the victim's name?"

Fred typed several key words into his computer, hit a button, and waited. "No follow-up," he said.

"Sure the information wasn't misfiled?"

"Nope," he said, "Nothing. The story was dead and dropped—just like the hooker."

Next I talked with Tina. She was still at her desk. Tina is a tall, handsome African American reporter who covers the city police beat. She could have risen higher at the paper, but she had no patience with the *CG* office politics. Tina liked writing and reporting and digging for facts. She hated playing games and toadying to editors. Police beat suited her. She did her job accurately and well. I pulled up a chair and showed her the "Police Notes" column.

"Sure, I remember that story," Tina said. "I

did a follow-up with the victim's name, and Hadley killed it."

"Why? Was he on one of his smut rampages?"

"You got it. Said the name didn't belong in a family newspaper. The victim's mother called Hadley up after the first item appeared and said she'd suffered enough. He told me he killed the story out of compassion for the mother. Ask me, he was looking for an excuse. You know how weird he gets about sex in general and sex and murder in particular. It wasn't a big story, so I didn't protest too much."

"Do you remember the victim's name?"

"No, but I still have the story." She checked her computer list, called it up and read from it: "Police said the victim was born Michael Delmer. His surviving relatives included his mother in Florissant. He lived with a roommate in the 3400 block of Crittenden on the city's South Side. Mr. Delmer was a female impersonator, known professionally as Maria Callous."

"Ralph was right! It was Maria, the Ass with Class!" I said, much too loudly, and a few heads turned at nearby desks. "That was the rest of her slogan," I said to Tina.

"I know," she said. "I wasn't even going to try to get that in the paper. I should tell you that her roommate was also her manager."

"Maybe the roommate-manager can help me," I said. "Maria disappeared during the Miss American Gender Bender Pageant, and most people thought she'd dropped out because she didn't have much chance of winning. Instead, the poor thing was murdered. You've been a huge help. Can I ask you one more question? Who did the autopsy for the Medical Examiner's office?"

"I couldn't forget that one," said Tina. "It was Cutup Katie. That's Dr. Kathryn Granito. You're in luck. She likes to talk about her work. She'll tell you everything you need to know. I have her number here somewhere." Tina rooted around in the pile of papers and old newspapers that covered her desk, pulled out a fat leather address book, looked up the number for me, and wrote it on a Post-it note.

"Thanks," I said. "I'll call her tomorrow and do lunch at the city morgue."

"Couldn't be any worse than the *Gazette* cafeteria," said Tina.

11

"I need to pick your brain," I said to Cutup Katie when I called her the next day.

"You've come to the right place," she said. "I've been picking brains all morning. Also freezing, slicing, and staining sections."

Katie is a pathologist with the St. Louis Medical Examiner's office. Her job at the city morgue gave me the creeps, but I liked Katie right from our first conversation. Tina told me she has a string of honors and medical degrees. But Katie grew up in the country, and it gave her a down-to-earth outlook about her job: People die. Sometimes it's sad. Mostly, it's interesting.

"I need to ask you questions about an autopsy you did last month," I said. "It's okay, there are no traps. It's not a high-profile case. In fact, that's why I'm getting in touch with you. This death hardly made the *Gazette* at all. All I want is information that's on the public record."

"No problem," said Katie. "My work is stacked up to the ceiling, but I can meet you for lunch."

I hoped it was paperwork Katie had stacked to the ceiling, but I was afraid to ask.

"I'll eat lunch with you," I said, "but not in your office. Tina said her last lunch with you there was disgusting."

"It was good," said Katie. "I had the daily special sent in from the lunchroom around the corner, and they have terrific spaghetti."

"Too bad you didn't change for lunch. She said those smears on your lab coat looked a lot like the daily special. She lost her appetite."

"I'm sorry," said Katie, and she sounded contrite. "I'm so used to my job, sometimes I forget how it affects people. Listen, if we go to lunch today, I'll trade my lab coat for a nice suit jacket."

"In that case, the *City Gazette* will take you to Kemoll's if you'll tell me all about the autopsy you did on a female impersonator named Michael Delmer."

"All right," said Katie, with enthusiasm. "A great lunch spot. An unusual case, too. I'll meet you at Kemoll's about one o'clock."

She didn't get there until one twenty, but I didn't mind waiting. Kemoll's is an old St. Louis restaurant that successfully survived a transplant to a new upscale location downtown. Now it was a favorite with the business lunch crowd. I sat in a comfortable chair and raided the bread basket while I waited.

I knew it was Katie coming across the room,

even without Tina's description. She looked the way she talked: smart and sensible. She had a no-nonsense brown suit and shoes, short brown hair, and brown eyes. She was about thirty-five, and as they say in her trade, she had "the body of a well-nourished well-muscled Caucasian female." These weren't gym-rat muscles. Katie played softball and pool. She drove a pickup truck, kept a big old dog, went deer hunting, and made her own gourmet deer jerky, which was so good the city kids in her office lost their reservations about eating Bambi. I'd never guess she was a doctor until she revealed her guilty secret: she loved golf with a passion that bordered on, well . . . the pathological.

We didn't discuss the autopsy until after we finished lunch. Katie held back out of courtesy so her shoptalk wouldn't spoil my grilled swordfish. It wasn't until the coffee came that Katie pulled the autopsy report out of her black briefcase. I looked at it curiously.

"Never seen one before?" she said.

Never. The report was fairly thick. The front page said it was "an autopsy on the body of Michael Delmer by medical examiner Kathryn Granito."

It also said, "In my opinion the cause of death was anoxic injury secondary to strangulation."

The manner of death was homicide. There was one more piece of page one news: The body had "an absence of genitalia, mutilated after death." At that bit of information, my swordfish did a flip-flop. The rest of the report explained how Katie reached those conclusions. She gave me the highlights.

"A homicide detective was present for the autopsy, but he was an old hand, so I didn't have to worry about him passing out. He told me the victim had one arrest for prostitution and one for loitering, but nothing in the last two years.

"The victim was strangled and the genital area was mutilated after death. Both are usually signs that it was a sex killing. But I'll get into that later. On the gross examination I noticed gynecomastia," Katie said, turning the pages in her report.

"What's that?"

"The guy was starting to grow tits. That's not such a big deal, no pun intended. Some textbooks say up to forty percent of normal men have palpable breast tissue . . ."

"What's that mean?" I interrupted again.

"You can feel it," Katie said.

"I think those same figures are true for women," I said.

"Certainly true for me," she said. "Anyway, a number of things can cause enlarged breasts in men. It can be a deficiency in testosterone. An increase in estrogen. A number of drugs, legal or illegal. Marijuana can give men bazooms, did you know that? I like to tell guys that little side effect of the weed."

"That's a reason for men to just say no. Might get women to say yes, though," I said.

"The other causes aren't as much fun. Tumors, like some lung cancers, and hyperthyroid problems can give men tits. Alcoholism can do it, too.

"Anyway, I did some checking on this guy to find out why he had breasts. The lungs, adrenals, and thyroid were normal. There was no evidence of marijuana use. The liver looked normal—no sign of cirrhosis."

"He wasn't an alcoholic," I said, brightly, like the A-student I used to be.

"Nope. When I did a tox screen I didn't find any drugs, but there were estrogen metabolites in the urine. Since there were no liver problems, adrenal disease, or tumors, and since the victim was dressed in women's clothes, it's real possible the guy was a transsexual, taking estrogen in preparation for a sex change operation. Which is what the cops guessed when they found the body. But we aren't allowed to guess until we rule out the other possibilities first.

"I couldn't examine the penis and testicles because there wasn't much left of them. The victim had been stabbed in the genitals seventy-eight times—at least I think so. There were so many cuts, they were hard to count. That's what we call overkill."

I nodded and watched the waiter pouring more coffee. I thought his hands shook. But maybe not.

"When someone is stabbed multiple times, it's either drugs, money, or sex. The assailant is frustrated: he can't get his drugs, he can't get sex, he can't get his money. There was no bruising or blood around the stabbing area, so the mutilation was done after death. There were no defense wounds on the victim's hands and arms, which is another sign it was done after death. I guarantee if you go after a live guy's gonads, there will be defense wounds."

"What was he stabbed with?"

"A small knife. A few of the marks seem to have been up to the hilt and running parallel to the blade marks. There are indentations of three millimeters on one side and seven on the other."

Katie caught my blank look. "That means it was probably a pocket knife. I can tell you that, but I couldn't swear to it on the witness stand. It could also be a kitchen knife or a small hunting knife, but I did notice those two ridges on either side, where the other blades would come out on a pocket knife. So my educated guess is a pocket knife.

"There was no sperm on the victim, so it's probably not some weirdo getting his jollies—unless he used a condom. Because of the overkill, I'd say the mutilation was done in anger.

"The victim was strangled, and that often has a sexual motive, too. He was strangled with his own chiffon scarf.

"The assailant fractured the hyoid bone. That's the horseshoe-shaped bone in front of the larynx that protects it. There was hemorrhage and some bad bruises.

"Strangulation is not a way you want to go. The cop told me the victim was a pretty little blonde, but not when I saw him. His head turned purple, his throat was bruised, and there were fingernail marks on his neck."

"The killer scratched him?"

"The victim did that to himself, trying to claw the scarf off. I checked the fingernails for hairs and stuff, but I didn't come up with anything."

"Could a small person strangle the victim?" I asked. At least I'd have some idea of the size of the killer.

"Easy. The guy only weighed a hundred pounds or so. Besides, if you get really mad— and whoever killed this guy was raging—you can strangle almost anyone. If you got mad enough, you could strangle a big guy like him," Katie said, pointing to our waiter. He backed away from the table.

"I think that's the end of the coffee," I said.

"Just as well, I have to get back to work," said Katie.

"One last question. Who claimed the body?"

"His mother. Now there's a piece of work. I'd like to carve her up—and she's still alive. You wouldn't believe the scene she made when she identified the body. The whole place was talking about it. Kept yelling, 'The shame! The shame!' At first everyone thought she was saying what a shame that her son died so young. Turns out she was ashamed of the way he died. He embarrassed his mother by getting strangled and thrown in a Dumpster."

The mother of Michael Delmer, also known as Maria Callous, the Ass with Class, lived in the suburb of Florissant, which was the end of the earth, as far as I was concerned. It took me forty-five minutes to drive to her house, and that's about the outer limit for a St. Louisan. I didn't have an appointment. I was pretty sure she wouldn't see me if I tried to make one. Maybe I'd get lucky and find her at home. Maybe I'd get luckier and find her gone.

The North County suburb started as an eighteenth-century French settlement. I liked the Old Town, with its ancient brick houses in mellowed soft shades of red. But most of Florissant was a sprawl of much newer ranch houses and split-levels, built in the sixties and seventies. Florissant had one other distinction: It was also the home of one of the newest Catholic saints, Philippine Duchesne.

Michael/Maria's mother lived in a newish ranch house off Shackelford Road. But she had plenty of old-time religion, too, and she proudly displayed it. The small front yard had a concrete statue of the Virgin Mary by the carport. The birdbath had a smaller St. Francis, with a concrete bird on his finger. A couple of pint-sized concrete angels perched in the gutters. I wasn't sure I'd want any angels of mine in the gutter.

The pale gray house with the black shutters had a wrought-iron eagle over the red front door, so I knew Mrs. Delmer was patriotic as well as devout. I rang the doorbell, and she answered. At least, I thought it was her. She was a small, trim, fiftyish woman in red stretch pants, a white turtleneck, and a red cardigan sweater. She wore enameled flag earrings and a red-white-and-blue belt to complete the ensemble. Her hair was set in a Jackie Kennedy pouf.

"Mrs. Delmer?" I asked.

"Yes?" she said, inspecting me like the dubious package I was.

"I'm with the *City Gazette*. I wanted to ask you a few questions about your son."

"Son?" she said, her voice shrill and hard. "I have no son."

"Michael Delmer?"

"He was no son of mine," she said. "I cast him out. He was an abomination."

"Please, Mrs. Delmer. Could I come in for just a few minutes?"

She opened the door. I wasn't surprised. I figured she'd be one of those people who liked to complain about how much they suffered.

The door opened straight into a living room. The place was so clean you could have performed surgery on the coffee table. The white ruffled Priscilla curtains were starched till they crackled. The blue braided rug looked like it had never been walked on. The milk-glass lamps with the ruffled shades were dusted and gleaming. I sat down on a blue Early American couch. She took the Early American recliner.

"You are quite a collector," I said, surveying the knickknacks on every surface. I'd never seen so many dust collectors in my life, and they didn't have a speck on them. She must spend hours dusting them. Mrs. Delmer proudly showed me her bronze, crystal, and china eagles. We stopped at a hutch full of Precious Moments figures. I also couldn't help noticing all the religious statues. Mrs. Delmer's religion was redblooded: The statue of Christ had a squishylooking bleeding heart, crowned with thorns. The picture of the Virgin Mary had swords run through her heart. The Christ on the cross had blood running down his arms from the nails, and deep gashes on his forehead and side. Her religion didn't offer much comfort, but what comfort was there for a woman whose son wanted to change his gender?

I figured it was time to get to the point. "When did you first notice Michael was different?" I asked.

"When he was six. I caught him dressing up in my clothes and hats. He even wore my lipstick. I knew it was unnatural. I beat him with a belt. I never caught him at it again, but I suspected he still did it. I would find a dress hanging inside out or a sweater folded wrong. I tried to reform him, but it didn't work. I made him play manly sports. I forced him to join the Scouts. I even sent him to the seminary, hoping the priests would straighten him out. Instead of finding God, he committed mortal sins with his fellow men. The seminary asked Michael to leave, you know. Because of his . . . his . . . because he was . . ."

"Because he was gay?"

"Those deviants have perverted everything, even that perfectly innocent word," she said. She sighed, then continued bravely. "But I guess it's the modern way to excuse sick and diseased individuals. Yes, Michael was a homosexual. And he dressed like a woman. What did I do to have such a perverted child? I gave him a good Catholic education. Why did God punish me with this unnatural son? I always obeyed the Church. I didn't use birth control, you know, because the Church forbade it. When I married, I promised at the altar I would do my wifely duty and care for any children God gave me."

Wifely duty? Mrs. Delmer made it sound like she made a deal with God and he delivered defective goods.

"I didn't see Michael for several years. I heard he was living with a roommate and dancing in those filthy clubs as a woman, Maria Callous. I was ashamed, but at least if he went by a woman's name, the neighbors would never find out. I'd always hoped he'd reform. Like St. Augustine's mother, I prayed and prayed for him to abandon his sinful life. Then one night, about two years ago, he called me. It was after midnight. He said, 'Mama, I'm in trouble. I've been arrested.'

"I asked what he'd been arrested for, and he said, 'Prostitution.'

"My son! A common prostitute. I was mortified. And he wanted bail money. He said he was scared because he could get raped in jail. I told him he was a disgusting creature and deserved what happened to him. If he dressed like a man he wouldn't make himself a magnet for carnal desires. People who are raped bring it on themselves by the way they dress," she said firmly. "Besides, you can't rape a moving target."

Oh, my god. I didn't think anyone still thought that way about rape. Especially women.

"I disowned him then and there. I told him never to call me again. Then I hung up on him. God was with me. The arrest didn't get into the paper."

More likely, the devil got into the night police reporter, and he missed the item. Or it was cut for space.

I wondered if Mrs. Delmer knew she'd lost her chance in the maternal saintly sweepstakes when she locked her son out of her life. St. Augustine's mom didn't give a hoot what the neighbors thought—and she certainly wouldn't have let her wayward son get jumped on in a jail cell.

"For two years, I had peace. Then two police officers came to the door, fortunately in an unmarked car, and told me Michael was dead. They wanted me to identify the body. It was horrible. Horrible. I was so ashamed that any son of mine would die like that."

"Like how?" I didn't mean to interrupt her, but I couldn't figure out why being strangled was shameful.

"Wearing makeup and women's clothes! I had to ride all the way downtown with those policemen, and they knew what he was! What must they think of me! And then the story got in the *Gazette*. How much more could a mother bear? At least your paper never printed his name. I talked with your nice managing editor, Mr. Harris, and he agreed not to do another story about Michael. There's some decency in this world. I just thank God his father was dead when it happened."

I bet Mr. Delmer was glad he was dead, too. Anything was better than a life sentence with this woman.

"I gather you've never accepted your son's lifestyle?"

"It's not a lifestyle. It's a defilement of the body, which is a temple of the Holy Spirit. The Church says sex should only be used for procreation. He shall be cast into a pit of fire."

What an understanding mom. "Do you know who your son was dating at the end of his life?"

"I know nothing about that filth. I don't want to. I know he was living in a flat in South St. Louis. His roommate packed up his things for me. I had them burned."

"Cast into a pit of fire?" I said. I couldn't resist.

"I was afraid of disease," she shot back. Mrs. Delmer looked at me shrewdly. After that smart remark, I was no longer welcome, no matter how much I admired her eagle collection. "It is time for you to go. I am confident you'll never write about this. Mr. Harris assured me there would be no further stories on such a revolting subject in his family newspaper. I know nothing about Michael's life. I don't want to. I only buried him to save myself public embarrassment, and because burying the dead is one of the Corporal Acts of Mercy."

She walked me to the red door. Just before she shut it, Mrs. Delmer made one last effort to get my sympathy. Her lips quivering, she said, "You must understand. Michael was my cross to bear."

Mother and son were even, then. I was sure she was Michael's cross.

Back in the car, I was so angry I was shaking. I speeded through the side streets to the highway, anxious to get away from that house. What an awful person. What a waste of time. I'd sure learned a lot from that visit: poor Michael/Maria had a real ball-breaking bitch for a mother.

Why the heck was I throwing my time away on this wild-goose chase? It wasn't getting me any closer to who murdered Ralph and Burt. I couldn't even write about what I'd discovered. Mrs. Delmer had my number: That nice Mr. Harris would never permit a story about Michael Delmer/Maria Callous in his paper.

But Ralph thought it was important, and Ralph was dead. Did he die because he knew something? What was it? Maybe there was a connection between this female impersonator and Ralph's death, but for the life of me, I didn't know what it was. I'd at least talk with Michael's roommate and manager. I owed Ralph that much. Then I'd put the whole thing aside. I had a column to write.

Going to see Michael/Maria's roommate wasn't a big deal. Maria's last address was on Crittenden, a mile or two from my house. Crittenden was a handsome street of old-fashioned brick houses and flats with big wide porches, near Tower Grove Park.

Todd, Maria's live-in manager, was a pretty boy who was fast becoming an ordinary man. The pale blond hair was darkening to a dull brown. A few more years and a few more pounds would turn that delicate Grecian profile into a round dumpling of a German face. The soft skin was already thickening and turning pale from too many late nights, too much junk food, and not enough exercise. The small frame was already carrying more weight than it should. Todd was dressed in the theatrical uniform: black turtleneck and black jeans. His black square-toed shoes had silver insets.

He had quite a talent as a decorator. He'd sponge-painted the walls of the flat turquoise and gray and then decorated it with fifties furniture. I always hated that period, but Todd made it seem witty and smart. It was a fantasy for a time that never existed. I admired the kidney-shaped table with the turquoise-and-tangerine inserts, the pole lamp, and the black couch with the wrought-iron legs, and I told him so.

"Flea market finds," Todd said, proudly. "Can you believe it?"

"They're in remarkable shape," I said.

"But you're here to talk about Maria Callous. That's what Michael wanted to be called. I gather you've met the mother."

"Saints preserve us."

"Girlfriend, have you ever seen anything like her?"

"She was god-awful," I said, "in all senses of the word. Poor Michael. Or Maria. She didn't have a chance, did she?"

"That's the sad part. I thought Maria was really turning her life around before she died."

"Who do you think killed her?"

"I haven't a clue. The police dismissed it as some kind of fag killing, but Maria wasn't fighting with anyone. She was extraordinarily happy the last weeks of her life. That's why I didn't report her missing when she dropped out of the pageant and didn't come home. I thought she was with her man. She'd talked about giving it all up for him. It would be like her to do something romantic. Then, the police called and said they'd found her body in the Dumpster. What a brutal end for poor, elegant Maria."

"How long did you know her?"

"We lived together about five years. We weren't lovers. Maria just wanted a friend to manage her. Once she started listening to me, her career improved. I gave her a lot of advice about her act. Did you ever see it?"

"No. I heard a little bit about it. Can you describe it?"

"It was different from most drag acts. That's what was good and bad about it. Maria didn't go in for sequins and glitter. She was fairly subdued, at least for a drag queen. It was part of her charm. She had this navy-blue designer suit—a genuine Chanel. It cost a fortune, even secondhand. She had a tailor take it apart and make it break apart for the stage, with Velcro. She added the little bow at the back. I thought it spoiled the lines, but it did set off her heart-shaped rear end. Most men have flat butts. Hers was nicely rounded. She was proud of her remarkable rear. No padding, you know. It was all natural.

"Onstage, Maria minced around for a bit in the suit, removed her white gloves, then got serious about stripping down to her lacy underwear. The crowd loved it. She'd leave the stage with her bra stuffed with tens and twenties. She could make three or four hundred dollars a night. By the time she perfected her routine and took it to the Miss American Gender Bender Pageant, she got Third Place. Maria was smart, though. She knew that was about as far as she could go. It really was a one-joke act. It wasn't a flashy, high-energy dance routine like some of the girls did. Her club dates were starting to dwindle. She knew she'd have to come up with something else, or get out of the business.

"She was working on a new act, but her heart wasn't in it. She really was a true transsexual—she felt she was a woman in a man's body. Part of her was like Maria Callous—she wanted to be classy and proper. Part of the act was a dig at her mother, who was so prissy she was half dead. A lot of people become impersonators to escape the poverty of life in the projects or the trailer court. Maria was running from the emotional poverty of life with her mother."

"Is that why she became a prostitute?"

"No. She did that for money, honey, and only for a few months. She was saving up for her sex

change operation. She was stopped once for loitering, but that didn't bother her. She thought
that was like a parking ticket. When she was
hauled in for hooking, it shocked her. Maria
really was a proper Catholic child. Her mother
refused to bail her out, so I went down and got
her. Maria was so frightened she never tried it
again."

"Are you sure she stopped? Maybe she just
told you that. Maybe she was killed by a john."

"Francesca, honey, we were roomies, remember? If she was hooking out of here, I'd know it. I
could tell by the phone calls and messages. She
had a boy friend or two, but she was giving it
away, like a good girl. Oh, maybe she wasn't
above taking a gift, but she wasn't selling it. That
arrest scared her. Besides, she didn't need to
peddle it all over town. She had almost all the
money she needed for her operation."

"Her mother said she called for help from jail.
It was a rotten thing for her to abandon Maria."

"It was," said Todd. "But she did Maria a favor
by making the break final. The more she got
away from her mother, the less outrageous she
wanted to be. Maria's goal was to have her operation and then pass as a woman. She could do
that for a while with her straight dates. She'd tell
them she had female trouble or say it was her
period, but eventually either they found out or
she broke off the relationship when she thought
they were suspicious. She was scheduled to have
her operation in a few months. She'd been
through the counseling and she was taking the

hormones. She just wanted to be a woman, and love some man."

"That's what most women want to get away from," I said.

"Old-fashioned, wasn't it?" said Todd. "But rather romantic. If she could have gone shopping at the Galleria and been mistaken for a West County doctor's wife, she'd have been in seventh heaven. I think with the right man she would have given up her stage act and settled down. And she would have made him a good wife—or an even better mistress."

"The guy would never have to worry about getting her pregnant," I said.

"Please, no breeder bias," said Todd. "I'm serious about the mistress part. Maria told me she was dating a married man. She knew he'd never leave his wife, but she thought they could have a long-term relationship."

"What was his name?"

"She never said. Maria could be very secretive when she thought it was important, and after the first date with this guy, she was madly in love. She said he wasn't handsome, but he was safe and solid and intelligent, all qualities she valued. I gathered from a few things she said that he was some kind of bigwig, maybe worked for a major corporation. She told me once that I'd recognize his name because it was in the newspaper."

"Todd, did Maria leave any letters or diaries or even an address book?"

"She had very few papers, and I never came

across any letters, except bills. Maria never kept a diary that I knew about. She did have an address book, but I gave it to her mother, along with all her clothes and papers and belongings."

"Her mother burned everything."

"Poor Maria. Her mother would, too, the miserable bitch."

"Why did Maria enter the Gender Bender Pageant this year if she was going to quit?"

"I think she still wanted some insurance she could earn a living if this romance didn't work. She was working on a version of her new act. She was going to perform it at the pageant. It wasn't quite perfected, but it wasn't bad."

"What was it?"

"She looked a lot like Princess Di, you know. Maria bought a knockoff of one of Di's ball gowns, and she was working on this dance routine with a guy who looked like Prince Charles. At least, he had big ears and a long nose. The new act was quite funny. Di and Charles fight onstage, and she pulls his ears, slaps his face, and boots him out, which is what most people wanted her to do to him anyway. During the fight, he strips off her long gown, and she does this hot dance in her bra and garter belt. I'm not explaining it right—it's better than it sounds. I wish you could have seen Maria. She was small and blond to begin with, but with the right makeup I could make her look enough like Di to get her into Buckingham Palace.

"I didn't tell you the best part of Maria's new act," he said. "She was talking about taking a new stage name to go with it. I thought it up. You know what it was? Di Tryon? Get it? Trying to be Princess Di."

"Or died trying," I said.

Todd told me a little about Maria. But not enough to lead me to the person who killed Ralph and Burt, and tried to kill me. Besides, something about Todd bothered me. He was pleasant and helpful and a hell of a lot more concerned about Maria than her mother. But if he really cared, and I think he did, why wasn't he worried when she dropped out of the pageant? He said it was because she'd gone off with the love of her life. But would she really leave him flat right before the debut of her new act, when they'd worked so hard together on it? Wouldn't Todd have called around to find out where she was? Or checked with her friends? Why didn't he get upset or curious? She sure didn't call and tell him where she was.

I needed to know more, and I suspected I wouldn't find it out from Todd. I called Jamie, Ralph's ex-lover. Ralph had introduced him to a lot of female impersonators, and Jamie stayed in touch with some of Ralph's friends. Maybe he'd know something.

I was lucky. Jamie was home. "It's my turn to cook dinner tonight," he said. "Roast baby chicken with baby squash."

"Sounds like child abuse. Ever eat anything that grows to adult size?" As soon as the words fell out of my mouth, I knew they were wrong. Jamie's snicker confirmed it. "Cancel that sentence," I said. "Let me start over. Hi, Jamie. I need your help."

"Hi, Francesca. What can I do for you?"

"Ralph left me some information about a female impersonator named Maria Callous. She has a roommate-manager named Todd. I need to know more about him. Ever heard of the guy, or Maria?"

"No," said Jamie. "But if it's important, I can do some checking."

"It's important. I think it may have gotten Ralph killed."

Now I had Jamie's attention. Even though he was happy with his new partner, the doctor, Ralph was still important to him. "I'll start checking now. I'm out the door."

"You can get me at my place," I said. "I'll be here all night. Should I call the poultry welfare department and have someone watch your baby chicken?"

"Screw the baby chicken. Domino's delivers. So will I," he said, and hung up the phone.

Two hours later, he was on my doorstep with a fey blonde in his early twenties—a discount David Bowie. His golden hair looked like a very expensive dye job, and *he* looked like a very expensive young man in a very old profession.

"This is Jordanne," said Jamie.

Jordanne gave me two fingers to shake. I wondered if I'd have to kiss his ring, too. He looked aghast at my grandmother's decor: the Naugahyde recliner, the lamps with the shades still in the original cellophane wrappers, and the slipcovered davenport. The eyes of the picture of Christ over the television set followed Jordanne around the room like store security on a shoplifter. I thought Jordanne's eyebrows would disappear into his hair at Grandpa's bowling trophies. Wait till I showed him Aunt Jemima hiding the toaster under her skirt in the kitchen. Unfortunately, Jamie ruined everything. "This is Francesca's grandparents' original decor," he said. "A New York decorator said this was the finest collection of kitsch this side of a museum."

"Or a garage sale," I said.

Jordanne allowed himself to give me a smile, but it was an effort. Still, he made it. After all, New York had blessed this room.

"Tell Francesca what you saw the night before Maria died," prompted Jamie.

"It was Underwear Night at a bar on Washington Avenue," said Jordanne.

"What's that?"

Jordanne looked like he couldn't bear to explain it to someone so unhip, so Jamie did. "You get free drinks at this gay bar if you wear only your underwear."

"I was with an older gentleman, trying to get him to go in," Jamie said. "He was from out of town, from Malden." Malden was a small, rich town in the Missouri Bootheel, an area not known for its tolerance of the gay lifestyle. I'd bet the gentleman had a lot of money. And a wife and kids.

"He said he wanted me to show him some fun, but he wouldn't go for Underwear Night. He said, 'Son, I'm fifty-two years old. At my age I pay to keep my clothes on.' I was trying to persuade him to try it, but he refused. He did agree to go in with me, and I could take off my clothes. About that time, I heard another couple arguing in the alley next to the bar, and their argument sounded so much more interesting than ours that we both stopped and listened.

"I could hear one person yelling, 'You're giving it away! Giving it away! I could fix you up with plenty of people who'd be happy to pay for your company, but you want to give it away.' Then we heard weeping, and the other person said, 'But I love him.'

"The first person said, 'He can't love you. And certainly not for yourself. Which self would that be, Maria? Does your man know you're still a man?'

"Well, at that, we couldn't resist. My gentleman and I peeped around the corner. And there was Maria Callous—I'd seen her act—arguing with her manager. She was dressed in her blue suit. Too bad they saw us. That ended the fight. But my older gentleman was thrilled by the drama, and he tipped . . . I mean, he was very grateful. I didn't think anything else about it until Jamie called. I didn't realize Maria was killed the next night."

Well, well. Maria's death was indeed a loss for her manager. And he was managing both her careers. I also guess that's why there was no address book. It was a trick book. Maria's manager/pimp got rid of that incriminating evidence before the police showed up to search her things. It was time for another little talk with Todd, and this time I didn't intend to be so polite.

Maybe that's why I didn't call when I went back this time. Or maybe I wanted to catch him off guard. He was at home, eating popcorn and watching a Judy Garland movie. He answered the door and gave me a host's smile. "Well. Francesca. Twice in one day. What an honor. What can I do for you?"

"Try telling the truth."

Todd started to shut the door, but I stuck my foot in it. I'd had practice. "I found a witness to your fight in the alley off Washington Avenue. You were arguing with Maria. You accused her of giving it away when you could find her paying customers. You didn't want her giving up her career. You were making money managing both. You didn't want to lose your income. You didn't give her address book to her mother. You destroyed it so the cops wouldn't get it."

"No. Yes. You don't understand."

"I do. I understand it all."

"No, you don't," he said. "Yes, I burned the address book after she died. I didn't want the cops pawing through our life. Maybe they know anyway. I know they didn't seem to care much that a fag died.

"Yes, we had the fight. But only because I thought he was bad for her. He was only going to hurt her."

"Sure. He was definitely going to hurt your income."

"I loved Maria. I liked guiding her career. I didn't want her hurt. I was protecting her."

"Oh, come on, Todd. If you were so concerned, why didn't you call the police when she didn't show up for the big number you'd been rehearsing? Didn't you realize something was wrong? Maybe you didn't go looking for her because you knew where she was: dead in a Dumpster. Did you murder her? Is that why you knew she wasn't going to call and tell you where she was—because she couldn't—she was dead?"

"No!" Todd almost shouted. "When she didn't show I thought she was still mad at me. I thought she was punishing me for our fight. I was mad at her for not showing. After months of work and that new outfit, it was all wasted. I was so mad I got drunk."

"Where were you the night Maria was killed?" I'd always wanted to say that.

"Drunk in the Dungeon," Todd said.

"The what?"

"The bar at the Louie the Ninth Motor Inn. I picked up a guy in the bar and spent four nights with him. We didn't leave the hotel. By then she was dead and buried."

"A terrific alibi. Too bad you can't prove it."

"But I can," said Todd. "We were fooling around in the hotel's hot tub and we got a little rowdy. By that time, we went through a lot of white wine, and several condoms. A guest complained that we were engaged in 'an inappropriate public display.' I remember that because the hotel security person could hardly say it. We started laughing and that only made him madder. He wrote down a report of the incident, and we were so drunk we gave him our real names.

"It's true. You can check," Todd said.

It was true. I had a friend who worked in PR at the hotel and she let me see the report, if I promised never to make it public. Hotel Security had problems spelling "inappropriate," too, but he got Todd's name right.

Francesca solves the Case of the Gay Deceiver. Francesca solves everything except whodunit. Somebody killed Ralph and Burt and tried to kill me on the parking lot at Uncle Bob's. He tried to run me down the day after I talked with Marlene. Maybe we needed to figure out what we said.

12

Tom the Cook was waving to me at the window as I pulled into the Uncle Bob's lot at noon the next day. I was going to dare to be different. I rolled down the window and yelled as I went by, "Make me a toasted cheese sandwich."

"Coming up," he said.

Success! My lips were set for golden grease.

When I got inside, it was waiting for me, its greasy gold calling to me across the room. It was a wrong number. Marlene was carrying a fried egg to my booth. "I told the cook you never ate toasted cheese," she said. "He must have heard wrong. And sure enough, that gentleman over there had asked for one. I told the cook you probably wanted a fried egg instead of a scrambled one." I saw the man bite into my toasted cheese. There was no escaping an Uncle Bob's egg.

"Aren't you worried about cholesterol?" asked

Marlene, as she plopped the plate on the place mat.

"Nope. I'm not going to live that long. Especially not if people try to run me down. Someone tried to kill me, Marlene. We know it's not the Aryan Avenger. It's not Todd, Maria's manager. His alibi checked out. I have nowhere to go and nobody to suspect. I watch my rearview mirror constantly to see if anyone is following me. I don't get out in any parking lot unless at least two people are around. I can't go on like this. But I have no leads. The only thing I can say is that the trouble started after we had that talk here at Uncle Bob's, and Babe listened in. My guess is it had to do with that conversation Babe overheard. He repeated it to the killer, and that's who tried to run me down on your lot."

"I can't see that we said anything to drive someone to murder, but let's try to remember what we said. I'm not real busy right now."

We went back over the Babe conversation again. "First, I trashed Babe's writing and then said maybe he had a boy friend," said Marlene. "I guess that was pretty nasty."

"Nah, everybody says that," I said. "I talked about his phone sex act."

"Then Babe would want to kill you," Marlene said.

"Nope," I said. "Babe wasn't the driver. He's too tall. And Babe would never wear a black-and-red ski mask with a beige coat."

"Then I talked about your editors coming into Uncle Bob's," Marlene said.

"At great length. And it was very informative. I didn't know Hadley was a cheap tipper," I said.

"I didn't say that."

"Yes, you did. You said my editor was a cheap tipper."

"I didn't mean Hadley, the managing editor. I mean that little squirt you work for—what's his name?"

"Charlie?"

"Yeah. Him. Sat in my station. This was a couple of weeks ago. Took up a booth on a Saturday night for two hours, drank coffee and left me a lousy fifty cents. I could have made ten dollars in tips during the time he camped out there. I should have charged him rent."

"Charlie never struck me as a coffee drinker," I said.

"He's not," Marlene said. "He was waiting for someone. A little blonde I saw Hadley with later. The classy one who looks like Princess Di with a better nose. Never did figure out what she saw in Charlie, but then I couldn't figure out why Di married Charles. The man looks like a blind date."

Princess Di? Suddenly, I could hear alarm bells going off. Was her Princess Di my Maria Callous? "Listen," I said, "could this pretty little blonde have been a boy instead of a girl?"

"I doubt it," said Marlene. "We get some transvestites in here, and I'm pretty good at figuring them out. Even when they're small-boned and have nice hands and feet, they don't hold themselves like women."

I'd better let Marlene finish her story, before she got another rush of customers. "Anyway, Charlie and the blonde were fighting, but they shut up every time I came over with more coffee. All I could hear was that Charlie wanted her to come to his house because his wife was out of town, and she wouldn't."

"You heard quite a bit."

"Well, yeah. I wanted to hear more. But Hadley came in with a blowzy brunette wearing black flats, black lipstick, and some sort of sleazy flowered housedress."

"That's the poetry editor."

"Charlie introduced the classy blonde to Hadley. The next time Hadley came in here, he was with Charlie's blonde. I don't think that romance lasted too long."

"They never do."

"After that, I saw Hadley with a frizzy-haired blonde who had to be fifty if she's a day. She smokes tiny cigars and says 'Fuck' every third word."

"Sounds like the etiquette editor." I bit into the yellow of the egg, and it gushed out onto my suit. I just got it back from the cleaners.

"Oh, fuck," I said.

"Jeez, I can't take you anywhere. Let me clean it up," said Marlene. She stuck a napkin in my water glass and began dabbing at the spot.

"So unless Babe wants to run me down for saying he has sex with a telephone, the only other thing we talked about was Charlie's latest squeeze. And I can't see where that's a big deal. It's generally known he cheats on his wife."

"She's prettier than most of the women I see him with," Marlene said. "But he wouldn't keep that a secret. I'm surprised he didn't hang on to her longer. Would he pass on his girl friend to his boss to advance his career?"

"You bet. The man was famous for organizing summer float trips in the Ozarks. Charlie got the rental canoes, the beer, and the 'sleeping bags'— the naive young women who were eager to sleep with newspapermen in the hope it would advance their careers. Needless to say, only male staffers went on Charlie's trips."

"Did Hadley go with them?"

"Oh, yes. Then he'd write a column about how he felt closer to nature."

"He felt closer to something," Marlene said.

"Charlie would brag that he tried out Hadley's girl friend first. He wouldn't kill to keep it quiet. The blonde has to be the key. I'm just not sure how. I don't even know who she is, but your Princess Di is beginning to sound a lot like my female impersonator, Maria Callous."

"I never saw her in here before—or since," said Marlene.

"When did you last see her?"

"Early February."

"About the time that Maria Callous disappeared. But that doesn't prove anything. Hadley and Charlie change girl friends as often as you change socks."

Besides, it didn't seem likely that Charlie

would make the same mistake twice and date
another Blow Job Betty. And if he did, he certainly wouldn't pass that mistake on to his boss,
Hadley. But maybe he was so eager to score with
his career he didn't keep Maria around long
enough to find out what she was. Or maybe he
found out a little too late, then had to kill her
before Hadley discovered his mistake. But I
didn't have a shred of proof. And that would be
too devious even for Charlie. Wouldn't it? I had
to ask better questions than that.

"I can't see what my Princess Di has to do
with your murders," Marlene was saying. "But
then, I didn't think Ralph and Burt were murdered until you told me, and even then I didn't
quite believe you. The next thing I know someone's trying to run you down in the parking lot—
and we still don't know why."

"All I've got are a lot of questions," I said. "I
need some answers." I took the final bite of my
fried egg. The last of the yolk that didn't wind up
on my suit dribbled down my chin. Marlene
laughed. "Just don't come away with egg on your
face," she said.

It was time for me to leave. After I paid, Marlene and Tom the Cook walked me to my car. I
saw them standing at the kitchen door as I drove
off.

I thought I should start at the beginning, with
Burt. He was the first death. I called Burt's wife,
Dolores, and asked if I could stop by her home
in South St. Louis for a talk.

Maybe it was my imagination, or maybe it

was March, but the brick flat looked forlorn now
that Burt was dead. The brown awning over the
front door had sagged after a heavy snowfall,
and no one had fixed it. Dolores's flower beds
were muddy and clogged with dead leaves. Inside was worse. Most of the furniture was gone.
The pictures, dishes, and knickknacks were
packed away in boxes, and I saw how scuffed
and scarred the walls were. The only thing that
stayed the same was the bank calendar. Saturday was circled and marked "MOVING DAY!!!"

Dolores was leaving the old neighborhood.
She'd lost weight since Burt's death, but she
didn't look good thin. Nature meant her to be fat
and jolly, and she wasn't either right now. But
she tackled widowhood as briskly and capably as
she handled the cooking at Burt's Bar. She sat
me down at her kitchen table, poured us both
some coffee, and told me her plans. "I've put the
bar up for sale," she said. "I'm renting the flat
and moving to Sunset Hills in South County."

"That's where South Siders go when they get
rich," I said, and smiled. But my mild joke didn't
register.

"Burt left me well fixed," she said seriously.
"He heard enough stock tips behind the bar. After a while, he became good at investments. I
can't stay here at the flat anymore. Every time I
look around, I see Burt. I see him sitting in his
big old chair in the living room. I see him at the
kitchen table, drinking coffee. I see him in the
hot tub." I looked at her, remembering what
Burt said about the good times they'd had in

that tub. She must have read my mind. She blushed.

"The new house in Sunset Hills is nice," she said, but she didn't sound enthusiastic. "It's bigger than this place. I want enough bedrooms for my grandbabies, so they can stay overnight when they visit. I'm getting new furniture, too. I had the Salvation Army haul off the old living room suite. When they took it away, I felt like I was burying Burt all over again. But if I'm going to make it without him, I have to get away from our old life."

Now the briskness was gone. Dolores seemed soft and sad and vulnerable. She and Burt had built a good life together, and someone destroyed it with a few thrusts of a knife. She missed Burt terribly.

"Dolores, what do you remember about the day Burt died? Was anything different? Do you know who was in the bar when Burt was closing for lunch?"

She shook her head. "It was just another day," she said. "We had a good lunch business, but most of our customers are gone by one o'clock. They have to get back to work. At one thirty, I saw a couple of tables were still occupied, but they were just businesspeople having a last cup of coffee. I didn't get a good look at any of them. There wasn't anything special to notice. I'd cleaned up my kitchen and my wagon was draggin'. I wanted a nap. Burt said he'd close up and I should go on home. I slipped out the back door. That's the last time I saw him. I didn't even say good-bye. I should have stayed. If I had, maybe he'd be alive. But I wanted a nap. Now it's all I do." She began to cry. I felt like a creep asking more questions that would hurt her, but I had to know.

"Do you think he was murdered for the money in the register?"

"Why else would anyone murder Burt?" she said, snuffling and blowing her nose. "He had no enemies. He was a harmless old man. I loved him all my life, but he wasn't important in the great scheme of things. He wasn't what Babe called a mover and shaker. He poured drinks for the movers and shakers.

"We were both grateful for what you wrote. Before your Best Saloon in St. Louis contest, Burt was just a bartender in an old city saloon, and some of the kids were kind of embarrassed by him because they'd gone to college and everything. Then you did those stories about Burt and everyone came to his bar. The Mayor himself drank there, and an alderman who wasn't even running for office in this ward, and Hadley Harris and a bunch of other newspaper people."

That got my attention. "Who else from the *Gazette*?"

"I can't remember his name, but he said he was an important editor there. He said he'd discovered you."

"What did he look like?"

"Short. Beer gut. Bald spot he covered up by combing his hair sideways. What was his name? Gary? Terry?"

It had to be that little rat, Charlie. Only he would have the nerve to take credit for my column while he tried to kill it. "I think his name is Charlie," I said mildly.

"I think you're right. That name sounds right, anyway," said Dolores.

"When was Charlie in the bar?"

"A night or two before Burt was killed, I think. He'd been in a few times recently, once with a real classy-looking blonde. Was that his wife?"

"No. His wife looks like a homely sparrow. That happens when you live with a crumb like Charlie."

"You don't like him, do you?" Dolores said.

I shook my head.

"Me, either. He tries to make himself bigger than he is, and I'm not talking about his height." She patted my arm. "I'm glad you think enough of my husband to look into his death, but I doubt that you will find out anything more than the police did. Be careful, Francesca. Don't let the small things trip you up."

"I haven't tripped over Charlie yet," I said, and we both laughed. "Dolores, I want to find out who killed Burt, but I think there's more to his death. I also lost a good friend, Ralph, the same week. I believe he was murdered. I think the same person killed Ralph and Burt, but I don't know why yet. Ralph is the person who first introduced me to Burt's Bar."

"I don't think I know him," she said. "But I kept mostly in the kitchen during the busy times."

"You'd know him if you saw him," I said, and brought out a picture of Ralph and me at a holiday party. She put on a pair of glasses.

"Oh, sure. I've seen him. Used to come in covered with dust and paint when he was rehabbing in the area. Nice young man. If he was really dirty, he would get carry-out, which was very considerate. Where was Ralph the day he died?"

"Working at that house on Utah."

"Did anybody see him, or notice if he had someone with him? Maybe that's a place to start, honey. Stay with your facts instead of your feelings."

"You're right, Dolores," I said, and gave her a good-bye hug.

She was right, too. Lyle and I had looked at Ralph's homemade appointment schedule when we picked up his truck. He was supposed to meet Ed at the Utah house. Who was Ed? Maybe Ralph's mother, Billie, would know. I called her and asked if I could see her again. Billie said she had a doctor's appointment and couldn't see me until later that afternoon.

I killed time by making a guest appearance at the *City Gazette* office. Naturally, the first person I ran into in the newsroom was Charlie. He was standing by the elevator. I noticed he was wearing a beige all-weather coat. Just like the person who tried to run me down. Just like thousands of men and women in St. Louis. He pulled out a pearl-and-silver pocket knife and began cleaning under his nails. Ugh. What a disgusting habit. I'd seen him do this at low-level staff meetings. I took it as a gesture of contempt. I never saw him give himself a manicure around Hadley. It made me angry. So did his next statement.

"I see you added two charter members to your Get a Life Club," Charlie said.

"I don't know what you mean," I said.

I knew exactly what he meant. I loved the offbeat people I wrote about. Charlie made fun of them, calling them the Get a Life Club. "Those two drunks who got married, Elvis and Edna, was it?" he said. I hated the way he sneered at them.

"They weren't drunk at their wedding. You should be careful about making slanderous remarks. I've never seen the bride take a drink," I said, truthfully. I'd seen the groom chug a few, but that was another story.

"Well, I found your column about the wedding a hoot, although I don't think that's what you intended," he said.

"I guess you would find something funny about two people who promise to love, honor, and be faithful to each other."

Ah! A direct hit. His face turned red. Even his ears were scarlet. Naturally, Charlie hit back. He went corporate. "That conversation you had concerning the management team in Uncle Bob's got back to us. Hadley was very upset that you were discussing company business with the little people."

"I don't know any leprechauns, Charlie," I said.

"That conversation you had with a . . . a waitperson."

"It's okay, Charlie, it's not politically incorrect to call a woman a waitress. And I wasn't discussing company business. I was discussing your affairs—which are growing more and more public. Even the little people are noticing you hang around with women who aren't your wife. But if you and Babe hadn't gone running into Hadley's office, I doubt that he'd know what I said to the waitress."

"You shouldn't have said anything. You're not a team player," he said. Charlie thought that was an insult.

"You're right, boss. I'm not a team player. Not your team, anyway. I'll stick with the little people—instead of giants like you." I patted him on his head. Charlie hated that, because I towered over him by almost a foot. A bell dinged, but it wasn't the end of the round. The elevator arrived to take Charlie away.

I figured he'd find some way to get me later, but it was worth it. We'd done more than trade insults. I'd proved one important point: Babe had reported everything to the *CG*. Charlie knew about the conversation I'd had with Marlene. He knew we knew about the pretty Princess Di blonde he'd been dating. But I didn't know why he cared.

I knew "Princess Di" was the nickname Marlene gave the woman who came into Uncle Bob's with Charlie. Because she was small and blond and looked like the real princess.

Burt had said Charlie was in the bar with a classy blonde. Dolores, Burt's wife, had seen them, too, and wanted to know if she was Charlie's wife.

Ralph had thought there was a connection between Maria and the mutilated man dressed in women's clothing in the Dumpster. The police called the victim a prostitute. Maria did some light hooking and had one arrest. Maria had breasts like a woman but genitals like a man. Until her killer stabbed them seventy-eight times. With a pocket knife. Like the one Charlie carried.

Maria had dropped out of the Gender Bender Pageant. Except she didn't drop out. She'd been murdered and dropped in a vacant lot.

It was starting to make sense. I knew now why Ralph had sent me those clippings. And I was almost sure that Maria Callous was the mysterious blonde Marlene called Princess Di. The woman who came from nowhere. The woman that Marlene had never seen before until she showed up with Charlie. And never saw again. Because she was dead. Because Charlie killed this dead ringer for Princess Di with her own scarf and then stabbed her with his pocket knife.

I opened my mail and I returned some calls and then I got out of there. Half an hour was all I could take at the *Gazette*. It was time to see Ralph's mother.

Billie looked a little better today. She still didn't look like beautiful Billie, but maybe her older sister instead of her mother.

"Billie, I'm sorry to bother you," I said. "But Ralph had an appointment with someone called Ed at the Utah Place house the morning he died. Do you know what it was about?"

"A little," she said. "Ralph was excited because some *City Gazette* editor wanted to look at his rehab work there, but he didn't mention that was his name."

There were no *City Gazette* editors named Ed. But Ralph used other abbreviations in that appointment book. Ed wasn't a name. It was short for "Editor."

"Ralph told me if the editor liked what he saw, he wanted Ralph to give him an estimate on rehabbing his own house—the whole thing. Ralph was thrilled. He thought it would be enough work to keep him going for the rest of the summer and fall."

"You don't know the editor's name?"

"No," she said. "I don't think Ralph ever mentioned it. He never told me where the editor's house was, either. He'd talked to the man briefly on the phone and seemed vague on those details. I think he was going to ask you about him."

Of course he was. He called me, but I let my answering machine take it, because I was too lazy to pick up. Suddenly, his rambling message made perfect sense. *Francesca, it's me, Ralph,* he'd said. *Listen, I forgot to ask you something tonight . . . I know for sure you know this guy 'cause you work with him, except work doesn't really describe what he does, does it? At least that's what you always say, ha-ha. Anyway, I'm*

pretty sure you can tell me if I should do this.
Come on, Francesca, pick up. I know you're there.
Yeah, Ralph, I was there. And if I'd picked up
the phone, you might still be here, too. At the
very least, I'd know who your killer was. *Work*
doesn't really describe what he does, does it? At
least that's what you always say, ha-ha. That's
what I always said about several top *CG* editors.
Mostly Charlie. That's who called you, wasn't it?
That's how he found out where you were working and took your inhalers. Did he use the same
pen knife he'd cleaned his nails with at the elevator to cut your "insurance" off your ladder? But
why? Why did he want to kill you? That's what I
didn't know.

I was going to need proof, and I couldn't get it
from Billie. That was all Billie could tell me,
though I kept rephrasing the same questions until she was tired of them and so was I.

The next person on my must-see list was
Todd. I didn't particularly want to talk to him,
and after our last encounter, I didn't expect him
to want to see me. That's why I didn't call ahead.
I just rang the doorbell. I was relieved when he
answered the door. There was no sign of the
pretty boy today. He looked like a petulant,
slightly pudgy man. He didn't invite me in. We
stood on the chilly front porch. "Well, you accused me of murder last time," he said. "What's
my crime now? Kidnapping? Arson? Armed robbery?"

"Todd, I'm sorry," I said. "You're right to be
angry with me. But I really am trying to find Ma-

ria's killer. You have no reason to want to help me, but I know you want to help her."

I saw that stricken look in his eyes. He shivered, but I wasn't sure it was from the cold. I wasn't the only one carrying a load of guilt. "I know you had to get rid of Maria's address book to protect her reputation," I said. I might as well let him have that. "Did she leave behind anything, even a phone number on a scrap of paper? I'd like to talk to her last boy friend, if I can find him."

"I wish I could help you, but I can't," Todd said. "I had to nag her to keep important numbers in that book. I put most of them in myself. If Maria had one fault as a roommate, it was that she never wrote phone numbers on the pad I kept by the phone. She wrote the numbers on the wall by the phone. It used to drive me crazy. I screamed and sulked and repainted that wall sixteen times. I told her she picked up that habit hanging around bars. But nothing broke her of it. If a man called, she wrote the number on the wall by the phone—'So I won't lose it,' she said. The only progress I ever made with all my nagging was when she wrote the last phone number from the guy she was dating on the side of the icebox. She said it would wash off. She acted like this was a big advance. Maybe for her it was. Anyway, I left it there, thinking it was better than the wall. You couldn't see that side of the icebox from the door anyway. It's still there. I couldn't bring myself to clean away the last trace of her."

I felt like I was in a dream. "May I come in and take a look at it?"

"Help yourself," Todd said, finally holding the door open for me. "It's on the side by the phone."

I sleepwalked into the kitchen. There was the number, written on the white refrigerator in blue ink. I didn't have to call the number to find out who it belonged to. I knew that number immediately. It was the main number to the *City Gazette*.

Maria was the woman Marlene and I called Princess Di. I was sure of it. The blond woman who was dating Charlie. A few more questions, and I'd have the proof I needed to nail Charlie. I drove back to Dolores's house. She was finishing up in the living room, surrounded by a stack of boxes, a pile of packing paper, and three half-used rolls of tape.

"Can I show you a photo?" I asked Dolores.

"Sure, honey, but make it quick. I got all this to pack away and the movers will be here before you know it."

I pulled out the Miss American Gender Bender Pageant program, and pointed to Maria Callous's photo. "Is that the woman who was in the bar with Charlie?"

"Let me put on my reading glasses. I can't see a darned thing up close," said Dolores. "Now where did I put them in this mess?" The wait was maddening. I joined in the hunt. We checked the kitchen table, the bedside table, the back of the commode, the top of pile after pile of boxes, before Dolores finally yelled, "Found them. Set them here on the fireplace mantel, next to my coffee cup. Can't find anything in this mess."

She put on her glasses and held the picture to the light, then took it over to the window. I thought I was going to crawl the wall, using my nails like rock spikes.

"Now, finally, enough light where I can see," she said. "Yep. That's her. No doubt about it. What is she, a model? What's it say? 'Maria Callous, the Ass with Class?' Is that nice-looking young woman a stripper?"

"That nice-looking young woman is a nice-looking young man," I said.

"You're shittin' me," said Dolores. I knew she was surprised. She never talked like that. "I'd never guess that nice-looking person was a guy. Wore such a pretty little navy-blue suit, too. Had a bow on the back. Real feminine. He was better-looking than most of the women we saw in the bar. Dressed better, too. Boy, you sure can't tell these days, can you?"

You sure can't. I needed just a few more facts to make my case against Charlie. I didn't want another Aryan Avenger. I knew Charlie carried a pocket knife. I knew he'd been to Burt's Bar with Maria Callous in her little blue suit. Now I wanted to know what Maria was wearing when she was found dead in the Dumpster. Cutup Katie would know. I called and got her. I could hear an electric saw going in the background. I shouted into the phone so she could hear me better. "Are they remodeling your office?"

"This place? Never. Who cares about an attractive morgue?"

"Thought I heard an electric saw."

"You did," said Katie. "That's a Stryker saw. The morgue tech is buzzing a head open so I can see the brain. Make this quick. I don't have a lot of time."

Me, either. In about two seconds, I was going to gorp. "One more question about that female impersonator autopsy," I said. "Can you tell me anything about the clothes Michael was wearing?"

"Yeah. They're in the autopsy report. You didn't ask about them, so I didn't mention them. Let me get it."

She was gone just long enough for me to get queasy again from the sound of the Stryker saw. "It says here the body was dressed in a woman's suit at the time of the examination. You know the weird thing about it? The suit was held together with Velcro."

"Michael used Velcro instead of zippers?"

"No, the suit had buttons and zippers in the right places. But the seams had Velcro fastenings, so the suit could come apart. I'd never seen a suit like that. I was curious about it. Usually, the only people who use Velcro doodads on their clothes are paras and quads, because some people in wheelchairs don't have the dexterity to do buttons and snaps. But that wasn't what was going on with this Velcro. I found out it was break-apart clothes like actors and strippers use on stage. But this wasn't any stripper's costume.

There was nothing flashy about that suit. You or I could have worn it."

"What did it look like?" I asked, although I had a pretty good idea.

"It was a navy-blue suit. Expensive designer suit, Chanel label, with a fitted jacket. But not too tight. Definitely not cheap-looking. Not what you'd think of as hooker's clothing. Had a cute little bow in the back."

"The back?"

"Yeah, on the butt. Just above it, to be exact. I'd probably take the bow off, myself, if I wore the suit, but that's just a matter of taste."

Maria Callous, the Ass with Class, with her little bow on her little blue suit, and Princess Di, the classy blonde with the little blue suit with the bow on the back. They were the same person. She was the woman Charlie had been seen with. The woman he'd passed on to his boss to promote his career. The woman who turned out to be a man.

The woman he had to kill before his boss found out and killed his career.

13

Long ago, I used to think Charlie was my mentor. Now I thought he was a murderer. What changed? Certainly not Charlie. Not in the fifteen years I'd known him. What changed was the way I saw him.

Charlie made no bones about what he did. He was the *Gazette*'s master of revels, illegal and immoral. Only a prude would object. He sold a little pot to the staff. So what if the price was jacked above street rate? He thought it was funny when someone complained he made a profit off his friends. "I took the risk," he said. "If I get caught, they won't go to jail for me."

He ran the office pools, and gleefully talked about how he broke the interstate gambling laws when he called his pals at other papers around the country. So what? as Charlie would say. Most offices had a little friendly betting. But most offices didn't print sanctimonious stories and editorials denouncing the evils of legalized gambling. The same writers who did the stories about the disgrace and disasters that befell bettors would go back and place a bet with a bookie who was a senior *CG* editor. Betting was bad for *them*, for the readers. It was okay for *us*, the *CG* staff.

Charlie bragged about cheating on his wife. Charlie had a sixth sense for which women were dissatisfied with their men or their marriages. He could see that Ms. X or Mrs. Y was feeling unloved and unappreciated. A joke or two, drinks at the Last Word, dinner if she really held out, and he'd generally have her. Often, so would his friends. He liked to say he was good at "breaking them in and passing them around." Several of his girl friends were passed on up the ranks to higher editors. It humiliated some. It helped the careers of others. One of Charlie's girl friends became a *Gazette* editor and another got a cushy reporting job. Charlie laughed at his infidelities until you did, too. Morals were for losers. Fidelity was for saps who couldn't get a little on the side.

Charlie wasn't especially good-looking. His complexion was red. He had a beer gut like a shoplifted bowling ball and a bald spot like a burnt-out lawn. But he made good looks seem like something for less fortunate men, because they couldn't have Charlie's smarts. Before Georgia clued me in on Charlie, I didn't run with his crowd, but I thought he was amusing.

Lyle hated Charlie. He was the first person who tried to straighten me out about the guy. I thought Lyle was being stuffy. One night, we argued about it after a *Gazette* party. I went to more of them in those days.

"Don't trust that man," Lyle said.

"I don't have to," I said. "I'm not married to him. What do you have against Charlie, anyway? He's kind of funny."

"He betrays people," said Lyle, seriously. "He cheats on his wife with that woman at work, Geraldine."

"That's his business."

"He's made it the office's business. He screws her in his car on the company parking lot, so the whole building knows. Then he cheats on Geraldine with those eager young journalism students who try to sell him their stories."

"They wise up fast. If I avoided people because they played around, I'd run out of folks to talk to," I said. "Charlie's rather lighthearted about his affairs. If his wife and Geraldine don't care, why should I?"

Lyle set his mouth in a straight line. I hated when he did that. He lectured me like the college professor he was. "With Charlie, it's not about sex, it's about betrayal," Lyle said. "Remember what he did to Peggy at the Christmas party?"

No one could forget that party. Peggy was the pretty young wife of Charlie's ex–best friend, a reporter named Josh. Charlie hit on her several times. She refused him. Charlie got Peggy drunk at the Christmas party—she was too dumb to know that the spiked fruit punch packed a wallop. Then he talked Peggy into doing a strip-

tease. Took it off almost down to the buff. Josh
was off talking in another part of the room.
Charlie had us all clapping and cheering and
yelling "Take it off."

First Peggy kicked off her penny loafers. Then
she pulled off her red cotton Gap sweater and
flung away her khaki pants. The cheers and
whistles grew more frantic when Peggy was
down to her rose-sprigged panties and bra. She
still had on more clothes than most people wear
on the beach, but we didn't think she would for
long. She looked pink and excited and very
drunk. We weren't much better, chanting "All
off! All off!"

Peggy was about to strip off her panties when
Josh, attracted by the noise, came over to our
side of the room. He saw his twenty-two-year-
old wife standing in her underwear in front of
the newsroom.

"Hi, Josh," said Charlie, wearing a boyish
grin. "We just wanted to see if Peggy is a natural
blonde." Peggy sobered instantly and burst into
tears. Josh wrapped her in his coat and they left.
Peggy never went to another *Gazette* party. Josh
never went anywhere at the *Gazette*. He and
Peggy eventually moved to the West Coast and I
lost track of them.

Even after the Peggy episode, I still didn't
catch on about Charlie. "You know," I said, set-
tling next to Lyle on the couch one night and
piling up some pillows, "Charlie's star rose after
that scene with Peggy."

"Showed he was management material," Lyle

said. He thought even less of the *Gazette* editors than I did. But I didn't want to fight about Charlie that night. I kissed Lyle and licked his cute little ear until we both forgot about anything else.

I felt sorry for poor Peggy. But I still enjoyed Charlie's accounts of his escapades. Maybe I hadn't left my parents' world after all. Maybe Charlie was some kind of father figure for me. I certainly thought Charlie was my protector at the *Gazette*. I was proud to have such a savvy mentor, and I followed his advice exactly. Besides, I liked going in to scream at Hadley. It felt good. I'd probably have screamed myself right out of a job, if Georgia T. George hadn't stopped me when I was about to commit career suicide. She was a type of editor I'd never encountered at the *CG* before: she believed in protecting and encouraging young talent, and stopping them before they did something stupid—like yell at the managing editor when they'd been set up by a false mentor. Once Georgia showed me his backstabbing memo, things were never the same between Charlie and me. Oh, I never confronted Charlie. Georgia told me not to, and now I followed her advice. To all outward appearances I was friendly with him. Friendly, but no longer admiring. I didn't hang around his desk listening to him talk about the people he screwed, literally and figuratively. I quit going to most *Gazette* parties. It was no fun watching the same tired people preying on each other. What happened to me

was an old, old corporate story, repeated endlessly at the *CG*, and plenty of other offices.

It didn't take Charlie long to figure out I'd
changed toward him. Nobody said Charlie was
stupid. He quickly went from a good friend to a
bitter enemy. Most of the *Gazette* staff blamed
me for the break. They said I'd turned on a man
who'd given my career a boost. That's certainly
how Charlie played it. Others knew better. But
they were members of a special club: they'd all
been betrayed by Charlie. He was destructive.
But so far, he'd only killed careers. Would he kill
people, too?

I knew Charlie could be violent. I'd heard that
he came close to killing Blow Job Betty. She's
the one I told Rita the Retiree about—the one
who hung around the Last Word, giving Charlie
and the other guys oral sex—until the cop told
them she was a he. When Betty made her next
visit to the Word, she was beaten up in the parking lot. Rumor had it that Charlie was one of the
people who hit her, and he would have killed her
if Terry, the bartender, hadn't stopped him. Why
didn't I connect Charlie and Maria earlier? I
guess I just didn't believe I worked with a murderer. Also, I thought Charlie was too smart to
make the same mistake twice.

What if Charlie found out he was dating another female impersonator? Would that have
sent him right over the edge into murder? Charlie wasn't the type to go into therapy and ask
himself why he was attracted to men who
dressed as women.

But why kill Burt and Ralph?

Why did they both die in the same week? What was the connection?

I knew Ralph drank at Burt's Bar when he was rehabbing in the neighborhood. Had Ralph been in Burt's Bar the night Charlie walked in with Maria? Would he have recognized her? Ralph knew a lot of female impersonators.

Burt couldn't answer that question. But his wife, Dolores, might know. I called her and apologized for bothering her again, but she was happy to take a break from packing. "My back is killing me, Francesca. I'm getting too old for this moving business," Dolores complained. But she sounded younger and livelier than she had since Burt's death.

"Was Ralph in the bar the night Charlie came in with the classy blonde?"

"Are you still digging around in that? Francesca, I'm warning you, be careful. The answer is yes. Ralph was in that night, and most every night that week. He was working on the Utah house and plaster dust made him thirsty."

"Was Ralph in the bar the day Burt died?"

"Yes," said Dolores. "Ralph was sicker than a dog that day, and came in for a bowl of soup to go. Chicken soup. Supposed to be the best thing for colds, and ours is made from scratch. I looked out of the kitchen and saw him for a minute. The lunch-hour rush had started and I was back there cooking. Burt was up front taking orders and fixing drinks. I saw Burt and Ralph talking together, but I can't tell you what about. Probably just ordering his soup."

That was the last piece to the puzzle. I had it all worked out now. But I needed to run my conclusions by someone. I called Uncle Bob's to see if Marlene was there. "She's working now, honey," said Sandie, the manager. "If you stop by in an hour, at seven o'clock she can talk with you."

I did. This time, we went into the back staff room, where Babe, the *Gazette*'s gossip columnist, never went. Marlene turned on the coffeepot so we'd have plenty of fuel. She poured us two cups of fresh coffee, and we sat down at a table. I pulled out the Gender Bender program with Maria's ad. This time, I covered up everything on the page but her picture. I was taking no chances. I didn't want any distractions. "Ever see this person?" I asked.

Marlene identified Maria right away. "That's her. That's the blond woman who was with Charlie."

"That's what I needed to hear," I said. "I think I've got it all figured out. Let me run it by you:

"Charlie murdered Burt and Ralph, and someone else, too. You've pointed out Princess Di, the classy blond woman who came in with Charlie. Well, she was a he."

"I'll be damned," said Marlene. "I'd never guess. Couldn't tell by the Adam's apple or the hands and feet. I guess because she was so delicate."

"She was so delicate she had a drag act called

Maria Callous, the Ass with Class." I showed her the rest of the ad.

"Good thing I'm sitting down," said Marlene. "I thought I was beyond being surprised in this business. Her bottom was a beaut. Not that I'm queer myself. Just checkin' out the competition."

"Well, Charlie was going out with Maria—maybe only once or twice, from what I can figure out. Then he hands her over to his boss, Hadley, to advance his own career. Except right after that, he finds out Maria Callous is really a guy and kills her. Maria wasn't his first female impersonator. Charlie already had a close encounter with BJ Betty. I told you about that one. And gossip says he nearly killed Betty when he found out."

"As much as he played around, you'd think Charlie could tell a girl from a boy. We had a few giggles over that one," said Marlene.

"So did everyone else. They'd have some real horselaughs if they found out Charlie made the same mistake twice. And even if they didn't find out, think how Hadley would take the news.

"That's why Charlie killed Maria and dumped her body in a vacant lot. He could lose his career. He certainly lost his temper—and maybe even his mind—but that's for the lawyers to figure out. He kills her before Hadley learns her secret. End of story. Nobody's going looking for someone like Maria. Even when she dropped out of the pageant, nobody asked a lot of questions. People like her disappear all the time. They're seen as shiftless and unstable. Then Charlie realizes Burt saw them together at the bar. Burt brags to his rehabbing customer, Ralph, that an important editor from the *Gazette* brought in a classy-looking blonde."

"Burt didn't brag about his customers," said Marlene.

"Okay. Burt mentions it to Ralph."

"He might do that."

"Ralph realizes the classy blonde is Maria Callous—the female impersonator who was murdered. He goes to Burt's Bar and they discuss what to do about it. Maybe Burt has some friend in the police department they can run their suspicions past. But before they can act, Charlie kills Burt and then Ralph. Now no one can connect her to him.

"It makes sense that Charlie went running into Hadley's office with the photos from the Miss American Gender Bender Pageant and whipped Hadley into a smut-crushing frenzy. I thought he was just causing trouble. But Charlie couldn't risk any more public exposure of the pageant or people might ask what happened to Maria Callous—and the questions might lead to Charlie, since he'd been seen with her."

"Didn't Hadley date her, too?"

"I think so. But he's not a hands-on editor."

"You know these people better than I do," said Marlene. "Everything you said makes sense to me. Except for one thing: How did Charlie find out that Maria was a man? Did someone tell him? Or show him a pageant program? You ought to answer that question first."

"We may never know the answer to that," I said. "Only Charlie can answer that, and why would he tell me?"

"Shouldn't you at least try?" said Marlene. "I think it's important. And maybe other people had a reason to kill Maria. Why don't you run your information past someone who would know? Detective Mark Mayhew is in here most mornings. You can ask him."

"Oh, no. When I first mentioned to Mark that I thought Ralph and Burt were murdered, he said I was crazy. Now that I've figured everything out, he'll come in and take the credit. Well, he's not getting the glory. This is my story."

"This is your career. If Charlie isn't guilty of murder, he'll kill that."

"He's guilty, Marlene. I'll stake my life on it."

"You may have to," she said. "How are you going to break the news that you know about these murders? We're talking triple murder here. Will you catch Charlie after work and say, 'By the way, boss, is it true you offed three people?' That would give him a good reason to make it four."

"Marlene, I'm not going to confront Charlie on my own. I'll go into the managing editor and present the whole case. Hadley will call in the company lawyers and get all the advice he needs. They'll do the dirty work and I'll get the credit. God, Marlene, this is so good, I can't believe it. I've finally nailed the little creep. Of course, it will be embarrassing to the *Gazette* to have a murdering 'Family' section editor, but the paper will weather it. What a scoop! It's mine, all mine, and it's a big one. This is a media Watergate. This is talk-show time. This is book contract time. This is my Pulitzer prize, and I'm not sharing it with anyone.

"It's a story with reader appeal, too. It isn't like Whitewater, where nobody can figure out what happened and if they can, they don't care. Everyone will identify with this story. Everybody hates the boss. Most workers know the person in charge is a mean screwup. But a boss who kills people! Readers will love it. The papers will walk off the newsstands."

"They do, anyway," said Marlene. "Yesterday, somebody put a quarter in the box outside the restaurant and helped themselves to fifteen papers."

"I've always wanted to do that," I said. "But I refrain, being in the business and all."

"Francesca," said Marlene, "I don't want to pour cold water on your acceptance speech for the Pulitzer prize, but what makes you think the *Gazette* will even publish this story? It's not going to make the paper look real good."

"They'll have to run it. They can't let TV scoop them. Besides, this is a national story. A newspaper with a killer editor! God, it's so good. I can't wait."

"So when are you going to commit this act of journalism? Are you going to tell Lyle first? Or that editor you like so much, who's helped you before, what's her name—Georgia? Shouldn't you at least run your plan past them?"

"I promise I'll try to talk with them both to-day," I said. I promised because I knew Georgia was taking a few days off, and Lyle was in classes until late tonight. Both of them would try to stop me, but I knew they'd be proud of me once I succeeded. And I would succeed.

"I'll tell Hadley tonight, before I go to the police. And then I'll write my prizewinning story."

Hadley went home around six thirty or seven most nights. But when he had to stay downtown for some big event, he always stopped by to look at the final edition, which came out about eleven thirty. Tonight was the annual Old Sports Dinner, a sentimental favorite for city baseball fans. By the time they got through all the beer, all the awards and teary speeches, Hadley wouldn't get back to the newsroom until almost twelve thirty.

I sat around at my desk at the *CG* and worked on Tuesday's column on gun control. Our department had emptied out hours before. It was so quiet, I finished writing the gun column and had time to answer some mail. I was nervous, excited, and full of energy. My mind and my fingers moved quicker than usual. Only the clock was slow. By twelve twenty-five, most of the newsroom staff had gone home and the rest seemed to be at lunch, or whatever meal night-shift workers ate at that hour. Hadley was in his office, his suit jacket off and his sleeves rolled up. I decided now was the best time to talk. His door was open, but I knocked anyway.

"Come in, Francesca," he said cheerfully.

He was in a good end-of-the-day mood. His

blue bow tie looked crisply tied, and I swear the man was wearing suspenders. All he needed to complete the image of an old-style newsman was a green eyeshade. He did have a green-shaded banker's lamp on his desk. It was the only light on in the room, and it made the place look more like a museum than ever.

In the shadows, I could see the headlines for the ancient newspapers. One was about the Battle of the Marne. Behind his desk were other journalism artifacts: Hadley's old California job case, the wooden recesses filled with Caslon type. The pica stick. The copy spike on its ornate green metal base. When did copy spikes disappear from newsrooms? When computers came in? I remembered them at the *Gazette* offices when I first started, but that was BC—before computers. In those days, editors hung strings of long wire-service stories on those spikes. The stories trailed over the sides of the desks, like long hair. An editor told me copy spikes disappeared when some federal agency outlawed them because they were too dangerous. I wondered if anyone had ever lost an eye on one. Hadley's spike looked deadly.

"I'm afraid I'm not here with good news, Mr. Harris," I said. Hadley listened intently while I told him what I'd found out. I told him about the classy female impersonator, Maria Callous, and how her dead ass had been found in a vacant lot. I told him how she was supposed to be in the Miss American Gender Bender Pageant. I told him that my friend, Ralph, and my reliable city source, Burt, were dead and I thought it was because they knew about Maria's death. Hadley looked stunned, as I knew he would. He didn't say a word as I kept talking. I built my case slowly and carefully. I told him about the people who identified Maria's picture, about the pocket knife, and about the message on the answering machine. So far, I'd told him just the facts, not the killer's name. I thought Hadley would accept it better if I presented the case as unemotionally as possible. I also thought I wouldn't mention that Hadley might have gone out—or have wanted to go out—with Maria.

"I believe, Mr. Harris, that the killer is a straight male who was horrified by the sudden knowledge that he was dating a female impersonator, instead of a real female. I think it made the poor man crazy. I believe he strangled Maria, then killed two more people, Ralph and Burt, because he thought they could connect her to him. I'm sorry to say"—actually I wasn't sorry at all, but I thought a couple of crocodile tears were called for—"that the killer is a *City Gazette* editor. That's why I came to you."

Now I was getting to the good part. I was just about to tell Hadley that the killer was Charlie. I knew Hadley would take it hard. Charlie was his boy.

Hadley's shoulders were slumped as if he expected the blow. His face grew grave and thoughtful. The scalp under his thinning hair reddened. Hadley turned his back to me and stared at his newspaper museum, as if for comfort, or inspiration. He rubbed the smooth wood of the California job case and touched the pica stick and ran his hands along the copy spike. I never realized how much that copy spike looked like an ice pick on a flat base. God, it was lethal looking.

Then Hadley grabbed the copy spike and went straight for me. He never said a word. Holy shit! Hadley was aiming straight for my eye. I put my arm up. It saved my face, but Hadley took a long stab at my arm. It ripped my brown-striped Donna Karan jacket from wrist to elbow in a long, vicious slice. I watched the blood ooze out of the cut. It stung.

"Hadley!" I said. "What the hell are you doing?"

But all of a sudden I knew. He was trying to kill me. The killer was a *City Gazette* editor. But it wasn't Charlie. It was Hadley. Hadley was the man whose career would be ruined if word got out that he'd been stepping out with a female impersonator. Mr. Morality with Maria Callous, the Ass with Class. He'd be a laughingstock.

He started speaking, slowly and softly. "Francesca," he said, "you have no respect for Family Values. None. No respect. I told you and I told you. I am tired of your smut." Now he was almost shrieking his rage. "Smut! Smut! Smut must be eliminated!" I was still standing there, stunned, blood running down my right arm, my left hand leaning against the desk, when Hadley struck again. He rammed the copy spike right into my hand, in the web between my thumb and forefinger. Oddly, it didn't hurt. Until he pulled the spike out and hit me upside the head with the base. That opened a cut in my head—I could feel something warm oozing in my hair. It also knocked some sense into me. I started moving, and fast.

"This hurts me more than it hurts you," he said in a soft, insinuating whisper, but I doubted that. "You won't obey me, Francesca. Why won't you obey me? You made me do this. It's all your fault. I didn't want to hurt you. You made me."

I made myself pick up a Steuben glass ashtray from his desk, a gift of the Jaycees, and fling it at his head. It bounced off his balding skull with a thunk that might have made me laugh under other circumstances. The ashtray stopped him. I saw blood on his forehead, but I didn't take long to look.

Hadley shook off the blow and slashed at me again with the spike. He missed. I ran out the door and down Rotten Row, Hadley behind me. Where was everybody? Why weren't any editors working late tonight? I tried a couple of office doors. Maybe I could get into an office and call 911. Hadley moved surprisingly fast, making strange noises, something between a grunt and a growl. He kept saying, "You made me do this. You made me. It's not my fault."

Why didn't anyone hear him? Why didn't anyone see us? Jesus, he was fast. He was close enough to slash again. Hadley put a rip in the back of my jacket, but he didn't get me. More office doors. All locked. Got to get help. Got to get away. Finally, one was open. It was the morgue. Good. Maybe Fred was in.

But he wasn't. He was on lunch break. He had his little sign out on his desk. I stopped just a second, but Hadley was behind me, overturning the bookcase behind Fred's desk. The heavy case toppled in my direction. As I jumped out of the way, fat reference books spilled on the floor in a dusty heap. They missed me, but Hadley lost his copy spike. It slipped from his hand and went bouncing down the aisle past me. As he ran toward it, I opened a file drawer and got him right in the knee. I'd been aiming higher, but a bruised knee stopped him well enough. He fell, landing on the floor on all fours. I grabbed Fred's copy scissors, ten inches long and sword-sharp, and stabbed Hadley in the closest hand, his left one. The blade went in. It felt like I was cutting chicken.

"You hurt me," he said, like a surprised child.

"I hope so," I wheezed. There was no point in being tactful now.

Hadley sat up with a grunt of pain and pulled the scissors out of his hand. God. I was sick. There was blood everywhere now, and some of it was mine. I could hardly see from the blood running down my face. My hands were sticky and slippery. Hadley was slowing down, too.

Then Hadley grabbed the scissors with his good hand and tried to slash me with them. I hit him in the head with Fred's phone, hard, hard enough to crack it. He sat there dazed, while I ran back to the rolling files. They were a Hadley special. The staff hates those rolling files, but Hadley wouldn't let the morgue expand into a larger space. He wanted the space for his office.

The rolling files are beige metal shelves that go up to the ceiling. They are set on tracks. The shelf units roll back and forth. Because they move, you can store eight aisles of files in the space of four. But you have to move one row of shelves to get to another. The shelves are moved by a big wheel, about the size of a steering wheel, on the side of the unit. It takes surprisingly little strength to get the shelves to start closing. Librarians are rarely built like Arnold Schwarzenegger. In fact, one of the selling points of the shelves is how easy it is to move something that big. Amazing. Also, amazingly inconvenient. The whole unit is about as big as an Olympic-sized pool. Stored inside are all the *CG* photos and old news stories that haven't been transferred to the computer.

The rolling shelves are a drag and a time waster. The library staff is constantly tripping over the metal tracks. One librarian was almost trapped in the rolling shelves when somebody started turning the wheel. Only her anguished squeals kept her from getting squished.

I slipped into one aisle, PHOTOS AR-CZ. Hadley was following, his walk slow and lumbering. But he was waving those sharp scissors with determination. The grunt had turned into a wheeze, and that sound was somehow scarier. As Hadley hobbled down the aisle, I slipped out the back of the rolling files, and found the wheel. Then I began rolling the shelves together, trapping Hadley.

"Arrrggaahhh," he said, a strange gurgling scream. He pressed on the shelves, but his strength was gone. The wheel slipped a few times because of the blood, but I kept turning and the shelves kept moving together. When Hadley couldn't move anymore, I jammed Fred's metal ruler in the wheel so the shelves would stay. Hadley had stopped screaming. Now there was only silence. I grabbed a phone off a small desk back by the rolling files, where the staff looked at old clips. The phone slipped out of my bloody hand. I grabbed it again and dialed 911.

"Help," I said, surprised it came out as a whisper. "I'm in the morgue and someone's trying to kill me."

"We don't have time for jokes, lady, and prank calls are against the law," said the person who answered.

I finally convinced her I was Francesca Vierling, calling from the reference library of the *City Gazette,* and I'd been attacked and slashed by a white male assailant. I was afraid to give out Hadley's name. She'd never believe me.

"Are you injured?" asked the operator, I suspect to keep me on the line.

"Yes," I said. "I've been cut on my head, and my hand and my arm, and there's a lot of blood."

A pool of it collected on the white Formica desktop and spilled over the edge. I watched the blood fall on the white floor tile. It sounded like rain. The room grew black around the edges and I passed out. The last thing I saw was my blood, dripping, dripping, dripping.

14

B y the time the police showed up at the *City Gazette,* I'd come to. It took them a few extra minutes to get upstairs because Jake, the night guard, thought the call was a prank, since nobody in the newsroom had called him about trouble in the morgue. The cops agreed, but said they'd better check it out anyway. Jake took them upstairs. Just about the time Jake and the cops arrived at the morgue, Fred came back from lunch. He took one look at the blood on Hadley and me and promptly lost his lunch, adding to the general disorder of the *Gazette* morgue.

After that, things got a bit hazy. I told the police what happened, but it wasn't easy. There were reporters all over, messing up the crime scene. Plus, once they realized who was trapped in the rolling files, a lot of police brass and high-ranking *Gazette* management showed up. I have no idea how long it took for an ambulance to cart me off to the hospital.

Lyle was the first person to visit me in the hospital. He found me on a gurney in the emergency room. "You look like hell," he said.

"Thanks, I needed that," I said.

"Oh, god, baby, don't ever do that again," he said, scooping me up in his arms. I felt so romantic and so cold. My hospital gown parted in the back, exposing my bruised rear end to the hall traffic. A nurse broke off this touching scene. "Put her down," she said to Lyle. "I don't want anything disturbing those stitches."

I felt pretty good, actually, between Lyle and the drugs. Legal drugs beat the street stuff any day. The nurse, a human pit bull, sent Lyle home after we got in a few more kisses.

When I woke up the next morning, I felt a lot worse. The last time I'd had a headache like that, I was twenty-one and had been drinking green beer on St. Patrick's Day. My head pounded. My arm throbbed and my hand ached.

At least I had something to look at besides bandages and bruises. Lyle had sent the most gorgeous peach roses. My first visitor that morning was Cutup Katie. The nurse, who'd been shooing curious fans out of the room, didn't dare chase away Katie. She knew from the white coat that Katie was a doctor, and she retired respectfully into the hall. Katie wore a clean white coat, too. I was honored.

"Hah. She wouldn't leave me alone if she knew all your patients were dead," I said.

"I like it that way," Katie said. "Cuts my malpractice insurance. Let's see what Hadley did to you. I saw you being carried out of the *Gazette* on TV and you had blood all over. But I figured anyone who could ham it up for the TV cameras had to be okay."

"I fainted when no one was around," I said.

"Good," said Katie. "I'd hate to have you wimp out in public."

I showed her where they shaved my head and gave me sixteen stitches in my scalp. "I'm going to have to comb my hair sideways over my bald patch for months. I'll never make fun of drapeheads again."

"Hope you got a tetanus shot for that hole in your hand. Nice long scratch on your arm, too. That's a classic defense wound. What was Hadley going for?"

"My eye."

"Straight into the brain. That's what I'd do, too," said Katie, admiringly.

"I wish you didn't sound so approving."

"You're fine," said Katie. "Look, I hear he's hired some tricky lawyer. There's no chance he'll get away with this?"

"Over my dead body," I said, and wished I hadn't.

Detective Mark Mayhew was my next visitor, a dazzling display of different shades of blue, from medium to dark. He showed up after they brought me back from X-Ray. I'd changed the hospital gown, which was designed by Frederick's of Festus, for one of my own. I was sitting up in bed, trying to look like an ethereal vision in pale peach satin. It worked pretty well, if you didn't count the big stupid white bandage on my bald spot where Hadley hit me. Lyle's peach roses added to the otherworldly impression. That impression vanished when the nurse poked her head in and said, "Have you had a bowel movement today?"

I told her that was classified information.

"It's not funny," she said. "We need to know if your system is functioning properly."

"It's functioning, it's functioning. Jeez. Elizabeth Barrett Browning never had these problems."

Mark laughed, then chewed me out for going after a triple murderer on my own.

"I didn't know Hadley was a murderer. I thought it was Charlie."

But Mark wasn't too mad. Not when he'd cleared three murders. With the lecture out of the way, he gave me the lowdown on Hadley. His scissors stab and head wound had bled like hell, and he was bruised from being trapped in the rolling files, but aside from that Hadley was in good shape.

When the police released Hadley from the rolling files, they must have loosened his tongue. "The man couldn't stop babbling," Mark said. "He refused any legal representation. I managed to Miranda-ize him before he got to the good stuff. By the time the *City Gazette* lawyers got there and told him to shut up, Hadley had confessed to everything, and he kept talking."

"Nobody tells Hadley Harrison the Third to shut up, especially not a rented mouthpiece," I said. "If he wanted to talk, he'd talk."

And the police listened to every word.

"Hadley said he went out with Maria Callous, a.k.a. Michael Delmer, once or twice," Mark continued. " 'It was not what people thought,' he said, looking like an Episcopal bishop. 'We never slept together.' And they didn't. She just gave him head in a downtown hotel room."

"Let me guess—the Riverside Inn," I said, remembering my close encounter with Hadley and Miss Mouse, the consumer-reporter-to-be, on the seventeenth floor.

"Correct. We found the credit card receipts. Also, Hadley put these encounters on his expense account—as a business lunch."

"No comment," I said.

"Anyway, after a few late-night lunches, Hadley saw Maria was getting serious about him, so he dumped her. Hadley didn't put it in quite those words. He says he told Maria, 'It would be better if we parted before things became too complicated, my lovely Maria. After all, I am a married man, and my first duty is to my dear wife.' "

"That sounds like him," I said.

"Maria offered to be Hadley's mistress, if he'd set her up in a house on the South Side. Hadley laughed at her and said she wasn't good enough. Maria said she'd tell everyone Hadley had been having an affair with her. Hadley said to go ahead. He'd heard that threat before from other women. Who would believe a nobody like her?

"That did it. Maria said he may have heard it from a woman, but not from a man. Maria told Hadley that she was actually a he—and she'd tell the whole city that Mr. Morality had been dating a man. Then to prove this was no cock-and-balls story she lifted up her skirt.

"Hadley was stunned. He reacted by strangling Maria with her own scarf. She spent her last breath begging and threatening. She told Hadley that Burt and Ralph knew about their affair and would make the details public if she died. The best we can determine, they didn't know a thing. Ralph and Burt were the last two men she saw at the bar that night with Hadley, and theirs were probably the only names that registered in Maria's poor oxygen-starved brain.

"Hadley insisted that killing Maria was a perfectly calm and rational decision. 'I did it to preserve Family Values,' he said. 'Then I dumped her like the trash she was.'"

"Adding littering to his other offenses," I said.

"You reporters are so cynical. Hadley had no explanation for why he sliced and diced Maria's genitals with his pocket knife. He threw the bloody pocket knife and clothes away in his trash can at home. The trash was picked up the next morning. They're probably six feet deep in a landfill by now. But he forgot two things. His shoes and his alligator watchband. We found blood on both, and it matches Maria's.

"The next day, he bought a new Swiss Army

knife on his way in to work. Told us he got one of the big ones, with the miniature can opener. Can you believe it? Like he was proud of his purchase.

"Hadley thought Maria might be lying about Burt and Ralph, but he had to know. He came into Burt's Bar alone at lunchtime. He saw Ralph and Burt talking together and got scared. We interviewed a customer who was sitting at the bar when Ralph was in. The customer heard what Ralph said to Burt. Ralph ordered chicken soup to go and then asked Burt for extra crackers. But Hadley didn't know that. He'd seen Ralph in the bar before, the night Hadley was there with Maria. He thought they were plotting against him.

"Ralph paid for his soup and left. Because Hadley was sitting alone, Burt thought it was safe to mention Maria. After all, Hadley had introduced Maria to Burt the last time he was in, which is usually a signal the gentleman will talk about his date. 'That sure was a pretty blonde you had with you,' Burt said."

"Poor Burt, he pronounced his own death sentence."

"Yep," said Mark. "Hadley took those words as a veiled threat."

"So he killed Burt after the lunch hour?"

"He sat there and drank coffee, waiting until he was the last one in the bar. Then he asked Burt for Ralph the Rehabber's phone number. Said he had some work for him. Burt wrote the number down and told Hadley where Ralph was working. When Burt turned his back to lock up the back door, Hadley stabbed him with his own knife. Dolores keeps her knives professionally sharpened. Burt was dead before he knew what hit him."

"Boy, never turn your back on an editor. Hadley seems to have a natural talent for murder. He killed Burt in a couple of clean cuts."

"He knew enough to wipe the knife, then put on his gloves and clean out the cash register," Mark said. "Although he didn't know to look under the cash drawer for the rest of the money—which made you suspicious."

"At least I was right about something," I said.

"You were right about a lot of things," Mark said generously. "We'd never have caught him without you." I keep forgetting. Mark really is a nice guy.

"Then Hadley put on his beige coat, pulled down his hat and let himself out the front door. The people in the office building across the street saw the killer leave and didn't realize it.

"When Ralph stopped by for soup, he sealed his fate, too. Hadley figured they were in it together. It was easy to kill Ralph. Hadley called and made a date to meet Ralph at the Utah Place house. Hadley had seen Ralph with the inhaler while he waited for his soup-to-go. Ralph was sick and needed the inhaler constantly. Hadley only had to be around Ralph a few minutes to figure that out.

"Ralph had been working on the ceiling for two hours that morning, and was already wheezing from the plaster dust. All Hadley did was lift Ralph's inhaler from the jeans jacket by the tool-box when he wasn't looking, and then cut the other inhaler off the ladder. Ralph never noticed. He was running around talking about his rehab work. Mother Nature, that mean mother, did the rest. Ralph had a fatal attack about an hour or two later, if you believe the pathologist's esti-mate. In case the plaster dust hadn't killed Ralph, Hadley said, he arranged to stop by the Utah house about seven that night to discuss the rehabbing job further. 'I had my new knife,' he said, as if that settled it.

"After Hadley left the house with Ralph's in-halers, he broke into Ralph's truck. He found two more inhalers and took them, just in case Ralph made it to the truck. Then Hadley searched the truck for any information Ralph might have about Maria. He didn't find any-thing, so he was satisfied that was the end of it."

"Good thing Ralph left the envelope with the pageant program and the newspaper clipping at his mother's house," I said. "Otherwise I would never have made the connection between Maria and the body in the vacant lot. Even if Ralph didn't know that Hadley killed Maria, in a way Maria was right. Ralph and Burt made sure peo-ple knew Hadley killed her. I have to ask: Did Hadley go back and check on Ralph?"

"Yeah," Mark said. "Hadley came back that night at seven. By then, Ralph was dead for hours. We found some plaster dust in Hadley's car and on his shoes, but we'll probably never be

able to pin that one on him. No one saw him at
the Utah house. The man had the luck."

"Why didn't the neighbor lady spot him? She
saw me," I said.

"She was at church," said Mark.

"Both times?"

"Yep. That man was invisible when he wanted
to be," Mark said.

"Was he sorry for what he did?"

"Hadley called Ralph and Burt's deaths 'regrettable.'"

"Regrettable? As if he could run a correction
on page two for his error. That's disgusting. Did
he try to run me down at Uncle Bob's?"

"Hadley drove the car that chased you
through the parking lot. He found out the way
you feared he would—Babe, the gossip columnist. Babe went back to Hadley's office reeking
of blueberries and repeated Marlene's remarks
about Princess Di.

"When we asked Hadley about trying to run
you down, do you know what he said? 'I panicked.' Then he smiled as if he was confessing an
endearing little fault. 'I thought I had to get rid
of her.'

"He wasn't too panicked, though," Mark continued. "He knew enough not to use his own car,
an easily identifiable black Mercedes. We found
a credit card bill that shows he rented an anonymous gray Chevy from Rent-A-Wreck the day
you were almost run down. He saw you leave the
newsroom and followed you. There were too
many people on Klocke, so he tailed you to Un-

cle Bob's. When he saw you were alone in the parking lot, he went after you.

"Hadley said he was glad you got away. 'She didn't know anything. She is only a reporter.'"

"I thought Hadley didn't know anything because he is only an editor," I said. "We made the mistake of underestimating each other, and we both paid for it. I'll have these reminders a long time," I said, showing him the cut on my arm and the hole in my hand.

"I was so sure it was Charlie," I added. "He dated Maria. He carried a pocket knife."

"It wasn't the only pocket knife in the world," said Mark. "We found out most *CG* editors carried them after Hadley pulled his out at an office party. The hostess forgot a knife to cut the baked Brie, and Hadley brought out his pocket knife and said a gentleman always came prepared. After he said that, every up-and-comer at the paper, male and female, bought a pocket knife."

"I missed something not going to those *CG* parties after all," I said. "I should never underestimate the editors' ability to brownnose the boss. When Hadley came back from one vacation with a beard, they all grew them. You never saw so much moth-eaten facial hair. Made it easier to identify who was going to sell us out."

"Must have been tough on the ambitious women," said Mark. "They couldn't grow beards. What did they do?"

"They grew mustaches."

Mark laughed. "Hadley seems surprised that we're charging him with your attempted murder. He said, 'It was a crazy impulse,' as if he was willing to forget it and we should, too."

"It was all crazy."

"That's what Hadley's lawyers decided. They think the *Gazette* managing editor is a bedbug, especially after he ignored their advice to shut up. They're trying to get that confession thrown out. Scuttlebutt says Hadley will plead not guilty by reason of insanity."

"A jury of his peers," I said, "if it includes any reporters, will probably agree. We think most editors are crazy."

"They love you, too," said Mark, and left me laughing.

Speaking of crazy, my dreams of glory were just that—dreams. I must have been as crazy as Hadley to think that my story would make the front page of the *City Gazette.* Even if I hadn't been out of commission in the hospital, the *City Gazette* wouldn't run headlines that said: WACKO EDITOR WHACKS READERS!

I'd hoped I wouldn't have to do much time in the hospital, but the doctors were worried when they found some blood between my scalp and my skull. They kept talking about a subdural hematoma. They took away my Tylenol Three, which almost wiped out the headaches, and kept waking me up and asking me what day it was and who was president. Finally, some bozo got me out of a sound sleep at 3:00 A.M. and asked me to count backward from one hundred by sevens. I told him I couldn't do that at high noon on my best day and he better fucking leave me the hell alone. He decided my level of consciousness was normal. After two days of this torture and a CAT scan, the doctors let me go. By the time I was well enough to sit down at my computer, I'd been scooped by five TV stations, twenty-one radio stations, and even the free throwaway shopper newspaper.

My story was severely mutilated by the *Gazette* lawyers. They claimed they did it out of compassion for the victims, but I think they were worried about being sued by the families of Michael, Burt, and Ralph. A newspaper that hires and promotes a killer might be liable for damages. My injuries, as the company lawyers reminded me several times, were covered by workers' comp.

The *Gazette* lawyers had a vested (and pinstriped) interest in making Hadley look as good as possible, which meant my story looked like it had been slashed by Hadley. The lawyers added so many "alleges," "presumes," and "police spokesperson saids" that nobody could figure out what Hadley did to me, but it might have been an improvement.

My favorite part was when the wimpiest company lawyer, a rabbit in pinstripes, was looking over my story. "Are you sure Mr. Harris meant to attack you?" the rabbit asked, blinking his pink eyes. "Maybe you tripped."

He was shocked and appalled at my response, and it wasn't physically possible anyway.

Fortunately, the other media in St. Louis made sure the story got out. The local TV stations, tired of Hadley's sanctimonious editorials on the moral decline of television, had a high old time showing Mr. Morality being led away in handcuffs by the police. Morning show DJs did a lot of routines about *Gazette* editors killing circulation, one reader at a time. The morning jocks said the *CG* was a dying newspaper, which was really too bad, because it had a killer staff. One enterprising morning show host dug out Hadley's editorials on family values, smut, and the importance of integrity. He especially enjoyed reading this juicy Hadleyism:

"Honesty and integrity are the cutting edge of journalism. It is my duty to stay as sharp as I possibly can in the service of my profession, to slash away at falsehood and keep justice as finely honed as a knife-edge."

Ouch.

I was right about one thing. This was a prizewinning story. The TV reporter who was at the *CG* that night won an Emmy for Spot News. I think the shot of me carried out on a stretcher, blood-drenched but giving the thumbs-up sign, made the story.

I saw Billie one more time. That visit made it all worthwhile. She quit blaming herself for Ralph's death. My search for the killer did some good.

Dolores quit blaming the neighborhood for her husband's death. Hadley was the killer, not the local kids. She got bored sitting around her splendid South County house waiting for the grandkids to visit, and went back to working at

Burt's Bar, for the guy who bought it. He's a handsome white-haired gentleman in his late sixties. He seems to dote on her. Rumor says Dolores may go out with him someday soon.

And Charlie? He's never stopped blaming me because I thought he was the killer. He constantly makes little remarks in the morning meeting, like "Francesca should do that story. She's *such* a good judge of human nature." Naturally, the story is a dog.

And while we're discussing animals here, Charlie landed on his feet like a cat. When word got out that he'd been dating yet another female impersonator, it only added to his cachet. Charlie's rat pack took it as a sign of his virility. "That Charlie will screw anything that moves," they joked at the Last Word, while he strutted and preened.

Some of the *Gazette* editors blamed me for the paper's troubles. They figured if I'd kept my mouth shut, no one would have known about Hadley.

If the *Gazette* editors were nasty, my readers were wonderful. While I was in the hospital, they sent cards, flowers, and teddy bears. Once I was up and around, they called and stopped by my table at Uncle Bob's to make sure I was okay. My favorite flowers, besides Lyle's exquisite peach roses, were a spring bouquet from Nettie's, an old South Side flower shop. The bouquet was sent by Rita the Retiree, and it had this on the card: "I told you so."

And so she had. It was Rita who insisted the

story of the dead dumped prostitute was a good
one. It was Rita who said that the murder of a
man dressed in women's clothes had a crazy sexual motive. "If the *Gazette* had any sense, they'd
hire you as managing editor," I told Rita.

"Hah. That paper hasn't showed any sense
yet," said Rita. "But now they got a chance to.
Any idea who they'll get as the new managing
editor to replace that Hadley person?"

"Nope. They announced a nationwide search,
though. It could take some time."

It took three months. I couldn't get any info
from my usual pipeline, my mentor Georgia, because she was one of the candidates. I hoped the
Gazette would make her the new managing editor. But I knew she didn't have a chance. The
Gazette didn't promote women. Especially
smart, tough, loyal ones.

The candidates for the ME job paraded
through the newsroom once or twice a week.
They all looked the same—grave middle-aged
men and an occasional woman, all in serious
suits. Charlie was tour guide for the candidates,
and Georgia joked that he'd finally found a job
he could do. I caught little bits of his tour. Once
I heard him tell an editor from Los Angeles,
". . . and here are the newsroom phone books.
We have a complete collection from cities
around the country." Wow. Wonder why the L.A.
guy didn't look too impressed?

We could tell the important candidates, because the publisher would fly in from Boston to be there on the newsroom tour. We could see Charlie, the visiting suit, and the publisher, checking out the computer terminals, the phone book collection, and the surly staff. After the tour, Charlie would take them to the Last Word. For some reason, the publisher seemed to like that place. Maybe he thought he was mixing with the little people.

Rumor had it that the candidates were whittled down to three. They certainly had impressive credentials. I thought any of them would be good, although I leaned toward the woman. One was an assistant managing editor at the *Chicago Tribune*. The second was an editor at *The Miami Herald*. The third was a woman from *The Washington Post*.

Finally, we got the announcement. The publisher would name the new managing editor tomorrow afternoon at 3:00 P.M. in the *Gazette* newsroom. All the reporters from the distant offices and bureaus began drifting into the newsroom about two thirty. No work was getting done that day. There was no point pretending it would until the announcement was made. Reporters and middle-rank editors collected on the edges of desks or leaned against pillars. I saw Tina standing by the fire extinguisher and went over to join her.

Since this was a major announcement, a podium and a public address system had been set up in the newsroom. At two forty-five the TV station cameras showed up and began setting up their lights. A couple of radio reporters arrived, too.

At two fifty-five, all the top editors with offices on Rotten Row, including the city editor Roberto, my mentor Georgia, and my nemesis Charlie, came out and stood close to the podium. I couldn't read Charlie at all. But from the look on Georgia's face, I knew she didn't get the job.

Promptly at three o'clock, the publisher came out, wearing an English-tailored suit and a set of cuff links that cost more than my car. He stood at ease at the podium and spoke in lockjawed patrician tones that made English sound like a different language. "The *City Gazette* is a great paper that will take its greatness into the next century," he said. "Because we are sound and strong, we have survived our recent problems. They were simply tests of our strength. We have put them behind us."

"I'll feel better when they put them in jail," I whispered to Tina. She kicked my shin.

"After a nationwide search," the publisher said, "we realized that the best managing editor for the *Gazette* was right here at home."

Maybe it *was* Georgia. I looked at her, but she seemed so glum. Maybe she was one of those women who didn't like responsibility.

"This editor knows the paper inside and out, every inch of the *City Gazette*, from the phone books to the dedicated people who consult them.

"But more important, he has captured the true spirit of the *City Gazette*."

He? Oh, god, Oh, no. Oh, please.

But then I saw the grin on that little ferret face, and I knew that the publisher was right. He had found someone who captured the true twisted spirit of the *City Gazette*.

"Now let me introduce your new managing editor . . ."

Charlie.